A Cord Of

Three Strands

With every best
wish Steve!

from

10/6/16.

Also by S. J. Haxton

Exposed To All Villainies

The first in the 'Pendennis' trilogy, which follows the fortunes of
three women; Grace Godwynne, Hester Phipps and Mary Carew.
Their tangled fates depend upon their past choices and the choices
they still have to make but they have one thing in common; they are
women in a man's world, which will leave them exposed to all
villainies.

A 2015 Nomination for the
Cornish Gorsedh Holyer an Gof Prize for Literature

Reviews for *Exposed to All Villainies*

"Steph Haxton draws the stories of her three spirited souls together
with such skill one can all but hear the beat of the drums that rattled
orders within the granite walls of Pendennis Castle."
WESTERN MORNING NEWS

"Highly entertaining, highly plausible, a remarkable narrative."
JOHN MORE, HISTORIAN

**The last *Pendennis* novel should be
published in Spring 2017.**

A CORD OF
THREE STRANDS

by

S. J. Haxton

A CORD OF THREE STRANDS by S. J. Haxton

ISBN 978-0-9929293-3-6

Copyright © S. J. Haxton 2016

Published by Boswell Book Publishing

COVER DESIGN by Claire Chamberlain
www.clairechamberlain.com

Printed and bound in Great Britain by TJ International, Padstow

And if one prevails against him, two shall withstand him; and a threefold cord is not quickly broken.

King James Bible Ecclesiastes 4:12

I Grace: A siege ends, peril begins

In that our circumstances leave us so insecure, having been exposed to all villainies, I deem it necessary to leave you this chronicle, my most cherished son, for none of us can now know what jeopardy might befall us.

Thus, I must tell you the circumstances of your birth, of the ties that bind you and of the precarious world you have entered, one turned upside down by civil war and man's inhumanity to man.

Though some will tell you your father was a pirate, he was not a murderer. In these lines will you discover where your trust might be placed and whom to approach with caution.

Read my words and know that the woman who writes this values your life more than her own. These words are the truth and the truth will serve you well.

You have Cornish blood in your veins and the sea in your heritage, indeed you were born under siege in Pendennis castle, on its wave-lapped promontory on the south coast of Cornwall. The beleaguered garrison was our home in the spring of 1646, our prison of choice, from March to August while elsewhere the nation bent to Parliament's will. As the newssheets and the pamphlets railed about the 'great malignants of the country' defying Lord Fairfax's summons to surrender, days and weeks turned into five long months. Rations, negligible to begin with, became pitiful. Eventually even the water in the wells turned foul. We endured all that … and the lice and fleas and the boredom … until at the end, there was but one barrel of salted horsemeat to feed nigh on a thousand souls. You were still a babe in arms then, too young to feel the cramps and evil lethargy that began to overtake even the strongest. Hester sustained you, against all the odds.

Looking back, I do not know how the last company of King's men and the pitiful following of wives survived, having occupied the high-walled fortress on the Fal though that sultry summer. It hardly seems possible that, near starved but unbowed, there were any of that ragged assortment of Royalists able to march from Pendennis Castle, reputations and pride intact.

At 2 o'clock on a thundery afternoon, the sky overcast, the air prickling with tension, our nerves jangling in accord, Hester and I were some of the last to step through into a world newly made by generals and commissioners, where the King was a captive; where nothing could ever be the same.

Colonel Lewis Tremayne's soldiers, having the honour of being the escort to the Governor, were in the vanguard. We did not know whether we would ever see that most principled man again, Lewis, your godfather, or his wife our dear friend Mary. He was one of the senior officers, the gentlemen graciously received by the commander of the Parliamentarian forces and Mary had been admitted to the infirmary, where we had to leave her. Though we were very feeble, Hester and I had not succumbed and were expected to quit the fort.

While I was determined to carry you out through the gates that had haunted our nightmares, I was too weak to manage for long. Hester took over as we, along with a miserably few women, tattered, bareheaded, straggled after the remnants of His Majesty's once-proud regiments. We were the lucky ones. So many of the camp followers, their men-folk as well, remained behind, too weak to stand let alone march forth.

There was a travesty of a guard of honour for the vanquished, men in blood red doublets two deep, either side of the dirt track from the drawbridge and down across the marsh. Even if I had held any hope of a friendly face in the crowd, which I did not, I was unable to focus on the blurry faces of the soldiers lining our route through the enemy lines. Hundreds of pairs of cold eyes marked our passage. Later we were to discover that, while one sympathetic gaze followed two unkempt, bareheaded women laden with a baby and some scant belongings, there was another individual in that crowd whose countenance I would have preferred never to

2

have to acknowledge. He, glimpsing a spectre from his past, made it his business that we would meet again.

The flourish of trumpets' fanfares echoing off the granite walls and the steady thud-thud, thud-thud, thump of the drum sustained our steps. The limp flutter of the Royalist's colours, barely stirring against the flag-staffs in the heavy air, mirrored our mood as we made our way to Arwinch Downs where another provisional camp had been set up by reinforcements to Colonel Hammond's militia. There we were to be documented, described, enumerated and given a pass with permission to pursue our uncertain prospects.

The first lie was the hardest. A lieutenant at his papers, beady-eyed and sharp like a rook, was untidily scrawling, sweat glistening on his brow. Another of the Parliamentarian officers stood beside him, looking less martial and quietly puffing on a pipe of tobacco as he watched, assessing each individual.

The officer scrutinised first Hester then me. He never asked, only assumed that you were her infant, as well you might have been. Then he turned to me,

"Your man: what is his name?" Tremenheere Sark.

"His rank?" Captain.

"What officer did he serve under?" Colonel Tremayne.

"What's his state – walking or sick?" Dead.

The first lie is always the hardest.

In my defence, I did not know then that it was a lie. His question mentioned no husband for I might have baulked at that and the truth might have prevailed. As it was, I became Goodwife Sark.

On the day that we heard that the fortress was to yield, Hester had asked me, shy and deferential, if I would like to accompany her to her dead husband's home. William Mattock, formerly a Dartmoor miner, was latterly a sergeant of pike in Colonel Tremayne's regiment. That unassuming giant had adored his feisty wife but had succumbed to the bloody flux only days before the signing of the Articles for surrender. Our chaplain had helped the dying soldier write his will, in which he left Hester his share in the business of the brew house in his village.

This she had shown to the official, stating with a conviction born of innocence that there was sufficient income to maintain herself, her child and me, whom she detailed as her housemaid. We would be no destitute women, vagabonds or burdens on the parish.

So, another line of ink was drawn upon another page. We were ready to be dispatched. We were given papers to allow passage without let or hindrance and two shillings each, an amount deemed requisite for our accommodation. However, putting down his pipe, the bystander stepped forward before the lieutenant could shout for the next in line. His voice was weary but kind,

"Good day, ladies. My name is Haslock, surgeon to the Army of Parliament. If you wish to travel to Devon, have you been told that you are to embark on a vessel? Ships are being provided for those who require them, no matter what rank or status." We must have looked askance.

"Do not worry, it will cost you nothing, though in your present state I would suggest neither of you have the strength for the ferry to Flushing, let alone to Yalme." Chivvying us, his arms gently flapping as if gathering his hens, he steered us toward two busy hearths, where lines of ragged soldiers waited, subdued, shoulders hunched. I recognised one of the gunnery crews and another soldier respectfully doffed his cap to Hester, bringing a tear to her eye. Surgeon Haslock placed us at the end of the shortest of the queues.

"This field kitchen has been preparing for just such an eventuality. You will be served some broth and bread, which should not be too much for your weakened constitutions to manage. Too much nourishment too soon could be to your detriment," he added, as an afterthought. "I'll come in a little while to see how you fare. Then we shall see whether you embark tomorrow or not." A frown on her face, Hester quickly asked,

"Sir, what are we to do tonight? Where do we sleep? The babe …"

"They will see to it that you and all the women here are given a safe place of repose. Until later, ladies!" Giving a courteous nod, he left us to wait our turn, while the acute pain of the aromas wafting from the cauldrons began to bite.

Each supplicant was given a makeshift trencher of rough bread. A very few still had their own bowls, the last vestiges of a soldier's kit, carefully carried in battered snapsacks. The cook doling out food was warily eying us all. Hester's own pack held the two prized wooden dishes, a wedding present from a benefactor and former employer in Barnstaple. I took them to the hearth as Hester waited to one side. As the cook slopped a ladle of the soup into each plate, the liquor splashed, burning my fingers. He gestured at a pile of loaves torn into lumps.

"One piece each!" he growled, adding, "Take one for the bairn if you must ..."

With that tiny morsel of compassion, I was dismissed and we were moved into a roped area, directed to join row upon row of the vanquished. Some were carefully picking at their food, others already greedily stuffing the last fragments of their meal into their mouths. A wild-haired preacher, with his Bible in his hand, was striding along the lines berating us all, who he proclaimed fallen angels. We were, he cried, ignorant in the face of the Lord's might, destined for a hellish confinement, everlasting incarceration. I suspect that few noticed the irony in the sermonising.

There were civilians moving among us too. A boy was struggling to carry a wooden pail of milk, offering a dipper to anyone who would take it. A few men, commonly used to leaving milk to infants or the aged, scoffed at him and turned away. We called him over and took what he could give us. Other hospitallers were carrying leather jugs and pouring liquor, which at first I took to be ale, into men's horn-cups or tankards but as the nearest to us approached I heard him call out,

"Water! Honeyed water! Surgeon's orders! Each man's to have water. For sipping only!" It made little difference: men gulped it down and called for more as if it was the best brew in the world. If anyone expected beer, he was to be disappointed, but the sweet water seemed to make men drunk anyway.

Suddenly, from among the men who had marched out and been processed first, there came a disturbance. Hester stood up, the better to see what was happening; she quickly sat down, looking worried. Men began shouting 'Poison!' as others staggered to their feet, preparing to defend a man upon the ground. Surgeon Haslock came running, shouting to the guards to stand back. We could not hear his words but he must have spoken strong reassurances, or else the anger of the King's men swiftly dissipated as their energy ran out, for everything went quiet, a deathly hush as it transpired. The doctoring could not save the soldier whose heart, rumour said later, had burst. Here was a horrid irony, a victim of England's new regime who died from eating too much, too soon. We took note, but Hester and I had barely picked at our ration for we had agreed to conserve our supplies for later.

I think we must have dozed, despite the unquiet commotion around us, for I remember little until, as dusk fell, the surgeon and two apron-clad assistants, came through the crowd, directing all the women and some men to wagons. Our cart bumped along the lanes to a church, where sympathetic villagers brought what blankets they could spare to make our makeshift sleeping arrangements more comfortable. Women were assigned to the floor of the upper room of the church house, Hester wryly remarking that we had left behind our luxury; Pendennis had afforded us a straw pallet where here it was just bare boards. Despite the fact that we were told to rest easy, we were once more kept secured, for the door was locked, the churchwardens taking turns to stand watch, a measure implemented for our safety, they said.

We were unlikely to sleep, even if there had been feather beds with silken sheets. The storm that had been threatening for hours finally broke as the church bell chimed one, forked lightening splintering the darkness and thunder rattling the glass in the leads. For what seemed hours, torrents of rain overflowed the gutters to splatter on the gravel paths below.

Eventually the clouds parted, letting in the light of a moon just past the full. Anyone who had managed to doze was startled awake by a thumping at the door that rattled the latch. An intense shouting followed, echoing round the churchyard as the intruder had discovered that their way was barred.

I cannot express the horror with which I recognised the accent, not quite Scots and un-mellowed by time, still authoritative, still callous,

"Open up! I have business with one who I know is billeted here! Open up, in Parliament's name!"

The man hammering at the door was my husband.

II Hester: To make a voyage

Well, here's a pretty pass. Just when I, that was Hester Phipps and is now Hester Mattock, thought I would find myself on the up for a change, here I am clinging on the rim of Fortune's wheel and mired in muck just as deep as ever. Servant, thief, convict, wife, camp follower, widow; 'tis how the wheel turns.

Still, I have more than I did at the start – my own skillet, some silver sixpences and a shilling or two. I have two books, some pieces of paper and I am even able to read my own name, given enough time and a scrivener who didn't make too free with his loops and swirls.

So perhaps then, things could be worse. We all have to wait to see what is to be, and what is to come, and as they do say, if a soul can get no lower then the only way to go is upwards.

If fortunes were to rise, t'was upward we would go, to Cornwood. In the months while I was following my husband Will, God rest his soul, I did climb up and down so many hills at Torrington to Launceston and all, enough to know the West Country is an uncommon hilly place, and Dartmoor, where we were headed, is summ'at steeper than most.

Mind you, even though I ached liked never before and was fighting weariness so heavy I could barely stand, I was so glad to get off the ship that the Parliament soldiers put us on that even if there had been a mountain to climb I would have thanked you for it. Hester Mattock's not made for seafaring. Not like Grace or should I say Mistress Fenwick or is that Goodwife Sark? I hardly know what to name her, though Goodwife Sark came easily enough when the soldier with his pen asked for her name to put on his list.

Grace ought to have been looking forward to some seafaring for there used to be a sparkle in her eyes when she spoke of ships; now she was in no mood to enjoy much at all a'cause of the black gloom that had wrapped her for months. That and the scare we'd had in Penryn.

Here I am though, running ahead with my tale. Let me start when we came out of Pendennis fort; what befell happened like this.

Once we'd been listed and done our share of waiting, they took us that first evening to the parish church that they said was closest by Pendennis. There was me, Grace and little Henry Charles, and just about a quarter of the other Pendennis womenfolk, shut in the church house at Budock. The rest were too sick and had been left behind. Mind, when the head churchwarden sat himself down beside the bolted door, I thought that we had gone from one locking up to another, for all his nice words and gentlemanly ways, but we came to be heartily glad of a locked door and a man who was strict about obeying given orders that night.

'Tweren't the first place Grace and I had shared a tiny bit of space. Now she, the babe, me and a score of other lasses lay head to toe and like pressed pilchards in the upper room, while the others lay in the room below, and it struck me that 'tis summ'at funny how life twists and turns.

See, Grace and me had been together like this in the Palmer's garret in Barnstaple back in '45 even though Grace had one time been my mistress at her family home in Bristol. In Wine Street, it was. It might have been a lifetime ago for all t'was only five years since. Truth to tell, I had been a right bad servant; no need for me to dwell on it but, suffice it to say I'd been 'moved on' by the time 'he' showed his face, the man who wormed his way to the family. Grace used to cry out the name in her sleep and not in a good way neither. I would soothe the nightmares, stroking her hair 'til she stopped sobbing.

She told me how this sea captain, Fenwick, courted her papa for Grace's hand and her inheritance as well. Her father, God rest his soul, was taken right in, hoodwinked and not all by honest deeds if what Grace read to me from a tattered book tells the truth. She keeps the thing hidden fast in what few belongings she carries, but it seems to me that book is a summ'at terrible burden if her husband once decided he wanted it back. And well he might a'cause it holds much that a man wouldn't want spread abroad. He sounds like a nasty piece of work does ship's master, Bartholomew Fenwick.

Anyways, just when I thought I might drift off that night, the thunder passed over and little Henry Charles - we do call him Hal - being suckled off to sleep, there was such a tumult down the stairs it was enough to stir the dust off the doorframe by my head. Grace sat bolt upright and grabbed my wrist. She looked terrified but before she could say ought we all knew the name of the fellow outside a'cause he was a-banging and a-hollering, calling out his rank, his ship and all, demanding to be let in under pain of Parliament's this and that. Our guard, a man who was particular about his authority, said ship's law held no sway here inland, especially with such unmannerly carrying on. Captain Fenwick's tone turned then, all silky tones and mollifying. He said there had been a terrible misunderstanding. His wife had been swept up in the day's events and was now shut up in this place by mistake. He was come to take care of her.

Now, that would never be the truth and both Grace and I knew it.

I could see her eyes, wide with fright, glinting in the moonlight. The other women, suspecting nothing, just muttered that he was a man who was moon-mad, but it must have smelled a bit fishy to the churchwarden. With some shuffling of his papers, next thing we heard was he, crying back through the barred door that there was no woman called Fenwick on the list.

"Medium height, slim, she's red-headed; she's got an infant with her! My ...daughter!" came the response.

He'd had half a chance of being right, and it sent chills down my spine to hear it. Grace's hand went to the matted mess of her chestnut curls.

"Sir, all of these poor wights are but skin and bone, may God help them! And no, there's no girl child here. There's a baby boy but his mother is Widow Mattock and she's swarthy, dark haired!" came back our protector.

Her hands now clenched tight so they were white at the knuckles, her eyes tight shut, Grace was quietly praying,

"Please, dear Lord, let the warden not mention me for, even under my new name, especially my new name, the fiend will know…" I clutched Hal, who was beginning to grizzle at the rumpus, rocking and hushing him as best I could.

Now, though I b'aint be a clever sort, I have had cause to ponder God and all His mysteries. I reckon that He, being awful busy, would not harken to a wayward, sinning lass like me, but I am sure He was listening to Grace that night, for next thing there was a right un-gentlemanly cursing. After a last two-fisted thump upon the door, the noise of footsteps on the stones outside gradually faded away, the horses' hooves clattered off into the distance until all was quiet again. The parish sentry down below called up,

"No need to alarm yourselves, good folk. You have nothing to fear in God's house and its environs." That was all very well, thought I, but what happens when we were beyond His walls? Grace and me lay awake with no chance of sleep from then on, holding hands for comfort.

In the early morning light, before the church chimes rang six, we heard a gaggle of voices approaching, women this time. The village wives had brought pots and bowls, all with a milky gruel. They said it would give us something for our bellies; help us face what the day would bring. Some had carried with them ragged garments, cast-off threadbare items, which they gave out where most needed. For us there was a handful of old but serviceable napkins, fresh wrappings for Henry Charles and a cap and some worn linen to serve as a head-wrap. I heard one woman, close to tears, ask why we should be shown such kindness. A Cornish accent, softly replied,

"My man, he was with Godolphin's regiment. He came home to me. But I look at you and think there but for the Grace of God go I," and, quieter still, added, "Long live the King!" Twenty voices answered, 'Amen'.

Not long after the villagers left, the churgeon who'd tended us arrived. He and his helper went among the women. He spoke kindly, asking all manner of questions,

"Are you managing to drink? Sweetened water…good but if you are offered food, eat but a very little at a time and slowly, slowly. How does your heart beat…regular and steady or fluttering, fast?" Some who were particular feeble he set aside. The rest clambered onto the wagons and back we went to the encampment. As we jolted along, I said to Grace,

"Why is it you and I still stand when others, better than we, are ailing badly?"

"I cannot say" she sighed. "Perhaps we have a hardiness born of having to endure difficulties even before we came to this place?"

"Not God's punishment, like the preacher said, then?" I asked. Grace's look darkened,

"What wrong did Mary Tremayne ever do that should draw down Heaven's wrath?" Now and then Grace was a tad snappish, but what she said was true. Mistress Tremayne was one of the kindest women I had ever met. She might have defied her family to marry the man she loved, and joined her husband at Pendennis when he bade her stay at home, but I thought God could not find fault in that.

The camp that had grown up to blockade Pendennis, yesterday thronged with folk, was much emptier now. Most of the soldiery had moved up to the castle. I decided that the red-coated regiments were welcome to have the flea-ridden billets we'd given up.

That morn was the first I had ever looked at the fort from a distance - from the land anyway. When I arrived by boat t'was on the other shore. There you could only see walls like cliffs above you. It looked so different from down here. Perhaps I was mazed with sleeplessness or just in a haze from lacking food, but it seemed to me that Pendennis, squat and solid on the headland, was watching us all. Not caring what King's men or Parliament's did, it just watched.

Still, I weren't too mazed to know that amongst the soldiers was a danger. We were in full view of everyone including Grace's husband; there'd be no hiding here. The soldiers were still checking on us and I had to get my papers out again, taking Hal from his mother to keep up the ruse we had begun the day before. We answered more questions. I hoped Grace would remember the fibs we had woven round the truth. Eventually, my head aching fit to burst, they sent us to another queue, to await a wagon to take us to a ship.

Just as Master Haslock had told us, the folk whose papers allowed them to return to Devon would go by sea, to Yalme. That could have been in Africk as far as I knew, but Grace said it was just east of Plymouth. From Yalme we would have to make our own way to our new life up on the moor. If we got there. I didn't trust the sea but there was another problem.

You could say that we had gone from a frying pan into the fire. We knew that one of the boats standing off Penryn was Master Fenwick's. If that was the ship with the orders to take us up the coast, and if his past actions were anything to go by, the chance of Grace and me making it any further than St Antony Head or Pendennis Point was as slim as a reed. Nay, slimmer.

So, what to do? Should we try to dodge the Parliament's men, maybe use womanly wiles to make our way by land? I'd rest easier for I did not like being on the sea. Yet in the spring, even before Parliament had tightened their hold on matters, when Mary Tremayne and me fled to our men at Pendennis Castle, it was plain to see how things would be with sentries posted along every road. Our papers would give the lie to anything we said, and stop us getting any further than the first checkpoint. I did not think that would be very far.

Could we fake some new passes? Well, Grace might, a'cause she could write. I could not, or not enough anyway, though t'wouldn't be the first time I had travelled on false papers. Me and Mary had made a reasonable job of meddling with an old permit to suit our ends when we needed it back in

March. Now though, we had no ink and to try to steal some from under a soldier's nose was plain folly.

"Shall I feign some sickness, do you think?" I said to Grace, as we watched other folk march off or climb into carts to be sent to heaven knew where. "I remember Mary and me tried out frebitachio fundementata on some soldiery when we ran away from Kestle Wartha ..."

Grace nearly choked at that. She was laughing but trying to hide it so as not to draw eyes to us. That sound was rare; I'd not heard my friend laugh for a long time. It may be she did not truly find it funny, being perhaps a little over-stretched with tension. Still, t'was proof she could still smile which was good enough.

"*What* did you say it was?"

"'Tiddn't a real sickness. We made it up, a reason to be on the road to seek a midwife when I was ...the babe, little Will..."

I wish it did not hurt to say his name, my little boy. He would have brought such gladness. They said he had died as he was born, never taking a breath in this world. That was why I was able to nurse Hal, when his mama's milk dried. Grace and me, we have uncommon bonds.

"No, Hester! I do not think that we could convince anyone of ...what did you call it? Frebid-what?" Her grin was catchin' and I giggled, sounding out the fancy words,

"Freb-it-ach-io fund-e-men-tata. We convinced one troop of Parliament's soldiers with it. They all said it was a catching disease and let us past! But you think it would not work again?"

"I do say so, and so would Surgeon Haslock, you ninny." The laughter fled as fast as it had come and Grace finished grimly,

"We will have to hope that there is some other solution."

We sat, the sun beaming down through new-washed skies, all the mugginess of yesterday cleared by the night's storm. Hal was wriggly, peevish. I tried to keep his little head shaded but it was a struggle. A screaming child would mark us out so Grace and I took turns to dandle him and walk about as far as we were allowed, which wasn't far. Everywhere there was a stench of folk, unwashed. I had never noticed it in the fort, but now it was so thick you could cut it. I suppose me and Grace didn't smell too sweet either come to think on't.

T'was on one circuit of the ropes that I overheard the orders for the little boats being readied to take us to the Devon-bound vessel anchored in the deeper channel. I tried not to be too obvious, bouncing the baby on my hip and pretending to babble to him but all the time listening as hard as I could.

I hurried back to Grace, sitting on the parched dirt, her head resting on her knees, arms clasped across the back of her neck. Getting down close beside her, I whispered,

"What did you say Fenw..." I dared not say his name for fear of being overheard by the company around us. "What is HIS ship called?"

"She was the *Ann of Bristol* when she was my father's; after Fenwick became a turn-coat they renamed her *Leopard*," she replied, heavily. It was the name we'd heard shouted the night before but, fuddle-headed, I had not been able to remember.

"Then, Grace, I do believe we may be safe. I could hear them talking. Our vessel is not the *Leopard*. It's the *Swiftsure*. The sailors are coming to fetch us in the row-boats. 'Twill be within the half-hour!"

In the event, it was more than that for some dimwit had muddled up the lieutenant's lists and all was confusion. Still, by evening we were aboard. When we asked to stay in the open air rather than take shelter, the sailors didn't seem to care one way or t'other and Grace did not mind that I would not go below. She knew the very thought of it brought back bad memories of the last time I was at sea.

As darkness fell on our second night of freedom, for all I felt zaundy with the rocking and bouncing deck, I was happy, for now we were on our way to a new life, to Cornwood.

III Mary: Correspondence from Pendennis Castle

Written this ~~17th~~ 18th day of August 1646
From my sickbed, Pendennis Castle.

Loving Papa,
I pray that when you receive this you are in good health. The dutiful and loving wishes of your daughter come with this letter. Forgive my errors or that which that I forget to write for my mind and body are weak. Our own surgeon Richard Wiseman did tell me that I should expect nothing less, it being the effect of deprivation on a gentle constitution but I wish that it were not so for there are so many here who want for care ~~and who I should be tending instead of lying abed~~.
I forget that it is no longer my duty but that of others. There is provision for the care of the sick and I suppose I must be counted as one of that number. They will let me ~~come home~~ leave here as soon as may be.
Yesterday we could hear the drums and trumpets sounding as Sir John Arundel led out those who were able of body at the formalities of the Surrender. Lewis went at the head of his men, much fewer now, but having seen to it that they were assigned their rightful terms under the articles he was allowed to return today. There is much official business to be done, and Lewis is still called on castle business, required to sign and countersign endless papers, being one of the old Council of War here who is still able.
We have new faces to tend us. They are kind enough, working under Parliament's Surgeon Haslock. He is a compassionate man who has provided the tools for me to write to you.
How are my sisters? Has Agnes finished the new coverlet for her bed? Tell her that ~~when I come home again~~ to stitch and spend our hours in gentle talk ~~will~~ would be my delight. Then I will tell her of the adventures of two women who I now

16

count amongst my dearest friends. The sweet and tender care and the companionship that we have shared these last months has bound us tight, ~~better than some real sisters~~. My own travels through the perils of the recent years seem as nothing to theirs. Yet, I fear that their travails are not yet ended. Should ever they need succour I beg that Mistress Grace Fenwick and Mistress Hester Phipps would find it at Penwarne, for my sake.

It seems our woes must continue unless matters now come to a good conclusion for His Majesty. The good surgeon tells me that the King is still with the Scots. Lewis says that he ~~will~~ might serve His Highness the Prince of Wales. He believes His Highness to be in Jersey but supposes he will soon go to Paris, to Her Majesty the Queen.

I know Lewis has hopes of news of his old commander, Sir Richard Grenvile. We know not where he is. With his brother Sir Bevil dead and Bevil's son John being with the Prince, the Grenvile's old house at Stowe must be too quiet.

Soon Trerice Manor will have the homecoming of Sir John and Richard Arundel though. The family will mourn John's death but Lady Mary will surely welcome Richard's wife; Gertrude and the children will make the old hall lively again. His wife will see a great change in Uncle John and will have her needle and thread out within minutes to put his doublet and breeches aright, for they hang like sacks, which of course would not do at all for Aunt Mary. Do you recall the stir she made over the suit of clothes he brought from London? She said they fitted only where they touched which in truth was not much. It has helped these months to keep in mind the family remembrances that commonly made us smile before.

~~Did I mention that the Parliament's surgeon Haslock is tending me?~~ Surgeon Haslock came yesterday late in the morning, before the marching out, because there was urgent need for care for Sir Henry Killigrew. Sir Henry has done much to keep tempers calm in these last days. Many desperate men with their officers, led by Digby, had plans to take much of the great store of gunpowder to blow up the

keep and under cover of that disorder, charge out and die with as many of the enemy as they could take. They would do that rather than surrender. Their hot-headed leader has often been rebuked for ungentlemanly challenges to our Governor. Sir Henry prevented that matter.

But Henry suffered an injury from the discharge of his pistol inside the keep, an act which was by way of marking the surrender with a flourish of bravado and an extravagance of powder. But it was carelessly done, whereby a great splinter of wood gave Sir Henry a wide gash upon his forehead. Despite his wound, Master Haslock tells me that his patient insists that he will take ship for France.

The ~~conquerors~~ officers with Parliament's authority have been into the infirmary with their lists to count us. They take our names and describe us in their register, our stature, colouring and so forth, even the women.

Dear Papa, this morning Lewis came to show me our pass to leave this place.

Richard Fortescue's signature lies at the foot of the page and that is so contrary when, in May, the very same Colonel and Lewis were bitterly in dispute over the wrongful detention of Lewis' father. They are most civil and deal with each other as if it never happened. Now though one is the victor and the other vanquished, which changes everything, of course.

I will tell you how our permit reads for only in such a way might I break my news more gently. The paper is small even though it contains such solemn matters:

"Suffer the bearer hereof Colonel Lewis Tremayne with his servants, arms, horses and goods quietly to pass unto St Ewe or any other place within the Parliament's quarters or beyond the seas about their particular employments without any search, plunder or injury, they also being to have the benefit of the Articles upon the Surrender of the Castle of Pendennis."

You see, Lewis has had to declare his intentions and I can no longer avoid that which I dread to write, for putting it in black upon the page makes it more immediate.

Lewis has chosen exile. Under the terms of surrender there will be a ship provided.

I cannot hope to be at Kestle Wartha where I wanted to make our home. We will be allowed to come to St Ewe, to Heligan and to Lewis' father, to stay only for as long as it takes for me to regain some strength. Yet I hope in those few days to be allowed to come the few miles to visit at Penwarne.

Then I will leave for I must go with him. I cannot rest here in the kind folds of Cornwall's southern coast, hiding like a fugitive and fretting from hour to hour. I need to stand alongside the man for whom I defied convention and with whom I have shared this siege. I have survived fear and famine and will do so again as long as I can be with him.

I truly hope that you can understand that, although it fills me with despair, the parting from those who I hold dear need hold no terrors for nothing is to be feared if I am by my husband's side.

I hope to be well enough to travel with Lewis, but if not, when he sends for me to go to him, to Jersey or France or wherever the Prince of Wales' Court is to be, then I shall go. While I am distant, my correspondence will keep us close. Honour, loyalty, pride - and hope - will inform my days and when you will read of me, you will know that the cords that tie us are unbreakable.

Your loving daughter,
Mary Tremayne
To John Carew,
The Manor of Penwarne
By Mevagissey in the county of Cornwall.

Written this 20th day of August 1646
From Pendennis Castle.
A packet enclosed.

Honoured sir,
I greet you with the hope that this letter finds you in the best of health.
Your son, Lewis was only able to write the enclosed few lines in haste but bade me inform you of how matters stand. For any omissions, I beg your forgiveness. My health is improving, for which I thank God and surgeon Wiseman who with the Parliament's man, Haslock, has come daily to oversee the care of the weakest.
Lewis received your correspondence which was graciously directed to him by Richard Fortesque.
It is to our regret that brother Philip refused all advice to return to Heligan. Lewis would have had at least one son return home.
It gives me great sorrow to hear that both Heligan and Kestle Wartha have suffered ~~at the hands of ill disciplined troops~~*. I suspected that our home had been ransacked for as I made my way here in March I saw the stuff of my bed-hangings fluttering at the tip of a pike-stave, which was a cruel mockery when Sir Thomas Fairfax had promised clemency to Cornish folk. My sister and I spent many hours stitching those cloths and to see them treated in such a callous way* ~~renders~~ *rendered me no friend to the Roundheads then.*
It would please me if you could let me know some specifics of the damage. It would help to while away the hours if I could plan how I might restore the farmhouse ~~in anticipation of our return~~*.*
But, dear sir, I stray from the reason for my letter which gives me as much grief to pen as it will for you to receive.
We were led to believe that we would be able to pass a few days at St Ewe, to restore our fortitude and to pay our affectionate respects to you; to Lewis' sisters and to those we love at Penwarne. This will not now be possible.

The vessels are now readying to take those who wish ~~to join His Highness~~ *to go to the continent. Some ships have already departed for Devon and to Wales. We will embark for St Malo. If it is of any consolation, our surgeon Mr. Wiseman will take ship with us so you may believe I will be in good hands.*

In the enclosed I believe Lewis has explained in as much detail as time allows. We now trust to the Lord's guidance and His mercy though we depart with heavy hearts.

I have little of worth to add and less that would bring comfort to you or my father except that there are a few of our lads to return to St Ewe, and Goodwife Morrish will be relieved to know that Hugh will soon be home with her.

There has been a strange occurrence and coincidence here. I am uneasy at it but Lewis assures me that there can be no harm. Yet I would also have you know how things are. You are wise and not unfamiliar with the contemptible ways of men.

You will recall what Lewis told you of that terrible episode in '44 when, were it not for the courage of Gunner Sark, Lewis would have drowned at the hands of Admiral Stanley and another, Captain Fenwick?

It seems that during these last weeks, one ship joining the fleet that blockaded Pendennis is that of the same man. During the time of negotiations, one of our envoys overheard a conversation which, when reported to Lewis, alerted him to the scoundrel's presence.

Being in no ways able to do otherwise, Lewis sent word to the man as an old acquaintance in an unfortunate circumstance, respectfully asking after his wife, though for safety's sake neglecting to reveal his own identity.

Fenwick sent civil words back but the strangest of all was that he insisted that his wife had died of the plague years before. Yet I have come to know Grace Fenwick. She is my friend and is very much alive, though the circumstance of our meeting will take more time to explain than this pen or my wits can presently stand.

Nonetheless, I state on my honour, that I believe that the depth of this man's evilness is unfathomable. His past actions are those of a monster. I can only pray that in time he will be brought to justice.

At present, I can give you no place to which you can send correspondence. As soon as Lewis has word you may be assured that he will write, until which time we remain, sir, your most dutiful and loving children.

Mary Tremayne

In haste: we have just heard we are to board this evening, the ship to St Malo is the Leopard.

Keep us in your prayers. MT

To John Carew,

At Heligan,

St. Ewe in the county of Cornwall

IV Grace: Of the past

You will never remember your first voyage, being but five months old, but we were blessed by reasonable weather and light SW winds, which made for comfortable sailing to Yalme. Despite this, poor Hester was desperately unhappy, which is not surprising, given her experience on the high seas. The only ship on which she had ever sailed had made its last passage from Bristol and was wrecked off North Cornwall. Hester was a convict, a thief, bound for the plantations. Yet by divine intervention, I believe true justice was done on that rocky coast since a young woman who had gone astray was given a chance of salvation. She survived because the shackles which should have held her slipped her wrists and so, though she was washed ashore half drowned, she was destined to live and we were fated to meet again.

It is little wonder that the thought of being aboard another vessel, once more heading into the unknown, made her uneasy.

Conversely, I felt better at sea than I had for months and was able to reflect that I had not been good company for Hester. Despite everything she was always patient with me. I knew that I would forever be grateful for her nourishing you. Now I had to remind myself that a future was Hester's gift to me too, no matter where that was to be. Ultimately, I owe Hester nothing less than my life.

I had to keep a watchful eye upon the crew who I saw eying us and our belongings and whose intentions I would not have trusted an inch. We made ourselves scarce, tucked tight into a corner between the steps to the fo'c'sle and a sail-locker, only stirring to collect our ration of broth with some biscuit-like bread and a piece of hard cheese. It had been so long since I had tasted something strong that when I bit into the cheese it seemed to burn the roof of my mouth. As Hester could hardly face food at all, I made some sops of the bread for her, remembering the surgeon's words of caution. The lumps of cheese I rolled into a spare napkin and packed away. Some gruel in the early morning helped her a little, but the hours could not pass fast enough.

Hester would be able to tell you of my father, Henry Godwynne, though she had left our house in Wine Street before his death. You are named after him. He was a gentle man, a scholar and a successful merchant. His trade would have been even more lucrative had the war not intervened for he had benefited from the proceeds of a voyage under Letters of Marque for the King.

I suspect that my father would have liked to command his own ship, but he suffered crippling bouts of sea-sickness. Only once did he take to the ocean. That was in a desperate attempt to flee the blackness that engulfed him when my mother died, taking passage on his own ship, the *Ann of Bristol*, with John Vickery as Master. John was a man who understood my father, who helped him to restore his faith in life. Father never got the chance to show him our gratitude for Captain Vickery was murdered so that another could obtain command of his vessel.

I had made the acquaintance of Bartholomew Fenwick - or I should say he made his presence known - in that period while father was away. The merchants and ship owners of the city were a close fraternity so, on reflection, it seems strange that Captain Fenwick should become so embedded in the community. He is not a West Country man, but from the north east of England, learning his trade on the collier ships taking sea-coal to London, moving into the trade in Welsh coal. It was but a small matter to exploit Bristol's opportunities. He was astute enough to know where and when to make his mark, so much so that father was persuaded that Captain Fenwick was the best replacement for John Vickery and also a man with whom he could invest his daughter's future.

It would not have mattered if either of my brothers, Henry or Edward, still lived. Henry and father had a bitter falling-out after the death of mother but father never disowned him, always loved him. He missed his son, always known as Hal, as you are. Father's death would have seen your uncle, my elder brother, by then an experienced factor in his own right, return home from wherever he happened to be. He would have run the family concern, and honoured father's memory. If matters had been different, perhaps they would have been reconciled, for Hal must have been returning to Bristol when he died.

It was an accident, they said, on the same voyage that the *Ann* made to bring armaments from Antwerp for the King's cause in August '43. And by then Bartholomew Fenwick was the captain of the *Ann*.

Edward, boisterous, energetic Ned, younger than Hal by a few years, would not have made a good merchant, I think, even though he also spent some time in London, apprenticed to one of father's contacts, a merchant of standing in the city. Ned, who had hoped to enter a college at Oxford to study the law, said that being sent to London had felt like an exile. It happened so very fast, father arranging it after an angry outburst when his black gloom was at its worst. Even in London Ned's gregarious nature could not be subdued for long and apprentices will find friends. When the storm between His Majesty and Parliament finally broke, the city raised regiments of the apprenticed lads to fight against the King. I knew that had set our father and Ned even more at odds, though father said nothing of it. Still, Ned wrote of the comradeship, his pride in his uniform and the skills he was learning with pike and sword. The pike and sword took him to Aldbourne Chase.

It was barely six weeks after the news of Hal's death had brought us to our knees that a letter from Prince Rupert himself told me that Ned had been killed in battle. Why a prince should be the bearer of our bad tidings is a strange enough tale to relate; that the same prince should apologise for the incident that brought about such a tragedy seems hardly credible at all. Yet men are often not what they seem and I believe the Prince to be a man with a good heart.

Thus your grandfather's other son was snatched from him. By then father was ailing too, from a sickness neither the apothecary nor the barber-surgeon could neither explain nor blame on wartime deprivation. His skin looked bruised and mottled. Though the bouts would come and go, there was no doubt that his health was deteriorating; he was eating less and less and yet swelling monstrously.

Father was anxious to ensure that I would have security but he had to submit to the conventions of the Society that ruled the merchants of our city: a daughter could not inherit his business. Since his appointment and more so after the start of the war, Master Fenwick had made himself almost indispensable, and he had been given permission to pay court to me. Though my father believed that the submissive, agreeable face that Fenwick presented in company at Wine Street was sincere, I had reason to think otherwise, as did others in the household. Nevertheless, he decreed that I should marry Bartholomew Fenwick.

Your grandfather did not live to witness the ceremony. I can tell you the poison that killed him. I have it, noted, in a book. And, although a battlefield wound took Ned's life, the same book gives me good cause to believe that your Uncle Henry's death was not an accident.

I once believed that I would live a quiet existence, with a good husband whom I would love, honour and respect, content to defer to him in all things. He would be a father to sons and daughters and I would devote myself to them and to him. Yet life is seldom the stuff of dreams. When I married it was to a man I could not love and life was anything but peaceful. Since All Saint's Day 1643, my husband has owned the assets of the Godwynne business but I will never defer to him. I cannot honour or respect him. Nor will devote myself to his son. For Bartholomew Fenwick is not your father.

V Hester: From the coast to Cornwood

I have never been so glad to feel the earth beneath my feet as the day I set down on the shore of the place they called Yalme. I didn't even trouble that when I clambered over the side I splashed into the shallows and soaked the hem of my skirts. What was a bit of wet and some fustian flapping round my shins? I was on firm ground without a drenching or a drowning so I was as happy as the day is long. Mind, I was summ'at weak and t'was strange how the earth beneath me felt as if it was rolling like the deck of the ship. Still, we were on dry land again and I had plenty to be grateful for. Most of all, I had that bit of paper that Will left for me, so despite everything, even with the empty place in my chest when I thought of my man, I had hopefulness.

Just as when we left Cornwall, t'was the small boats that rowed us to shore. Sailors have a mighty rare sense of humour for they called the ship's boat the jolly. Other punts, boats much like the ones I'd watched when I lived in Bideford, came alongside and were loaded according to folk's destinations. Those who had the furthest to go shipped first. Cornwood was quite near, the officer told us, a dozen miles or less, so it was mid morning before I had to face the slimy rope ladder down the ship's side. Fumble-fingered with fright and knees a-knocking, I slipped the last rung, landing on my backside in the bottom of the boat. The oarsmen sniggered. I couldn't think of anything sharp to say so I just glowered. I can tell you, there was nothing jolly about me just then.

With Grace, the baby and our bags stowed safe, they rowed us to a small scattering of cottages that seemed hardly big enough to need the name of a harbour. It felt summ'at odd as we got bustled through the village. There were watchers in every doorway as the Parliament's men made sure we went on our way. I've never been one to trouble about going to new places and so maybe it was the time spent closed up in the castle which had changed me, but I thought to myself that I would have to get used to meeting strangers again and quickly, for where we were going I knew nobody.

Anyways, the three of us set off up the hill on the road inland. We took turns either carrying Hal or the rattling pack of scant belongings we shared. Grace didn't have anything very useful; that battered book, a horn-backed brush and a blanket. The book and the blanket had a rancid smell of boat-tar that made me feel like being sick every time I caught a whiff; the hairbrush she treasured as if it was made of gold, being panicked if it wasn't to hand. Not that Grace is vain, but it was a gift from...well, suffice to say, it was a gift. In a separate knot, Grace had tied up a pair of breeches and a doublet, threadbare clothes she'd worn when she adventured through Wales after her husband tried to drown her. She said she'd kept them against the season when an extra layer for warmth might be welcome or a few pennies could be got by selling them. There are laws against a lass wearing a man's clothes: mind, there are laws against husbands drowning their wives too.

We headed north following the traders' track that led to the skirt of Dartmoor. Occasionally we caught a glimpse of the moor in the distance, all grey and hazy looking for all like a sleeping giant wrapped in a rust-stained cloak. 'T'was surprising we met no soldiers on the road, but on the outskirts of Yealmpton - which was busy enough - a picket blocked our way, manned by smart fellows in almost-new red coats. I could sense Grace was all edgy. The sergeant looked an ill-favoured lump, round shoulders and sagging belly, the cut of the bright doublet doing him no favours.

I expected a deal of questions a'cause the pass must have shown them where we had come from. Yet the chap barely glanced at our papers and there wasn't even a raised eyebrow, he just waved us on, almost friendly and not at all what I'd expected from a battle-hardened Roundhead. As we walked away, I nudged Grace's arm, pulling a face, chayneeeyed and blowing a puff of relief. She shushed me, shaking her head,

"Not here! We're not safe, not yet!" but I was pleased to catch the twitch of a grin on her lips. By the church, we set our bundle down for a while. Hal was sleeping. While we rested in the shade, we pondered the strangeness of us passing unremarked.

"'Tis not a'cause there was no fighting in these parts," I said, "for I once knew a lad who marched from Bideford. We heard later that he was at the fight at Modbury and that's not too far from here a'cause I overheard one of the lads on our boat say that was where he was going."

"And Plymouth has been a Parliament stronghold since the outset of the war, besieged for years. Yet those lads looked as if they could barely manage a skirmish, let alone a battle."
I had an unkind thought and spoke it,

"Perhaps them's just laggards?"

"Or maybe conscripts with no real convictions, merely new jackets?" Grace added, wryly. "On the other hand, the war has been over for many months for everyone except us. Perhaps all of England is a now tranquil place? We must hope that this mood prevails wherever we go." Amen to that, thought I.

A young girl, with a shallow tray perched on her hip, swayed her way towards us along the street and a'cause she smiled as she passed, I smiled back. I caught sight of pots of scalded cream in the basket and I'd have spent some of the coin Parliament gave us on a dish of the thick sweetness but, remembering Surgeon Haslock's warning that our stomachs needed gentling, I thought better of asking. I didn't fancy the cheese or the bit of bread we'd saved. There was nothing to ease anyone's belly in that, for sure, since both were so hard that David could have used them to sling at Goliath.

Grace must have been thinking the same, for she asked the dairymaid where we might buy some simple fare. But it seemed that Yealmpton's welcome didn't stretch to selling victuals to strangers. She told us right directly that there was little to be had, nobody selling anything anyway and if we were travelling, we had best aim to be with our kin by suppertime. Pointing out the road we should take, she hitched up her tray and scurried down a narrow lane between two cottages.

In the event, we did find a small alehouse where a goodwife with a face like a walnut skin agreed to sell us a farthing's worth of small ale. I reckoned it was short measure but as beggars can't be choosy, I kept quiet. We drank the bigger part between us which was enough to quench a little of my thirst. The rest we used to soak the bread to a pulp. It hardly made for fine eating but at least it didn't risk our teeth. The cheese was left in its wrapping.

The sun was well past its highest when we picked ourselves up and set off again. I was minded to ask Grace if she recalled the day a'cause I had lost track, being sick at sea and all. She was some moments thinking before she pronounced that she thought perhaps it was Friday, maybe Saturday but she was sure it was not yet Sunday, the end of the third week of August. She asked me why I wanted to know.

"I was just wondering," I replied. T'was little matter but that today would have marked my birthday. Nobody but my husband had ever thought to mark it.

Anyways, up and down went the road, us passing fields striped with country folk, bringing in the harvest. Despite the blue sky, there was a hazy ring around the sun, a sure sign that the weather was on the turn, so the farm-hands were too busy to take much note of two scruffy women passing by.

Once I'd have thought nothing of a day's walk, ten miles and more. Now, by the time we were trudging through the valley winding toward Cornwood, I could barely put one foot in front t'other. Grace was no better. I could think of nothing but food, no matter how I tried. And my poor feet! The holes in my socks were sticky with blood from the broken blisters. Late in the afternoon, we stopped so I was able to suckle the babe and though I was sorely tempted to dangle my feet in the cool water of the river I dared not. If I took off those shoes I knew I'd never put them on again. It was only faith in

Will that kept me going. That and the hope of a kind word, a place to call home.

We dragged the last mile and reached a little bridge below the village where the road forked. A church bell clanged someway off up the hill. It was a doleful chime. The light was getting dimmety now and harvesters would soon as like be returning from the meadows. Feeling a proper lummock, I had no notion of which way to choose. Will never told me just zackerly where his home was, all'us expecting to be taking me there himself so I had no notion of where to look for his ma's place, where he'd lived before the war.

Another clanking, a working sound, was ringing from along the lower lane, so I chose that road. It led past a forge. The smith, a brawny fellow, was using the last of the light to finish shoeing a scraggy mare. I saw him take the measure of us over his shoulder, the horse's hoof still clamped between his knees. I thought he would surely know Mistress Mattock so I reckoned I would ask. But when I went to speak I could say naught. My tongue went dry so all I could do was croak.

'Hester,' I said to myself, 'What ails 'ee! You must do better than that!' The blacksmith must have thought the same for he turned back to his work, only setting the nag free when Grace stepped forward. She spoke to him quietly, Hal in her arms,

"Good even', sir. We seek for Mistress Mattock, William Mattock's mother. We would be grateful if you could you direct us to her home." Grace must have had summ'at about her and so he acted a tad more respectful, answering gruffly,

"Will went from this village a long while ago and his mother's had nary a word of him since." He cocked his head side-a-ways, eyes narrowed. "And what business do you have, that I should send you to trouble Goody Mattock?" I could just imagine Will's poor ma, shrunken and wrapped in a shawl, mourning her lad but all the whiles hoping he would walk though the door. My eyes filled with tears, but less sentimental, Grace weren't one to beat about the bush,

"This woman is William Mattock's wife."

The man just shouldered the hammer he was wielding, tipped his head back and guffawed,

"Oh, aye! And I be the King of Sweden!" His tone turned nasty. "Look-ee, mistress-whosoever! Peg Mattock has her own burdens, without two twily churns carrying a brat darkening her door. And we'll have no beggars here! Move on or I'll fetch the constable!"

I found my voice then,

"I pray, sir, don't do that! We b'aint bad women. My friend tells the truth. I *am* William's lawful wife! See! Here ..." and I started to struggle to unpack the Bible where I kept my precious papers.

"If 'tis so, then where is 'ee?" scowled the blacksmith.

"He was soldiering but I was with him ... he was made a sergeant, a King's man, and we were at Pendennis fort and I... he ..."

I faltered, stopped hauling at the baggage, all my strength suddenly gone.

I had begun to cope with the stillbirth of my son. I had even found the heart to raise the occasional smile even though my husband was dead. I had an inheritance of sorts, though I would need to learn quick if the brew house was to thrive. I wanted to do whatever Will would have done to help his ma, even if I had to make a new start in a strange place. Truth to tell, though I had nowhere else to go, my resolve was fast ebbing away.

I just managed the words,

"I was Will's wife, sir. Now I am his widow!" before the tears came, and to save my life I could not stop them. I sank into the dust and wept as I had not wept in all that wretched year; since the terror of fleeing, heavy with child, to seek my man; since the death of my baby; through the hunger; the sickness; and the misery of losing the gentle giant who won my heart. I could no more have stopped the flood than Noah did.

Grace told me later that the oaf, in turns shamefaced and surly, kept mumbling,

"God's nails, hush wench! You'll frighten the mare! You be mazed as a brush!" She reminded him that all we had asked was for directions to find Goodwife Mattock. He still looked sour but under his breath said,

"Reckon he died fighting for a cause ... honourable enough in a fellow, no matter what ... and you being a woman ..." He grudgingly swung our pack onto his shoulder, and led us, me snivelling, Hal grizzling, along the road.

Before long, under trees where two lanes met, he pointed to a low, shabby building, the roof sagging and the canopy over the door all skewed. It looked for all as if it would fall down at the slightest tap, only propped up by two rough tree trunks. It hardly looked a thriving sort of place but then, if this was Will's home, there'd been no man here for years.

Our guide slowed his pace, letting us walk on. Then as if he didn't want to be overheard, he muttered,

"There!" and began backing the way we'd come, saying, "You'll need to knock hard, for it's as like she'll not hear you by this time of the day and the girls are still in the fields." Then he turned on his heel and scuttled back to the forge.

We stood there for some minutes, me trying to compose myself, trying to think what to say to Goody Mattock. I imagined all manner of dire things happening when we broke our grievous news. What if she was part addle-pated with age? It could send her quite mad. What if she suffered a fit of the palsy? I knew it had happened to Mary Tremayne's pa when he learned that his son had died. What to do? I was a cat's whisker from turning around and walking away when the door opened.

Raucous shouting echoed round Cornwood coombe. A wiry little man dodged out, clutching his hat followed swiftly by something metal, flung through the air. It barely missed his head. As he made off down the lane, a woman came appeared. Bent almost double, she hollered and cussed at the runaway, threatening to tan his nether parts the minute she caught up with him. He didn't tarry to see if she would keep her word, but lifted his heels and made off into the gloom.

33

She scanned the roadway, and slowly picking up the tankard, gradually stood upright, unfurling like a hedgepig, and just as prickly. Now her shoulders were level with the top of the door, standing with her hands on her hips, patched skirts swaying as she teetered slightly. Then she let out a girt big belch.

I needn't have worried about fright, nor palsy, or a frail old lady trembling with dread. 'Twas only the one person whose dear face had ever born the same wild eyebrows as the woman across the way or whose stature matched hers inch for inch.

Sticking out a dimpled chin, bristled almost as bravely as her son's, she let out another belch, then, spying Grace and me flinching in the shadows, she leered forward and bellowed,

"God's dines, what now! You over there with a face like last week's jakes! Who d'you think you're gawping at?"

The woman duddered with drink and glaring at me through the twilight was Goody Mattock, my mother-in-law.

VI Mary: An exile writes home

Written this 23rd day of September 1646
St Malo
At the sign of the Fiddle and Tabor

Dearest Agnes,
I hope that this letter finds you well, also too my sisters
Bridget and Grace. I would that you give them both a fond
embrace on my behalf. Does Candacia still lodge at Antony?
If she has returned from Aunt Carew's domain ~~then I should~~
~~be pleased if you would pass on my regards~~ I trust she ~~is well~~
~~arrived safely   has lost her mean spirit~~ is well.
How is papa's health? I fear that the shock of Lewis and I
having to take ship so quickly might impact upon him, and
nothing would weigh heavier upon me than my family suffer
as a result of my actions - though the good Lord knows, it is
far from being within my power to change matters.
Much of what I write will be of a rhetorical nature for I know
that there is only a small chance that you will receive my
letters and less chance that any reply will find me. If they
remain intact it will be a miracle.
Lewis says that we shall soon make shift to join the Prince of
Wales. That is not any state secret so I may tell you. He
hopes also to be reunited with Sir Richard Grenvile in His
Majesty's cause. You see how unlikely it is that our
correspondence can be frequent.
And yet, dear sis, I will write while I can. It may be that my
exchanges will reassure if not entertain you.
To date, three ships have voyaged from Cornwall to France
with a miscellany of His Majesty's army, a few soldiers but
mainly officers and gentlemen. We have heard no word of
Philip, which is a matter of great concern.

The passage across was unpleasant, so different from the last trip I undertook by boat, though my emotions ran as high. Mevagissey to Looe is nothing more than a skim across a lake in comparison to crossing the channel, though I am happy to say I was not overtaken by sea-sickness as others were. Even battle-hardened men were laid low, hanging over the ship's side to puke, their faces the colour of Goody Butland's pastry dough.

I thought the passengers would be imbued with heavy hearts but it was not so (sea-sickness apart). There were many pledges to return, armed and with every resource to bring the King to his own again.

If wishing it were so could make it happen, then His Majesty would have been at Whitehall by Michaelmas.

Lewis would, I think have preferred to land at Jersey or Guernsey, but since His Highness, the Prince of Wales, who Lewis would serve, left there two months since and looks not to return, then he will of necessity need to travel to St Germain near Paris, where Her Majesty and the Prince now are. There he can expect some orders as to where his services might be most welcome.

But, to tell of my experience as an exile, the experience of which is not yet as alarming as my imaginings had it to be. When we reached St Malo there was much business trying to find accommodation. I was glad that, though I neglected many of my lessons as a girl, I did recall much of Mr Cobb's instruction in the French language for, though I am less than competent, it made asking for the essentials for a lady's toilette considerably less embarrassing than it might have been. I even have some lavender scented soap of which I am sure you would approve. After months of scant attention to such matters, a jug and ewer of hot water, a fresh huckaback to towel my skin and this soap was such a simple pleasure but one which brought tears to my eyes.

I will not regale you with detail of the many infestations we endured in Pendennis. I saw more demoralising wounds

*inflicted by the creeping and crawling enemy inside the walls
than ever the Parliamentarian army could inflict. We had no
means to combat them for the ground around the fort was
bare - scarcely a blade of grass let alone yarrow or fleabane.
I know that the surgeons begged the governor to add vinegar
to the requisitions when he sent to the Prince, for we had
nothing to resemble it, except the last dregs of some vile
wine. However, ~~Mssrs Digby and Bligh, dropping their
incessant personal feuding for once~~ some officers persisted
that the stuff was fit for drinking, which was truly not the
case and they would not agree to release the stuff to the
infirmary where it might have been of some use.
But, enough of fleas and lice for the merest thought of them
now makes me itch.*

*My health improves daily though my courses have yet to
return, a matter that I am assured is due to the prolonged
want of good nutrition which, as yet, we still have here.*

*Resumed on 28th instant
Sister, forgive me for the tardiness with which I return to my
pen.
I now have a sad occasion to report. Sir Henry Killigrew,
who took a wound at the siege, yesterday slipped this earthly
existence. John Haslock had done his best to attend to him,
but to no avail. Two Killigrews, father and son to perish by
the sword, is more to add to the tally of Cornwall's losses. I
feel his poor wife will take this hard. Jemima has barely
recovered from mourning their son and Ince will be a
beautiful but empty home without Sir Henry's lively spirit. Sir
Henry's last wishes were that he be buried in Jersey. ~~Cornish
earth under the parliamentarian boots was not to his liking.~~*

*Yet in the midst of death there is life.
I told you that I had been missing my courses. Today I felt a
strong quickening which even without surgeon or midwife's
expertise I know now to be not the effects of near starvation
but that I carry Lewis' child. This is a blessing that I had not*

37

*looked for in such difficult times. I can scarce believe it and I
dearly hope that we shall be at home again, with all our
present uncertainty merely a memory, when the babe is
delivered This I think might be by Christmas but it is difficult
to say, as I have not expected it so have not read any of the
common signs.
Perhaps you would tell papa for me? I think that he will be
happy to see his grandson at Penwarne and should it be a
boy then Heligan will have another generation to roam its
lovely valley.*

*A boat leaves for Dartmouth in the hour, and so I finish in
haste so that the master will carry this missive. ~~Lewis says
they also have business at a landfall west of that destination
so~~
I remain, as always,
Your loving sister,
Mary*

*To Agnes Carew,
The Manor of Penwarne
By Mevagissey in the county of Cornwall*

*In haste, postscript, Lewis suggested that I adjust some of the
sentiments in this missive, and so I offer my apologies if you
read offending words.*

VII Grace: Of past friends

You might have been raised a Devon man, and a moor-man at that, but for the fact that William Mattock's mother gainsaid the notion. She would not accept that her son had made a valid last will and testament so Hester could not stay: if Hester had no place to stay, then neither did we. It was not matronly grief on Mistress Mattock's part nor a vehement denial of her son's death, but more that she challenged Hester's claim, convinced that the church courts would not enforce it. We were to discover that she was right, though it was not due to her scheming. When there are no proper civil authorities and the church is disregarded, a particular type of lawlessness ensues.

It would not be unkind to say that Peg Mattock was stupid, merely an observation close to the truth. That she was a wilful, unscrupulous harridan was something we came to discover. Not one of her family resembled the kind-hearted William in temperament. I watched Hester, fingernails bitten to the quick, trying to be what she knew Will had wanted: a good wife and dutiful daughter-in-law, but circumstances tested her resilience to the limit. If Hester had not found the home she hoped for, we would eventually have to take to the road again and that would be a trial for there were no options; we would be expected to go back to where we came from, Bristol.

I have glimpsed the essence of foreign lands in the bales, sacks and casks that filled my father's warehouse, always understanding the world to be wider than my own horizon. I did not expect to broaden that horizon any wider than any merchant's daughter ordinarily might, perhaps become a wife with a home in another county at most. Yet through Bartholomew Fenwick, my perspective shifted and I have seen things that no woman should see, on an odyssey that sounds incredible, even to my own ears. As I have travelled, I have come to know people who I shall cherish my life long. I have no regrets. On this journey, it has been my friendships that have sustained me, which have protected me and inevitably have saved me. The war has made enemies of old associates, so it is well to know where you can place your trust.

I can think of nobody to whom you might turn in Bristol, for the city has been riven by disease and by conflict. The man to whom my father entrusted my moral welfare, along with many of his commercial concerns, was my godfather and his oldest friend, Robert Yeamans. Parliament hanged him as a traitor.

In our own household, our steward was a man in whom one could confide, on whom one could depend. Yet Matthew Allerway was lost to the battlefield, forced to march to the beat of the drum. My beloved maid, Jinty, who sustained the Wine Street house in my absence, was faithful to the last, but succumbed to the sweating sickness in July of 1645. I could not even stay to give her any comfort in those last hours, because my fortunes then depended on the goodwill of a man who I barely knew and his wife, who I had come to love dearly. I will tell you of them, as I believe that, should you ever need assistance, then Sir Richard Fanshawe would be a man to whom you could turn.

I had met Lady Fanshawe while she was still Ann Harrison. Her father was the richest man in London, yet in '44 she was living in a tiny, mildewed garret in the city of Oxford. My accommodation was just as bad, despite the fact that it was obtained on letters of recommendation from a prince. With the Royalist court and high command crowded into the city, Oxford was a seething mass of people. A constant stream of soldiers bled the city of any healthy humours, infested it with filth and everywhere there was the stench of humanity. It was in these grim circumstances that I lost my first child, a miscarriage, and yet God forgive me, I cannot say I grieved for that poor lost soul, the offspring of Bartholomew Fenwick.

Ann nurtured me through that illness and knew of my trials. She was wed in the same spring. There have been times when I have envied her the warmth and trust that she and her husband share, yet I will confess that when I knew that she had divulged all my miseries to him I was alarmed. However, Sir Richard Fanshawe is a perfect gentleman and unruffled by the details, he made enquiries as to how my situation might be resolved. Not easily, as it transpired.

The Fanshawes had an infant of their own within the year. He lived but ten days. Sir Richard had been sent with the Prince of Wales' Council. When Ann was told to join him, I have never seen such a transformation in spirits, for the uncertainty of biding in Oxford, the loss of her baby and not knowing how her husband fared weighed her soul to such an extent that the death of their son was felt a hundred times harder.

When she heard that the Prince of Wales, his councillors and retinue, were to make their headquarters in Bristol Ann would brook no argument. As Bristol was my birthplace, I was to travel with her, the house in Wine Street again becoming a home of sorts. Ann and I had become close. She knew my mind better than I did, but the truth is that without their generosity I was destitute.

I cannot yet bring myself to state in black on white the events that took me from my home, to south Wales, to Shrewsbury and thence to Oxford. I will only say that my husband believed - indeed hoped - I was dead. That being the case I had no recourse to any money. As the wife of a traitor, I would find little sympathy anywhere in the hard-pressed city of Bristol; as Grace Fenwick I no longer existed. Although he could not return to the city to realise his assets while Bristol was in the hands of the King's men, the house in Wine Street was maintained with monies held in trust by Fenwick's lawyer. So it was that, officially, our lodging was requisitioned from Captain Fenwick, turn-coat. The fact that a lady's companion travelling with the party was that man's wife was not made general knowledge. My only childhood friend and the person who might have raised an eyebrow,

Beth Yeamans, had died of the sweating sickness the previous winter. Bristol was a sorry place.

However, my sojourn there was not to last long; the heir to the throne could not stay in a city where plague threatened as it did in July of '45. Where the Prince went, so did the Fanshawes. I had no option but go, to leave Jinty to die alone. We sailed from Bristol, our destination Barnstaple, for through the West Country lay the Prince's route to safety. The voyage ... my voyage to freedom ... I will leave aside, for there is much you need to understand and perhaps it is yet not the time.

In Barnstaple fate conspired to bring Hester and I, ex-servant and ex-mistress, together again. Later, we were to go our separate ways, destined to meet once more at Pendennis Castle. We are unlikely companions in adversity it is true. However, God had placed us where He best thought we should be and neither Hester nor I would question His mysterious ways. Certainly I had no right to judge her, and there was not one jot of ill-will in Hester Phipps, as she was before she was wed.

Barum, as Hester called it, was another town overcrowded first with the influx both of the Parliamentarian army who had successfully garrisoned the place for months, and latterly the Royalist troops, who had recently succeeded in capturing the port. The royal entourage only added to the turmoil. We had been placed in a house in Cross Street, the home of the Palmers, who were Parliamentarian by inclination but who bore the vicissitudes of civil unrest with stoicism and good grace. We were in such close quarters in the lodgings that there was no space for even a splinter of antagonism.

For a few rare weeks in that summer, the Palmer's house was home to an extraordinary contradiction of women: the courtier Lady Ann Fanshawe; the Puritan Mistress Palmer; the convict, Hester Phipps. And I, Grace Fenwick, the greatest contradiction of all: stateless but married, deceased but not dead, unfaithful but totally, completely, gloriously unabashed.

I had been given in marriage to a man for whom honour meant nothing, his nor mine. I did not like him and would never have come to love him, but, until ordered to join him on the *Ann,* I could not have imagined the corruption in his soul.

Though my words must seem like those of a shameless woman, in time I hope that you will come to understand the circumstances that led me to behave as I have done.

Do not condemn me yet.

VIII Hester: A cool reception

I know they do say 'tis wrong to speak ill of the dead but there have been times in the last months when I felt right folshid about my husband's will and wished I'd never seen that wretched bit of paper. The chaplain at Pendennis had been so sure 'twas right and proper and would make my life easy. He'd certain sure never been to Cornwood then.

I have cursed at Will, God rest him, and wept then a'cause I felt guilty for my bitterness. All the while, Grace heard all my rantings with such patience. We are both in this pickle together but 'tis all my fault we're in this cawtch.

At first, you could have blown me down with a sneeze when I saw Will's ma. I stood with my mouth agape until she started her ranting. I soon moved myself just in case the pot in her hand came a-flyin' my way.

"God give you good 'een, Mistress Mattock!" says I, ready to duck.

"And what's it to you if it be good or no. And how is't you know me? Your face ain't from these parts and you've the look of a progger…and her," she leered, poking a bony finger in Grace's direction, "what's she, with her face like a dun cow?"

There was naught to do but come straight out with it, for all that the woman had plainly been sampling the wares from her own brew house.

"My name is Hester, and this is Grace … er … Sark, and her infant, Henry Charles." Ma Mattock raised an bushy eyebrow and opened her mouth to speak, only letting out another foul belch, so I hurried on, before I lost my nerve,

"I have some sorry tidings, and I wish it were not so, but I am the widow of your son, William, who went to fight for His Majesty in '43. He died in the King's service these three

44

… nay two weeks hence at …" She didn't let me finish, but leaning against the doorpost, started shaking. She bent forward till her gnarled hands rested on her knees, and let out such a snort that I wondered if she was indeed to have a fit after all. But 'twasn't a fit, for on the next breath she straightened and out came the start of a wheezing snigger, then a snort, then more wheezing. Ma Mattock was laughing.

"Nomye, stop or I'll split my sides! For the life o'me! Or tell me another for 'tis enough to make a dog laugh! Oho-ho!" and she grunted and wheezed some more.

Grace tried her best civil voice,

"Goody Mattock, please, could we step inside? What Hester says is true and I feel sure that it is only the shock of the tragic news that makes you answer so. Perhaps you might sit …" Poor Grace got short shrift though and now my in-law started to look fierce,

"Ye must think I don't 'av ort between my ears, come tellin' me a hunkin' pile of fibs like yon! And as for coming through these doors to sit, the only folk to cross this threshold are they that have the coin to pay their way!" Without thinking, I ducked as she brandished the pot in her hand again.

I could hardly credit that Will had suffered this harpy all his boyhood days yet bore no trace of it. I cried out,

"Will *was* my wedded husband, and I have the lines to prove 'tis so, and 'afore he died he wrote his last will and testament that I should find a place to bide here. I bore his son, who would have been your grandchild but the infant soul died 'afore…" The tears were starting to come again.

"I'll whapp your whorish hide for you if you come any nearer! If you think you can just wring a few sly tears out and pass off a yarn of a by-blow, expecting me to settle you because of some shifty penman's scrawl, you must think I was born yesterday! Yah! Go'rn! Yaaaaah!"

There was a clatter and in a flash, quicker that I thought a woman in her cups could go, Goody Mattock lunged. But now she was hefting a club, studded with nails, grabbed from behind the nearest doorpost.

I pushed Grace behind me, and started to back along the lane the way we had come, thinking there was nothing I could say or do but knowing I'd let myself be beaten to a pulp before anything should happen to Hal. Out of the corner of my eye, I could see two girls, their hay-rakes over their shoulders, strolling towards us along the road the fleeing man had taken. Seeing there was trouble, they picked up their pace and began to run. Trouble was, they weren't to come to my aid but their ma's. And that was how I met Will's sisters, Daisy and Rose.

Screaming and swearing they threw down the tools and began lash out with their fists. The only good thing about this was that Goody Mattock backed away and left them to it. I laid about me with my baggage, feeling the rim of my skillet hit bone beneath one skirt hitched up for field-working. One girl howled which made the other sister Mattock madder than ever, so she hurled herself at me even harder, kicking and biting, while the other hopped and cursed and rubbed her shin.

Hal was howling, Grace was screaming and the rooks in the trees were cawing and crawing and adding to the din. I began to feel as though my feet were in clay boots, so heavy and leaden that, try as I might, I could no longer shift to defend myself. I could feel myself begin to topple but I was past caring. I just hoped that if they could beat me they would leave Grace alone. I shut my eyes, expecting the sick thud of more blows that I couldn't fend off.

Instead, there was a girt sploosh, and then a screetching. I felt a splattering of wet but the battering stopped. Instead, all around me was different shouting, men's voices raised with a no-nonsense tone ringing above them all, a voice I recognised filling in the gaps.

It seemed that the blacksmith, who was a good-hearted man under all that bluff and bluster, had told his wife about the newest local legend. She had scolded him for sending us to Mistress Mattock without protection, hastily bidding him fetch the constable, the vicar and a few Cornwood chaps to see what was a-doing. The two pails of water that they flung over the Mattock girls had stopped them in their tracks. I d'think they saved my life. I certain sure felt near dead, afeard and zaundy and close to being sick.

The smith took me by the elbow and right gently helped me to my feet as I looked around for Grace. Two lads with staves were guarding her, though they were so slight that Ma Mattock could have flicked them down with a finger. Still, they were there.

Over by the doorway of the cottage, a middle-aged man in minister's garb stood behind a fellow who we found to be the constable, with two more men, like buttresses, beside him to give him the chance to have the last word. They were shoving the three wrestling women back into their home, threats of whipping, cart-tails and the stocks ringing around the scene. The door slammed, cutting off an order that had the weight of a battlefield command. It went very quiet after that, the rooks settling in the high branches to chirk and chark about what they'd just seen.

I just sat in the dust, gathering my wits. When Grace ran over to me we hugged - well, as much as the pain would let me- and I decided that there were no bones broken though I reckoned I would have a girt black eye and some pretty bruises by morning.

The vicar slipped out from the alehouse, scuttling and scuffing dust around the hem of his long black coat. He had the most terrible stammer, so the greeting took some time,

"G-g-god g-g-give you g-g-good d-d-day, ladies. M-m-ay I introduce m-m-yself. Reverend Henry S-s-smyth, vicar of this p-p-arish. T-t-his is n-n-not the w-way C-c-cornwood c-c-customarily g-g-greets v-v-vistors." I could not help but feel for him - and for the parishioners who would have to sit through his sermons every week. It was clear that he was trying to make amends for the assault,

"I shall p-p-personally see to it t-t-hat you are f-f-f ... g-g-given ac-c-com ..." he was struggling but eventually, squeezing his eyes shut tight, spat it out, "s-ssomewhere to s-sstay." Not wasting any more energy on words, he signed that we should follow and strode off up the hill.

For the second time in under a week, we found ourselves in a church house. The sympathy of the blacksmith's wife didn't stretch to finding us a bed that night but the vicar seemed to think that the brew house being at the bottom of the hill and the church house being at the top would at least check the Mattock women for the time being. What the lady from the smithy did do though, was bring thick slices of gammon, some bread and a pottle of cider for our supper, with some goat's milk in a jug for Hal, saying Grace didn't look as if she could feed an infant herself. We explained that I was wet-nursing the lad. At that she raised one eyebrow but didn't pass comment, only saying,

"Well, by the look of 'ee, y'could do with a month of good meals. By the by, I'm Sarah, Sarah Beale, and my man's known as Jet." She added with some pride, "He be blacksmith, farrier, and ironmonger - if 'tis formed of metal, Jet will handle it. Mind, Jet's not his given name," she winked, "but Jehoshaphat's too much of a mouthful for everyday calling into the forge and he comes in from work as black as that stone, so Jet is how he's known! Now then, settle yourselves and I shall bring some pottage and more milk tomorrow!" and chuckling, she left. At least there was one soul in Cornwood who had a kind heart, I thought.

The church house lodging was light and dry but hardly full of homely comforts. Someone charitable brought us the makings of a bed. Whoever it was, they didn't want to be seen so left the old sacks and a scruffy blanket at the bottom of the steps. I was shown to a stable, the vicar saying that I could take hay to fill the sacks, which made the floor a tad easier on our frames.

Every morning the vicar and churchwarden checked up on us, with Sarah bringing what she could spare from her own board, always with milk for Hal, and she'd return with some bread and meat or pottage in the evening.

I would have liked it if we'd had a few more days before we faced the nosy stares of the parish at the Sunday service. My face must have looked liked a bag of mashed mulberries, with an egg yolk or two thrown in for good measure. We made our way into the church well before the congregation started to arrive a'cause I was hoping to find a dark corner to hide in but this wasn't a church for dark corners. Every time another Cornwood worthy arrived we were shuffled to another pew, got a frownsy 'tut-tut' or were just glared at. 'Twas not much of a Christian welcome, until Sarah and Jet with their children arrived and bade us sit beside them.

There was a real show of unpleasantness when Ma Mattock and the girls arrived, and we heard some hissing and muttering. I was right glad that they has seats at the back of the place, near to the door, and that we were near the middle; there were enough folk betwixt us to prevent another attack. From what I'd seen of Goody Mattock I wouldn't put it past her to pick a fight in the House of the Lord.

We had filled little Henry Charles with as much milk as we could, both my own and some goat's milk from a spoon, suspecting that the sermon would be dire. It was. I think the babe knew it too. He grew ever more fretful until, during Job's lesson on sharing morsels with orphans and a particular bad phrase with too many 'n's, he let out a huge wail and began to cry so hard that Grace had to wriggle past our fellow worshippers and rush outside. There was a general rumble of disapproval and a cackle from the direction of the Mattock family. So much for charity and goodwill, I thought, or for us hoping to go unnoticed. Still, in the following days nobody except Sarah came near us and we slept whenever we could. My strength began to return as the bruises faded. But with that came the worrying.

On the morning of the fourth day there was a rat-tat at the door and in marched the churchwarden and constable with Reverend Smyth dodging in behind them. The constable took charge, for which I am sure all present were grateful. I thought him to be an ex-military man as just like Will's first sergeant of pike, he puffed out his chest before he spoke. 'T'was almost a bellow and sounded summ'at terrible and important. He began.

"With the powers bestowed on me, James Triggs, by the Justice of the Peace, in this, the parish of Cornwood, in the

Diocese of the Bishop of Exeter, within the Archdeaconry of Totnes, as Constable and Overseer of the Poor I require you to submit to this inquiry into your circumstances." He took another girt breath,

"With the authority of the Reverend Smyth and the wardens of this parish, I am required to establish your means; whether you be impotent poor, or destitute, indigent or the responsibility of any person or persons in this parish." He made a weighty pause, sniffed disdainfully then finished with a growl, "or are simply idling vagrants." It was quite plain that Cornwood would have none of them in their bounds.

I laid out my papers on the table before them. It felt like nothing as much as the court in Bideford, when I had faced the town's authorities accused of witchcraft back in '43. That had only been a nod away from a proper trial. This felt like my future depended on it too. I suppose that was the truth of it, and not just mine either.

The Reverend's eyes nearly popped out of his head when he examined my Bible, with its list of dates alongside the names: my marriage, the birth of my son, the death of my husband. The constable passed the will across for both vicar and churchwarden to pore over. They muttered amongst themselves for some time before the constable began again,

"Until this document is proved then you have no right to the inheritance to which it refers. This will require due process of the Court of Archdeaconry." I didn't like the sound of that one bit but he rumbled on,

"With the present ... ehem! ... distractions, that may take time." I knew he meant the war but had no notion of how bad things had become, that even the church was in doubt. He carried on, all self-important sounding,

"Yet it is evident that you have a claim against this parish for outdoor relief. To whit, this panel has agreed that each of you will be supplied with provisions amounting to one half-loaf, ½ lb dried peas or beans, a quart of small beer daily for a week, during which time we will see fit to find you useful occupation."

Grace and I bobbed a curtsey, relieved as anything. It was poor fare but more than we had survived on in Pendennis. Besides, I knew that I could turn my hand to any domestic task they gave me. It would be summ'at new for Grace but I was sure that hard work would trouble her none if she and Hal could rest quiet and safe at night. The next matter was where we would lodge. Reverend Smyth seemed to read my thoughts,

"G-g-gentlemen, I have s-s-spoken with M-m-mistress M-m-mattock. She is a-adamant that she will n-n-not have these women beneath her roof. Therefore, I p-p-propose that, in order to avoid f-f-further c-c-confrontation, they remain lodged here until f-f-further notice. It is far from ideal but there is ..." and there the constable interrupted,

"Aye, but 'twill keep that hell-cat and her kits off my back ... begging your pardon, reverend sir. I mean, it will keep the peace of this parish until matters can be resolved."

The men, having disposed of matters to their satisfaction, pushed our papers back across the table, got to their feet as one and left.

Later, sitting on the weathered slab of a grave enjoying the quiet of the warm dusky evening, I asked Grace if she knew aught about proving a will. She did not, never facing such an eventuality herself, for her husband had made sure of that, but she thought there would be a deal of to-ing and fro-ing, perhaps to Exeter where the Bishop's court would be held, or perhaps, as the constable had hinted, to Totnes, which I knew was nearer.

I sighed. In my head, it had all seemed so simple; I would present my bit of paper and I would take over where William had left off, helping his ma brew and sell the ale we made and making a life and livelihood for us all. 'Twouldn't be riches, but 'twould be honest work.

'Well, Hester,' I said to myself, 'it just shows how much of a dawcock you can really be. Still, there's naught to be done except follow the path, whatever the good Lord sends.'

As we settled down to sleep that night our bellies felt a little easier than any time in the last month and Hal's gentle snoring lulled me to a fitful sleep. I dreamed of papers, in stacks and piles, in chests and boxes heaped high all around. Faceless clergymen in purple robes poked at me with bleached bones, wordlessly mouthing questions I could not hear while I tried to dust around them all with a goose-feather. As the questions came, more and more urgent, I dusted harder and harder, until at the last the papers flew up and around, blowing around me like a blizzard until all of a sudden they whisked away, leaving me in a black empty space, alone.

IX Mary: Of a reunion

Written this 13th day of October 1646
St Malo
At the sign of the Fiddle and Tabor

Dearest Sister,
I pray this letter finds you in good health. I thank you for
yours, which I received this morning. You need not apologise
for brevity. Any correspondence is a joy and today especially
so for it greatly relieved the sadness of Lewis' most recent
duty.
The last tide saw his return from the ship that bore Sir
Henry Killigrew to his chosen resting place. Lewis knew that
Cornish hands should carry him aboard the little vessel, if
not lay him in Cornish earth, and it was Cornishmen who
stood the watch while his body lay in state at the Constable's
house at St Helier. The voyage to that place was not as easy
as it might have been for the vessel was harried by enemy
shipping as well as by bad weather. Lewis said that he was
pleased that they were not bound for the Tamar after all
because the winds were so contrary. Of the little vessel I
shall write more anon.
Many of those at Pendennis through the siege wished to pay
their last respects. Given express permission by the Prince of
Wales, Richard Wiseman attended ...you recall, he was our
army surgeon ...And before I close I really must tell you of
the conversation Lewis had with Wiseman ...
Pendennis garrison's own Reverend Gatsford preached the
funeral sermon. I had heard tell that before he died French
priests had pressed Sir Henry to declare he was of the
Catholic faith but he cried out for a preacher of his own
church. Mercifully the Reverend was still in St Malo. Sir

*Henry's remains were interred nine days ago in the 'Temple'
in St Helier. May God grant that he rests in peace. Amen.*

*I am grown much bigger in these last weeks. Lewis says it is
because I eat enough for three. I admit to having cravings for
sweet custards and apple cake but I think I may be forgiven
for that. I cannot eat rich meats for those greatly disturb my
digestion. The baby kicks strongly and any way I lie,
particularly by night, he has knee and elbow, or so I suppose
them to be, pressing to my ribs or poking outward. Lewis is
the most assiduous father-to-be.*

*Reverend Gatsford being with the Prince's party, and close
to Sir Edward Hyde, I asked Lewis if he would ask him for
news so that I might convey such to you to reassure you. I
have none.*
*Yet I do have something of extreme cheer to report, of the
boat that sailed hence to Jersey bearing the Killigrew bier.
You will no doubt know well enough, from the fishermen at
Mevagissey and Portmellon that there is still a fleet of vessels
that manages to ply its trade - and the King's - beneath the
nose of Admiral Batten. St Malo is a frequent port of call,
though not a safe haven. A ship called the* Dolphin *is one of
these, with letters of Marque, and operating along this coast,
from Jersey and even Ireland I am told. But St Malo is where
the* Dolphin *was berthed when called upon to do the sad duty
to Sir Henry.*
*When Lewis boarded he discovered, among the crew, all
West-country men, our old friend and fellow Cornishman,
Sark.*
*I could have wished to be there at their reunion, for Lewis
owes his life to this man. No less brave was his valiant bid to
bring relief to the fort when he swam out. Hearing nothing
more, we had thought him lost, drowned in the attempt. It is a
matter of great joy to discover him. I hope to have an
opportunity to offer Sark some hospitality here before we
leave for Paris, no matter how meagre.*

I think Lewis must have spoken to him of Grace. And Hester, of course. It is a delicate matter to explain but Sark will want to know as much as possible of Grace, and ~~his~~ the baby, Hal.

Thus, by reunions amongst the losses, we are buoyant despite the hardships and tragedy.
I remain your affectionate sister,
Mary

To Agnes Carew,
The Manor of Penwarne
By Mevagissey in the county of Cornwall

Post Script: Sis, I grow forgetful. I have no time now but I will write that which I promised but have omitted in my next letter.

X Grace: Jeopardy

I have told you a little of some of the people who would love you for my sake, people you can call friends. Now I should tell you of the dangers that are implicit in my situation, and show you the nature of my choices. I know that marriage is a sacrament, ordained by God, and I must bear the guilt of resisting His will yet I would have you understand how it was. I will be honest. I do not wish to turn the world by its heels and I would not choose to break the laws of God or man. The law is a body by which every man and woman should be ruled. We challenge it at our peril for without the rule of law we can be sure of nothing. This war has taught us nothing if not that. Yet the legal chains that keep our world secured often become as entangled, even in moderate times, just as a length of twine bundled in your pocket becomes knotty. Then all is confusion, offering no clear direction. Yet again, sometimes the edicts' effects are simply cruel.

Hester would have to grapple with the law, though her situation was the very reverse of my own. William Mattock had made good provision for his wife, a timely last will and testament witnessed by the chaplain to the regiments in Pendennis fort. Will died assured that he had done the best for his beloved. He believed that the law would uphold her entitlement, and so it should have done. Yet for all that, we were to discover that the scales of justice in this land swing unsteadily.

Both Hester and I might wait a lifetime before we see them righted. Sir Richard Fanshawe, with all his knowledge of the law, could give me no assurances that there would be any remedy for the sorry position in which I found myself. I recall his words,

"The church and the words 'till death us do part' are most likely to prevail, unless your husband's traitorous acts bring him to justice and the executioner." For the man to whom I was married was indeed both a traitor to the King's cause as well as a murderer. Death did not part us, for although he thought me dead, I was every bit a captive as if he held me bound hand and foot.

I have two books in my keeping and have read to you from one battered volume, a Shakespeare folio that your grandfather bought before I was born. Do you remember the tale of the Roman emperor, Julius Caesar? There are words that your grandfather would sometimes quote, 'The evil that men do lives after them; the good is oft interred with their bones'. The poet's words resonated for him because my father wished to believe the best of every man. The reality might brand him innocent, naïve, perhaps even a fool, for in the man to whom I am married I truly believe there is no good, nothing to redeem him, only evil.

Yet I have something which belongs to Fenwick which, given time, may bring him within the reach of the law and to proper justice. It is the evidence of his perfidy and malice against my family and others. As for the cruel and monstrous acts he has performed against his fellow man in the name of Parliament, there are witnesses to a deed that would condemn Fenwick to the gallows. One is Lewis Tremayne and the other is a man most people simply know as Sark. There were more on board ship off the coast of Pembroke on that February day who, if they can sleep quiet at night must have sold their consciences to the devil. Or to Bartholomew Fenwick.

The evidence is concealed in the pages of the other book, tattered and watermarked, which I keep close and hidden. Open it and you will find that the pages detail a seafarer's log of voyages, a rutter - notes on landfalls, currents, tides, trading accounts and all manner of right and proper records for a ship's master. However, look more closely and the journal contains so much more. A man - or woman for that matter - might keep a diary, a memoir or simple record of finances. I kept such a book for the household in Wine Street. Yet, Fenwick's rutter is more than a seafarer's diary and contains entries that should make an honest man's blood run cold. How I came by it is no easy tale to relate, the memory brings back horrors I would prefer to bury deep. You need to know, so I will tell you.

I was married but my husband left the same day, his business keeping him away. If the *Ann* happened to be in port, then he chose to sleep on board and not at Wine Street. I cannot say otherwise; I was relieved. Matters did not stay that way. I was forced to join the ship, a peremptory command not a companionable gesture. A few personal necessities were provided but I took no belongings, except my dog Patch who would not be denied. My husband does not like dogs, and for Patch the feeling was mutual. I thought I had lost him forever when he escaped from the cabin. Fenwick would have killed him if he or his minions had found him.

That night Fenwick came to ... claim his conjugal rights. It was a cold deed. His ardour was plainly evident ... but it was not for me ... there was someone ... it was ... I am ashamed to say more except that the church and state both deem it an unnatural act. Towards me, there was only malice, a satisfaction in my humiliation, the lust of possession. I endured it four times. Only once was he ... clumsy with his seed, siring the pitiable infant I lost in Oxford.

Made to wear breeches and doublet, I knew I was the subject of the sailors' scorn. Even the cabin boy would not pass the time of day. Barely ten years old, he looked terrified if I even looked at him when he bought what passed for food. There were good men on the ship though. The gun crew caught and hid Patch; skinny, bony, leggy Patch, my canine shadow. They fed him and kept him safe, abetted by their gun captain, the man they called Sark.

Sark and Fenwick: I had first seen them together in Bristol and firmly believed him to be Fenwick's man. Yet I discovered that you must not read a man the way you would a page. The playwright noted it, for he wrote that 'there are daggers in men's smiles.' He had no advice upon how to read men's scowls. Sark seemed perpetually scowling, more often than not at me, and so I assumed that he was ... to Fenwick's taste. It is ridiculous now, but then hindsight makes matters so much clearer. Fenwick had insisted that Sark and a particular bo'sun be signed on the *Ann* when he became our ship's master and so Sark seemed everywhere, more in evidence than ever, on board, on the quays or at the house, even dining with us.

Sark brought his own gun crew with him, loyal men whom he could trust. My father's ship, like all merchantmen, had always carried guns to protect against pirates but the war elevated Sark's profession even further. I know that he spent time with Prince Maurice's army in the summer of '44, but he is not a landsman and soon returned to the King's service at sea. He joined an independent vessel, a small, fast ship called *Dolphin*. Her master, Pasco Jago, is a privateer who had joined Sir Nicholas Slanning's fleet to harry the enemy on the south west coast, running supplies for the Royalist cause. I doubt if Jago made any loss in the business either.

Jago is a man who is large in every way and his wife who sails with him is even bigger. If I describe Fenwick as tall and lean, translucent grey eyes, with thin, slick hair then Pasco Jago is everything that is the opposite; squat and brawny, a mass of black bristles at every point that a man could have hair and flashing eyes, almost black, always ready with a laugh. You hear Pasco long before you see him. He knew and liked my father well, extending his affection to me. Goody Jago could not be better matched to her man; huge in every respect, especially her heart, and they are folk to whom I have entrusted my life, and would do so again.

I was reunited with Patch thanks to gun captain Sark. The circumstances are a catalogue of betrayal and treachery, for the ship my father had entrusted to Fenwick to work for the King's cause, had secretly been working for Parliament. On that fateful voyage, we had picked up passengers, Royalist troops returning from Ireland. When we reached the Welsh coast, Fenwick made rendezvous with two Parliament vessels then revealed his duplicity. On the orders of Admiral Swanley the soldiers - and their women too - were cruelly dispatched, thrown over the side to drown. It was an opportunity Fenwick seized and I went with them, bound back-to-back with the major in command of those poor men. That was Lewis Tremayne.

He had recognized Sark as a fellow Cornishman, Lewis' bonhomie overcoming Sark's testiness and they quickly established a rapport. It seems that Sark had overheard something, or perhaps knew Swanley's reputation, but Sark and the Major had rightly anticipated trouble and, between them, had hatched a plan. They play-acted their roles as brute and victim. I believed every word and gesture. A barrel in the ship's boat went unremarked, while the Parliamentarian gunner ostensibly went about the business of ensuring those in the water would drown. Yet in truth, he was cutting as many bonds as he could manage, and when the major and I hit the water, he tipped the skiff over and, out of sight, beneath the stern of the ship, Sark released us. Thankfully I knew little more of the ordeal for Sark knocked me unconscious. I now know it was for my own good, but the last thing I recall was seeing that the ship I had known as the *Ann*, named for my mother, had been renamed. It is now the *Leopard*.

The barrel had contained my beloved hound, subdued with poppy juice. Also, wrapped tight against any leakage of water was a packet. I awoke on a beach with Patch almost sitting on my chest, unruffled by his adventure. The packet I received many weeks later, in Oxford. It contained the rutter, stolen in the turmoil of those last minutes on board. I know by heart the message Sark slipped under the oilcloth wrapping:

'*I came by the enclosed book by dishonest means but nevertheless I would justify the action in any court in the land. I confess that I had knowledge of some of the events it details. My perspective now being somewhat different I deeply regret that I stood by and did nothing to resist. As the fortunes of a seafarer and a man of war are uncertain, if you should ever find yourself in need of security against Bartholomew Fenwick, the evidence hereby incorporated may stand you in good stead*'.

He wrote more and there is so much more to explain, but this is what is most important now. The book carries both security and danger for the contents damn the man to whom I am married. It is irrefutable but if ever Bartholomew Fenwick discovers I am alive and that the rutter is in my possession, then he will destroy anyone in his path to get it back.

XI Hester: An uneasy place to bide

Honest work was soon sent our way. The good rate-payers of Cornwood and Lutton weren't convinced that two strangers were entitled to any village charity, however willing the cleric or constable was to believe us. Every Monday we did the vicar's laundering, cleaning and the like; there always seemed to be much to do in the Reverend's house. His wife was not in good health and there were six children to see to, and the only servant he kept was an old deaf fellow known as Cled who was not much good for ought really. Smyth must have been a good sort of vicar though, a'cause it seemed the parishioners were happy to provide domestic niceties for him, even though a living was hard to get on the edge of the moor.

Other times we would be brought mending, usually darning - blankets and the like, nothing fancy. The smith's wife often needed a hand with this and that. Then a weaver down by the mill sent drop-spindle work to keep his loom in yarn a'cause his wife had a newborn and with other little 'uns at her skirts had less time to spin his fleeces. There was all'us work to hand. We got no payment in coin, but I would get a slice of something wrapped in muslin thrust in my hand when I took our handiwork to the cottage doors. Sometimes there'd be a little butter, occasionally eggs, and one day there was a small jar of potted meat - pigeon or summ'at like - with the brisk warning to 'bring back the pot!' On the little hearth we had, I could make pottage. We could collect herbs, berries, or nuts from round and about - I would eat mushrooms but Grace would have none of that, mindful of what poisoned her father I suppose. We did well enough though.

Still, every day there would be some niggle from my in-laws, usually harsh words a'cause even they were wary of being disrespectful of church property. Only once someone did thrust cow dung through an open window. I regularly had stuff lobbed at me in the street. One day a rotting apple, tossed from behind a hedge, hit me on the back of the head. I couldn't see who threw it, but it didn't take much to guess a'cause the ninnies couldn't help cackling from their hidey-hole. 'T wasn't pleasant but 'twas mainly harmless.

Then, after a few weeks, we got less ale and a jug of cider took the place of the other drink. I supposed we were in the season for apples but it weren't as wholesome as ale. Eventually the gossip reached us that Mistress Mattock had disliked the thought of sending any generosity our way and had refused to sell her brew unless the parish paid double the going price. So we got ale, just not as much.

I did try, once, to pay my respects. I knew it was what William wanted and reckoned that if I went first thing of a morning, Ma Mattock wouldn't be so much in her cups and maybe would let me tell her of me and Will and the babe and all. Well, that was a faint hope! I didn't get within twenty paces of the alehouse, let alone to the yard where the brewing shed was, before I could hear her. She'd got the sound of one who'd already been a-guddlin' her own wares and she was berating the maltster's mule, a sorry looking beast hung about with heavy sacks.

The mule, not being wise to his customer's sensitivities, had dropped a girt pile o' dung in the alleyway to the courtyard. The poor animal, ears down and the whites of its eyes showing right scarily, had then backed up to try and get away from her dudder, right through the pile of shit, kicking it all over the place. Then Ma Mattock started on the poor maltster, who had been hiding behind his mule He was a weedy chap not cut out for a quarrel with the likes of she. What man was? Anyway, not staying to hear the end of the matter, I put thoughts of any peaceable talks with the Mattock women right out of my mind.

There would have to be summ'at done though. We needed to find a roof over our heads. The church house was never meant to house folk month on month - only when they had truly fallen on desperd-hard times. Will wasn't the only man not to come home to his hearth and there were men maimed with families needing help, though none homeless like us. We had already shuffled up our makeshift quarters when Grand'mer Toms, toothless, tattered and stinking, arrived after her hovel had collapsed around her ears.

On my way back and forth through the village I'd seen her roof, a rotting mass of old heather thatch. It was a wonder that the smallest gust of wind didn't fetch it off. She was too old to work on it herself and too poor to get it fixed. There didn't seem to be family to do it for her and nobody else cared to turn their hand to the repairs, so the winter frosts then summer rain had done their worst, washing chunks of mud wall away in a slide.

Grace and me tried to do what we could for her and once we'd persuaded her to a bit of a wash and dried out her clathers, knocking the clops of muck off, she weren't so bad. Still, each morn there'd be a puddle round the chamber pot, and as the days went on the poor old maid got more addled, sitting by what little fire we had in the hearth, rambling to herself under her breath. The strange thing was that Hal took to her, and he'd chortle and laugh at her jabbering, and she doted on him, which let Grace and me get on with whatever piecework we had in hand.

And, o'course there was the matter of the papers. Reverend Smyth promised that he would send a letter to the churchmen at Totnes about my problem. I asked Grace who this Archibald-whoever was, and why he would help with the will. When Grace stopped sniggering and looked to see if I had grown cloth ears, she explained it was the Archdeacon's office, he being a churchman a bit lower in importance than a bishop. Cornwood parish came under the ruling of Archdeacon Cotton of Totnes and he would be the man to decide about my inheritance. I was summ'at glad that, back when the parish worthies had been settling us, I hadn't opened my mouth about it. I would have been the laughing stock for sure. But then, my experience of churchmen was only on a Sunday, and the man who wed Will and me. There was one preacher who got too close, back in Barum in '44, a wolf in cleric's clothing you could say but he was hanged for pretending to be someone he wasn't, not for what he did to me. How was I to know about church laws?

Anyways, I had been told that long before there would be any chance to see a church lawyer, I would have to deliver my papers in person so that they could be picked over. That was one trip to Totnes. Then I would need to go myself to this court when they did their business. That meant I would need to make two journeys, there and back, and my broken shoes would hardly take me two miles let alone to town, twice. Still, it mattered very little for we heard nothing for weeks.

Eventually, Reverend Smyth arrived late one foggy afternoon while Grace was out delivering a basket of spun yarn. His black gown was furred with fine droplets from the fog. He had news of a sort and not helpful either. Shaking off the damp, he nodded a greeting then began, very hesitantly,

"M-m-mistress Mattock," he was wringing his hands and looking for all like a girt sorry crow, "I … t-t-today … this morning, in fact, I … received word in response to my enquiries on your behalf." He paused then it all came out in a rush, almost without stutter at all, "There is some hiatus regarding the … ahhem! … authorities and the Archdeaconry C-c-court." I wished he would talk in plain language so I could keep up, to be able to tell Grace.

"What's a hy ... one of them?" I put down my knitting, the better to listen but he spoke even quicker,

"There is to be some inquiry into Archdeacon C-cotton being rector of Duloe, of B-b-bridestowe and of St Peter T-t-tavy simultaneously." I knew that meant all at one time and I could see there might be summ'at in that, the places being scattered across Devon and into Cornwall too. The Archdeacon chap must be a clever fellow if he was to be in all those parts on a Sunday. Come to think of it, Will was garrisoned at Bridestowe, and we never saw a sign of a clergyman, let alone an archbishop.

'Concentrate, Hester!' I said to myself, as Reverend Smyth rattled on,

"One of Parliament's new c-c-commissions intends to seek into the validity of all church patronage," Now I got the feeling our vicar was a tad anxious, "and it is very unlikely they will s-s-stop at the Archdeacon. I regret to tell you that the next sitting will not now take p-p-place until the spring and until then all wills must wait, unless supplicants are prepared to apply direct to the Archbishop of C-c-canterbury …" I gasped. That was no good to the likes of me.

Our vicar didn't seem to care and without any of his usual courtesies he turned on his heel and scuttled away, muttering under his breath in a very un-churchy way,

"Damned C-c-ommittees … an a-a-affront … G-god's ord-d-d-damnation- dained!" He was practically running as he passed through the graveyard, but I could hear that angry stammer spitting out something about canons and Exeter, patronage, fathers and bishops. When Grace came in at dusk I told her what had passed and sat ourselves down to consider what it all meant.

It was now well into October. There was no point to thinking of ought but a long wait until the probate court. We had a house to find and if we were to keep that roof over our head, we would need to earn our keep. Taking stock of what we had between us, it wasn't over-much.

I had carefully unpicked the little pocket I had sewn into the back of my bodice where I'd hidden what you could call my dowry. It had moved Will to tears when my kind-hearted master had pressed those two silver shillings into his hand on our wedding day. I'd been robbed once before of some pennies I had sewn in the hem of my skirt, so these I had stitched into Will's doublet for safe keeping but when he passed on I'd had to find another place. Feeding Hal, at my back was about as secure as a pocket could be.

"I still have our wedding gift from the Palmers, and one shilling, eight-penny three-farthing of the surrender money." I piled up the coins on the table.

"I have … one shilling, two, three shillings … thr'uppenc ha'penny," declared Grace, adding her money, "and this."

She pulled off her wedding ring and rolled into the stack of coins.

"You can't count that! 'Tis sacred!" I croaked, horrified. My ring was only a tiny brass band, worthless, 'cept I wouldn't part with it for the whole world.

"It means nothing to me, even less than nothing, Hester, and we are desperate. If I can sell it for a decent price then we might have a little leeway; it might even pay rent for somewhere tiny, at least for a month or two. This is not for me; it's for Hal and if it's for Hal then it is for you too." There was no arguing; I had seen Grace determined before and knew the signs. She went on, "I am going clean up the breeches and doublet, mend the seams, and see if I cannot get a few pennies for those too." Thinking aloud, I said,

"Hal is taking sops now, and the goat's milk gives him a bit more than I can. One of us has to be at hand for the lad, but, if we could find a place, maybe I could take in paying work? We could ask about once we have a place ..."

So, we were agreed. It felt better to have a goal. It wasn't much of a plan, but it was something. We had nearly seven shillings, and some hope in our worldly goods. Added to that were two stout hearts and strong hands not affeard of hard work. At least it was a start.

XII Mary: A daughter's dilemma

Written this All Saint's Day 1646
St Malo
At the sign of the Fiddle and Tabor

Esteemed Papa,
I thank you for the loving wishes conveyed in Agnes' last
packet.
~~I am happy to hear that the wheat fared better than you~~
~~feared~~ How do matters fare in Cornwall?
Do I know any of the new County Committee who will
govern? Have all of the old Justices been dismissed, even Sir
John Trevanion?
I am as well as may be in trying circumstances and in my
condition, which I cannot say I bear with any equanimity. But
it will be as God wills it. ~~I always believed exile to be~~
~~bearable if I was at my husband's side.~~ Amen.
I shall write at the first opportunity when Lewis returns from
Paris with news of when and where we are to find
accommodation. I will be sorry to leave here.
St Malo has an advantage in that there are many ships
calling and being an inn closer to the quay - though not
sufficiently close to be a haunt of the worst sorts because
Monsieur out host is wary of strangers - this house is known
as a lodging for those loyal to His Majesty.

You will recall I have spoken of the surgeon Richard
Wiseman. He was briefly here again recently, on matters
pertaining to the Prince's household where he now holds a
permanent post. He was recommended by Lord Hopton
himself and as he is younger than Lewis, his appointment is
all the more impressive.
~~I wish to write of something which, while not of~~

Please

I have something to recount and in your wisdom, I beg you take whatever steps might be possible to act upon it if conditions allow. I promised to Agnes of this matter, but forgot. I ask that you to recount it if you will, or let her read this missive.

Just before Lewis' departure, we dined with Richard. He is a good man and a friend. He and Lewis were to travel to Paris together. He is a sociable man, ingenuous and entertaining. He takes each man at face value. This is of course entirely as it should be, for a medical man must treat each individual the same. However, I think he may have unwittingly given information to a man I deem a personal enemy ~~as well as him being a Parliament man.~~
He was regaling us with stories of the chaos and tedium surrounding the Queen's household. One of his favourite remedies is to expound upon his peculiar theory, which even the most unforthcoming companion is unable to resist. He gave us an account of this cheerful diversion, to wit, using a chain of acquaintances of no more than six individuals, Richard maintains that there is a particular association between Prince Rupert of the Rhine and every person in England. It is a piece of nonsense and our friend admits that he could just as easily choose Socrates or the man in the moon, as his purpose is only to stimulate conversation; I personally think he should have done. Innocuous as our friend's anecdote seemed the possible repercussions are disturbing.
I think you know that we had no choice as to the vessel we were to board when we left Cornwall, despite Lewis' attempts to secure an alternative.
As polite convention dictated, the ship's Master extended his hospitality to the officers, gentlemen and their ladies but Lewis and I did not attend, giving my ill health as an excuse. Wiseman had attempted to dispel the awkwardness at the supper with his particular anecdote. He is a good raconteur

and until the implication of this story struck me, I confess our companion's performance was engaging.

"I have never met His Highness" he declared "but I know him by six degrees of association. It goes thus: I very recently attended a patient, sadly deceased." At this point, surgeon Wiseman ruefully noted, there had been expressions of derision regarding his medical skills but he had persevered undaunted, ignoring the jibes, "And this man had a wife. Thereby we have two associations." His said his audience grudgingly acknowledged this so he continued,

"This goodwife had lost her own infant, stillborn into this world by my hand; three, (This to expressions of condolence), but she, a kindly soul had become wet-nurse to another woman's son, the fourth link in my chain (polite cheering followed). The mother, number five, knew well a man who had been promoted by none other than His Highness, Prince Rupert of the Rhine! And there we have it, ladies and gentlemen! A fait accompli!"

His audience immediately complained that Wiseman had deployed a chain of seven, but the ice had been broken and the conversation had then moved on.

Engaging his guest later, Captain Fenwick had politely marvelled that there were mothers giving birth within the fort and had asked a great deal about the women of whom our friend had spoken. The surgeon expanded upon the courage and fortitude of all women, tactfully including those who had become legend in the defence of Parliamentary towns like Lyme as well as detailing the experiences of his Royalist patients. I ought to be flattered for he particularly remarked on my capacity as his assistant, in the infirmary at Pendennis. He applauded the bonds of adversity which led one female in those terrible conditions to not only offer succour to another's infant but afterwards to provide a home and hope to a woman whose life had been ripped asunder by the tragedy of conflict.

He had not dwelt upon particulars in his example of women's capacity for endurance. He had only used their Christian names. There will be many called Grace, a handful of who might come from Bristol. But few will have survived near-drowning.

As we dined last week, Richard confessed to being troubled by the exchange, not being able to say why. It was after recounting the episode to us that he identified the reason. His host, he now realises, had been subtly interrogating him and, without Richard proffering any information on his patients' appearance, it had been Fenwick who had mentioned that one of the women had a head of copper curls.

Lewis thought better of acquainting our friend with Fenwick's treacherous nature at that point, though I made him promise to enlighten him en route to St Germain.

Papa, I truly believe that, should her husband wish Grace further harm and I believe he might, he now knows without doubt that she is alive. ~~Can anything be done to ensure the safety of my friend? I wish that I could What could be done to~~ Lewis thinks that I am overwrought due to my condition and the tensions of our circumstance.

I can but pray that his seafaring obligations keep Fenwick occupied on Parliament's business. ~~I would wish for shipwreck, but it is cruel as others would be endangered thereby~~.

Please tell Bridget that the best recipe to fricassee a rabbit is written in the back of my receipt book, kept on the shelf in the still-room. Agnes will know where to look.

I remain your loving daughter,
Mary
To John Carew,
The Manor of Penwarne
By Mevagissey in the county of Cornwall.

XIII Grace: The man named Sark

It has been hard to talk of the life I led before you were born, filled as it was by incidents marred by anguish or sorrow. However, it was not all gloom. Though many would call it folly, name me a bawd or lewdly perverted, I chose a path that was for a time full of joy and contentment. To choose and not to simply do my duty to father or husband was a rare and fleeting freedom. Those memories alone are treasures, and you are the most precious gift of all. Friendship too is a gift. Friends in adversity prove the dearest, as close as family; the names of such friends as we have you now know, people on whom we both can rely. The dangers of our position you are beginning to know too. I will pray to God daily that you need never ask for protection.

Yet, there is one more individual of whom I must speak, a man about whom I want to convey so much more. The man is gone; lost, and the more is my sorrow for you will never know him. I have mentioned him already. It is the man known as Sark.

Any stranger might save another's life, though Sark was no stranger to me when he saved mine. He had been at Wine Street for the Twelfth Night revels in '40, though for a long time after he and Fenwick barely crossed my path. Still, I remembered that young man, or at least his eyes. Neither was he was a stranger before my marriage, being closely associated with Fenwick and the ship's crew.

I was suspicious of his perplexing involvement with my husband-to-be; Fenwick was obviously in authority, yet I had often heard Sark challenge his superior, almost as an equal. I remember Sark's presence in the shadows at the church on the day I was wed. Only later did I learn why he deemed it necessary to be there: he could not prevent Fenwick's scheming and remained aloof but he had privately resolved to watch over me.

Voyaging on board the *Ann of Bristol* to and from Ireland, while we still thought her a Royalist's ship, I often watched Sark train his men. It was a diversion amidst the uncertain and squalid nature of my circumstances. I began to be aware of the respect with which the gunners and sailors treated their leader and noted that it was not out of fear as it was with, for example, the bo'sun or indeed Fenwick himself. I doubt if his men knew him well, for I think nobody will ever know Sark well, but I came to realize that they liked him, which was to me a paradox. I remained wary of the man who had spoken hardly a handful of civil words to me in all the time I had known him. It was therefore especially odd when first he tried to tell me that Patch was safe. He spoke using an obscure code, words hidden in such a random conversation that it took me a long time to grasp his meaning.

A further revelation occurred when Lewis Tremayne joined the ship. Sark could not resist Lewis Tremayne's gregarious nature. It would also have been ill mannered to rebuff a man who was your senior in both rank and status. Whatever else he was, Sark was not ill mannered. Until that point, his accent was something I had never even registered, his intonation merely in contrast to my husband's northern tones. Nevertheless, Tremayne, recognizing something familiar in Sark's inflection, promptly established the enigmatic man's roots and his given name, Tremenheere, as well as the reason for his reticence to use it. Lewis Tremayne is the only person I know who was ever truly at ease with gun captain Sark. He called him 'Men'; every morning on our tramp from Tenby to Shrewsbury he would comically declare 'Forward, Men!' as we set off. To me his name was always Sark.

His innate cordiality being irresistible, Lewis discovered that the gunner was born near Penzance, that he never knew his father, a sailor, and that he had a Spanish ancestor in his mother's family, all this being revealed within ten minutes of their meeting. I came to know later that our gun captain was no boor, but a man who could speak in several languages, including his native Cornish. He could discuss playwrights and poetry. His skill with charcoal or pen could capture a likeness in a few strokes, and at his ease, he would discourse intelligently and without tedium on any topic you cared to mention. My escort to Oxford, on the orders of Prince Rupert of the Rhine, was this same man and the journey was a revelation.

When the time came for us to leave Bristol matters were urgent. Ships had to be commissioned to take the wives of the Prince's retinue, and their few servants, by sea to a safe haven. By then Sark was part of the crew of the *Dolphin*. The first time I sailed on the *Dolphin* as a passenger, Pasco Jago did not know me as his old associate Henry Godwynne's daughter. Later, when I had the choice to follow the fortunes of the Prince or make a voyage into the unknown, I chose the latter. I too become part of the ship's crew, to join Sark.

He taught me well as I worked my share of the daily tasks with him on deck or in the galley with Goody Jago. I swiftly grasped the mathematics of navigation and took great satisfaction in the calculations, which seemed to please Sark. I learned the handling of the vessel, the effects of wind and tide as well as taking my share of the menial jobs. I even enjoyed working with the canvas; you will not find your mother happy with her embroidery silks, but put a sail-maker's palm on my fist and I will mend your torn staysail as neatly as you like, better even than I can make you a shirt. Sark taught me all this. Nor was it all work, for Jago did not run a gloomy ship. Our captain was a man who loved to laugh and play practical jokes alongside his tall sea-stories. Sark, as ship's gunner but also Jago's old friend, was always a willing accomplice, being both witty and prone to surprising bouts of tomfoolery.

Even though I spent days, weeks in his company, there is much mystery about that man. I know little about his youth, his early years at sea nor even how he came to know Bartholomew Fenwick. I only asked once and, though he changed the subject with a lighthearted quip, I sensed there was a resistance not simply a reluctance to divulge his past.

He was a man whose innermost thoughts remained locked away.

Once, when we were plotting a night sky, and taking sights on the stars Sark quoted words from my father's book of plays, 'It is the stars, the stars above us govern our conditions' and asked me if I agreed. I told him that if it was so then it was at odds with his admiration for the works of men like Copernicus and Galileo and his belief in the power of truth and science.

Goody Jago claimed there was much that was true in a man's horoscope. Her elaborate performance with a pack of macabre cards regularly entertained the crew and, in some ports, earned her a reputation as a seer. She considered herself a competent astrologer and was prepared to wager that Sark was born under the sign of Aquarius. It was a memorable occasion when, after too much rum, she held forth on the subject for nigh on an hour before falling asleep where she stood. He would not reveal the date and time of his birth, and Sark kept his own counsel as to whether he thought her observations were accurate.

Would my fortunes have been different had we stayed on board *Dolphin*? I cannot say. I only know that Sark was a man who could see to the heart of an issue, for whom the common sense path was always the obvious one. When it became evident that I could no longer stay on board the ship, he saw Pendennis as an immediate and apparently sensible alternative. Sark's logic was irrefutable. The castle was a stronghold, and reputed to have supplies for a twelve-month. It was strong for the King, a cause for which he had fought for years. I would find security there with his protection. What other discussion need there be? Pendennis Castle was a refuge, but it was also a symbol of his principles but it would be his principles that would separate us.

You know of this nation's recent history, the crisis in which the last of His Majesty's western army found themselves in '46. Matters were desperate even by late June, so the scheme to send a messenger to the Prince of Wales, a plea for assistance, was born of desperation and the task had been assigned to Colonel Tremayne. However, on hearing the plan the gunner was adamant, arguing that Lewis' men needed their leader and that Sark was far better qualified to undertake the mission himself.

We all knew the risks and the penalty for being caught. Hester and Mary believed that I should beg him not to go. I knew more than anyone what Sark was sacrificing, but I could not do that. His independence and sense of honour were characteristics deep-rooted in his nature: to beg for something that I knew he could not give up was unthinkable. We both knew that any dreams of a future together had always been illusory. Perhaps that was another, private reason behind Sark's decision to slip into the dark water on that sultry July night. I will never know if he had tired of me. We never even discovered if he survived the swim across the dark waters of the Fal, he and Patch.

Much of this man will forever be an enigma. He was often stubborn and could be authoritative; but his men respected him. He would play the clown simply for the delight of making men laugh, but could confer with a prince and have his opinion valued. He was generous, imaginative, yet often could seem remote. He helped me to rediscover the joy in life, to trust in humanity again. He showed me how man and woman should be together and he opened my eyes. I think Sark knew me better than I knew myself.

This man I will love until my last breath. This man is your father.

XIV Hester: Some surprising kindness

If I look back to the winter of '46 all I can remember is mud; mild weather, rain and more mud. There was always mud on my hands, mud on my feet, and mud all over Hal. But then, the muck had its good side too for 'twas also the walls of our new home. It happened like this.

Blacksmith Beale and his wife proved good Christian folk and not just in church on Sunday neither. Most days something would come up from the forge, maybe a handful of fresh-dug vegetables or a few leaves of kale from their smallholding. Once there a wrap of salt all done up in a little package, which was right welcome for we'd no spare coin even for such a simple thing. It might not seem much, but 'twas all a great kindness. Time was a-passing and yet they had never once asked us to do mending or the like, which we neither of us thought was fitting.

So, after church, the Sunday before Advent, Grace asked if there was anything we could do to repay them. They did look at each other, seeming a little awkward - more particularly as Daisy Mattock had just barged between Goody Beale and her children, knocking the littlest one off her feet into a puddle. I thought we were going to get short shrift. Instead Jet bowed, all correct and stiff, which didn't seem like him at all, and bade us join them for evening prayers and supper. I was that taken aback, 'twas as much as I could do to bob a curtsey and mumble my thanks, though Grace has her good manners in hand, and accepted with all the proper politeness. We had brushed ourselves up as best we could for church, yet we spent all that afternoon trying to get ourselves looking respectable enough to go a-visiting.

The Beales were strong in the Puritan ways, though they all'us attended the parish church a'cause Reverend Smyth took pains not to offend his flock by word or deed. Mind, their faith did not require that the couple keep a mean house nor, once the prayers were over, a sombre one. I was a tad uncomfortable in case Jet and Will would have been at odds in the recent strife. What he chose to read to us from his Bible put my mind at ease; 'Behold, a king shall reign in righteousness'. Seemed he'd been for the King too, though never bore a weapon, managing to dodge both armies' draft. I wondered how but didn't care to ask.

Listening to him took me back to the days in Bideford, when old Ezekiel Judd would instruct his children and me from the great Bible he kept on the shelf, but there the likeness ended. Judd had snuffed out all candles when he closed the good book whereas Jet and Sarah Beale lit all the tapers on their table and we sat down to eat. Meals with meat had been so rare on my platter since … well, for a long time … that I wondered how to do proper justice to this hospitality. I noticed Grace only took a little of what we were offered so I did the same and eventually, amidst the family's cheery chatter, I began to rest easier.

Once the boards were drawn and the children settled head-to-toe in the box-bed at the back of the room, Jet drew out his pipe and bade us take our seats by the fire, but it was Sarah who cleared her throat,

"Jet and me, us have been planning to speak to 'ee for some whiles now on a subject of some … well, 'tis only one way to say it, 'tis a shameful matter."

I didn't know Goody Beale well, and couldn't imagine why we would receive a welcome before a scolding, but I didn't like the sound of this one bit. I looked at Grace, whose expression said as much as I was thinking.

There came a 'Harrumph!' from under a cloud of 'baccy smoke. Goody Beale started picking at the burrs on her skirt, not looking at us. She took a deep breath, and then the words all came out in a rush,

"'Tis Grand'mer Toms!" I must have looked mazed as a brush, Grace looked just as baffled so Sarah gabbled on explaining, "She's my cousin! That is, my ma's sister's girl…" then, just to be sure, she added, "there was eighteen years between Aunt Ellen and my ma."

I couldn't think of Grand'mer Toms as a girl, she looked as though she had all'us been wrinkled. True enough she was aged, and not well in her wits … but why that should cause Sarah Beale to be so upset I couldn't think. It soon became plain.

"She is my kin. By right, she should be in my family's keeping but the pity of it is there's nobody living now 'cept me. And 'tis to my eternal shame that I cannot look after her as she deserves." Goodwife Beale was wringing her chapped hands, "Yet you, seeing the straits she finds herself in, you share what little you have and show her great kindness. Verily you are like the widow who gave in her last two mites to the alms box at the temple." I didn't think there was that much of a likeness, but Sarah had got into her stride now.

"Jet and me, we can't take her in here. Though it is my debt to God to see to her needs, we have no space." That much was true. The blacksmith's home was tiny. No matter what the reason though, failing to do her Christian duty went hard with Goodwife Beale.

What came next was like a thunderbolt. This time it was Jet who spoke, firm and strong where his wife had been all a-bivver,

"Mistress Mattock, Mistress Sark; winter is near on us. With no satisfactory conclusion to yon legal matters of yours likely before May Day, I have taken the liberty of … spoken to … landlord …" He faltered a bit. Jet Beale wasn't a man for fancy talk, for all he tried, so after a pause he shrugged his leather jerkin more comfortably on his shoulders, took a deep pull on his pipe and finished,

"Look, if 'ee want it, there be Grand'mer Toms' old place, for two shillings rent for the year from Quarter Day coming, payable to the Constable, if 'ee be willing to work to make the place habitable … and if 'ee give the old lady a place back at her old hearth."

Grace and me were struck dumb. We must have looked like rocks, which he mistook for ill feeling. That couldn't have been further from the truth. He became intent on attending to the dried weed for his smoke, not looking at us as he rolled the leaf on his palm. By way of explaining, he pressed on,

"Don't 'ee worry, there'll be some help. 'Tis a scrap of glebe land and the good Reverend will take the doing of repairs as a substitute for folk's tithes. Woody Hillson has pledged some lumber and coppiced hazel; he, and Jake's lad from the mill and me, we'll set the timbers up and mend the wattle a bit to form the old lean-to into another room. That'll make up the two. 'Tis not big but you'll be as well with the extra space. We'll do what we can to get the roof weather-tight and get that cob-wall fixed. But it'll need to 'ee to set yon hands to fixing up the daub, paint the render ..." By the time his pipe was glowing to his satisfaction and he looked up, his message had sunk home, and the face of every woman in the room was awash with tears.

The blacksmith was as good as his word, and even with the short daylight hours, he and a good number of the village men, notwithstanding Ma Mattock's disapproving looks, set to fixing up our new dwelling. Grace and I collected heather, with the oldest Beale lad to help, and then we set about with the mud-and-straw mix for patching the walls. We were lucky with the only dry spell that season. I doubt anyone would ask us to do the same for them, our mud-walling not being the best of finish, and none too thick, especially the very last bit, out the back. 'Twas typical of the Mattock women that, just when you would have welcomed a delivery of dung, they'd not oblige you. Still, we managed. Nobody 'cept me seemed to wonder why the parish couldn't have done all this for Grand'mer Toms before, but I kept that notion to myself.

When we had finished, I thought it deserved better than to be called a hovel, though it was no palace either. Sarah Beale's home was small, but with the forge next door and four stout stone walls, it was at least substantial. The glebe-house wasn't quite that. Still, freshly lime-washed inside and out, our lodgings were clean and bright, kept off the rain, kept out most of the wind and, once I got the measure of the fireplace, kept us from freezing too - me, Grace, little Hal - and Grand'mer Toms, with her gappy grin there for all the world to see.

So it was that on Quarter Day, what would rightly be Christmas 1646, Widow Mattock and Mistress Sark became tenants in the parish of Cornwood, Devon, with a lodger at our hearth, and all at the bargain rent of two shillings a year.

XV Mary: Of France and of family

Enclosed as a packet:
Written this day 29th December 1646
Rue des Abbeyes
St Germain-en-Laye

My dearest sister,
This will be of necessity very brief for I am tired and Lewis
had ordered me to rest. My confinement has not been quiet
for as you can see we are now moved. Our new home is near
to Her Majesty's court at the palace. It is hard to think she
has been here over two years now. We arrived before
Christmas but I have not yet been called to pay my respects
to the Queen, my condition preventing it, though Lewis has
been formally introduced to the Prince of Wales.
I think I shall be keeping a quiet season, and the court is
much reduced in their festivities, being embarrassed for want
of money.

And Agnes, I never thought to say it but at this moment, I
care little for all the grand court concerns. I only wish that
my impending ordeal was over for I am heavy and lumpish
and tired and I confess, afraid. I would give a fortune - which
I do not have, but I still wish nonetheless - for any one of the
gossips of Mevagissey to reassure me that all is as it should
be. There will be no familiar goodwives' faces when the time
comes for the birth. Lewis says he will seek out an
experienced woman to assist, but I think there will be little
comfort in that. I wish I knew my future.

I suppose that I had become too used to my old lodgings,
though I knew them to be temporary. They were not as
splendid as here but I had come to like the tavern-keeper's

wife and her serving girls well. They were kind. Madame
Condeleu reminded me of Grandmother Dewnes being very
tiny and sprightly. She would have been a good midwife I
think.
The journey from St Malo was horrible, the carriage smelly
and the roads rutted so badly that we were stuck twice. I
thought the wheels were likely to come off their axles.

Did I ever speak of Loveday Yendacott? I think I did not,
because it is a strange tale and I ~~feared your reaction might~~
~~be to think it witchcraft~~ thought that you might be alarmed.
Goody Yendacott was a villager, a healer, from
Drewsteignton, and Grandmother Hillman knew her well and
trusted her. When I first arrived at Coombe Barton I was
ailing and Loveday treated me. She knew, without being told,
that it was not all my bodily wellbeing. Of course, it might
not have taken a seer to know that, for Dewnes had quickly
discovered my fears; about Aunt Carew's cruel scheming;
about Lewis and about our hopes of being together. When
Loveday read my palm she told me things that put my mind at
ease. Her predictions did come true even though she said that
she could see no further than the gates. You might think me
rash, but I would that I had her gift of vision now, be it magic
or no.

I can report some news that I am sure will bring a smile to
my father-in-law's face. Lewis has spoken strongly to Philip
about returning to Cornwall. The brotherly intercession was
not met warmly as you can imagine. The argument that
Heligan was in want of at least one of its sons to keep up the
estate was not well received either. Philip called his brother
condescending, arguing that it is poor recognition for his
service in Lewis' regiment. With mutual requests for
forgiveness, after a long and frank debate, they parted on
good terms and I understand that Pip should soon sail for
home, going via Jersey on some business for an 'eminent
person' whose identity I am not supposed to reveal. It is the
discharge of part of a debt I believe, nothing more.

*There are gentlemen from the King's party arriving every
week, but they are not all amicable. Lewis tells me they were
not so even before the present predicament despite being on
the same side. Prince Rupert and Lord George Digby were to
have dueled in la forêt. Quel surprise! Apparently Digby has
always had a habit of being able to aggravate people. In the
eventuality, Her Majesty heard of the matter, and they were
both arrested. I have not heard if there are to be
repercussions. I cannot think that the Queen will act too
harshly; she should treat them like badly behaved boys. Like
all boys they need something to occupy them for I think the
King's cause still blazes in them, unsettled as it is.*

*I will write anon or if I cannot then Lewis will send news of
my well-being.*
Pray for me, all at Penwarne and Heligan.
I remain your loving sister,
Mary

To Agnes Carew,
The Manor of Penwarne,
By Mevagissey in the county of Cornwall.

To John Carew
At Penwarne Manor
By Mevagissey Cornwall
31st inst.

Honoured Sir,
*I write in haste having intercepted the messenger to add this
but my respects due to you are none the less for that. God be
praised! Your daughter, my wife Mary, was safely delivered
of twins, girls, last night. She is weak and very tired but I
think will do well. We have called our daughters Mary and*

Honor. Mary is by far the louder of the sisters, and a little bigger. They are fair, like their mama and I think them both perfect and beautiful.

I am sure Mary will have more to tell her sisters of infants, and all womanly matters pertaining to babes-in-arms and she will be able to write in due course.

I have given the carrier an extra shilling. I will be pleased to reimburse you should you add to his reward if the delivery of this letter has been expedited with the speed I have instructed.

I remain, Sir, your most respectful son-in-law,
Lewis T

This and the enclosed packet with all possible haste to John Carew
At Penwarne Manor
By Mevagissey in the county of Cornwall.

XVI Grace: Fortunes changed

I cannot say whether to speak of fortunes lost is to stir emotions that are better left quiet. Nonetheless, it perhaps is well that you know the extent of matters. My inheritance, now my husband's assets, included full ownership of one ship, 200 tons, the *Ann of Bristol*. Shares were also held in varying degrees in four other ships, all profitably trading out of Bristol and Dartmouth. Of property, the deeds to the house in Wine Street, both the freehold and the fabric belonged to the family. It is a handsome double fronted house with carved jetties and coloured glass panes in the parlour window and eight chambers with hearths as well as three garret rooms and kitchens, cellars and a small walled garden.

In addition, there is a four-chambered house in Small Street which, when I was last in the city, was leased by a tailor at an annual rent of eight guineas. Our warehousing on St Nicholas Back would accrue rents, the income being variable, dependent on trade patterns. There was also, at one time, a small-holding in the parish of Keynsham, the land bounded in part by the river Chew. It was secured as my mother's jointure many years ago though I could not say in what condition it is now.

Coffers of coin; the wares in the cellars and holds; furniture, Turkey rugs and curtains; some silver and our pewter tableware - or what little was left after the forced contributions to the war - I could continue, but to do so would be mere speculation. For all I know the city of Bristol and its environs have been razed to the ground and everything we ever owned turned to dust. All this was my inheritance, and my dowry.

There was no provision for a jointure made on my behalf. There are supposed to be laws to protect the weaker sex, yet there was scant hope of a remedy before the King's cause was lost, and now there is no hope at all. Even if there was ever any real prospect that I might live a long and comfortable life as a merchant-captain's wife, I have forfeited it. To dwell upon former prosperity will only make us bitter, for Fortune's wheel turns for everyone. I have no regrets.

What of the future then? What choices did we have and where were they to lead? Whatever wealth might have been in coffers elsewhere, it was inaccessible to me now, and our current situation required an income, no matter how reasonable the rent for 'Toms Hall', as our lodging laughingly became known. Our small pile of coin would not last long and although I had still had the expedient of my wedding ring, there was the small problem of how to go about selling it. Bringing to mind Sarah Beale's comment about her husband's association with all things metallic, I decided to call upon his expertise. Jet was the man most likely to know where I could get a good price, or at least an honest goldsmith.

Jehoshaphat Beale's manner in church or at board contrasted with the tough pragmatism of the man in his workplace. Gone was any gentility. Until I made it clear that I wished to sell the gold, Jet Beale was disinclined to engage in any conversation. His reaction to the possibility that I wanted him to condone usury was prickly and he was none too sure that disposing of my wedding ring was the right thing for a respectable widow to do. However, when I was adamant that it was necessary, he said there was a man in Ashburton who he would trust, though he admitted he was not likely to give me the best price.

After a few minutes working a piece of iron over the anvil, he turned back to me. I sensed the offer was made reluctantly, but if I could delay a little, Jet said when next he went to Plymouth to see about a new shipping of black-metal he would make enquiries on my behalf. He strode over to the hearth, plunging the bar back into the coals.

I was relieved and more than happy to put the matter in his hands. It was but a few weeks to wait and we could manage that long. However, as I was reluctantly leaving the warmth of the forge, a parting remark took me by surprise, especially as he was shouting above the noise of the bellows,

"Do 'ee know that there's work up on Stall Moor, if you've the strength for it?" I shook my head, and, as he had returned to beat the red hot metal again, I stood waiting for him to finish hammering the curving blade. "They reckon they'm going to try one old seam again. Ask me, I think 'tis a fool's errand, but, either way, one of the blowing houses wants folk to break the stones," he went on, thrusting the piece into a barrel of water.

"Surely, there are men who ..." I began. Amidst the steam I saw him shrug.

"Never so many. With the paltry price of tin, mining's been dead these last years. The men who'm still fit for it have gone to seek a wage elsewhere. And anyway, women have all'us dressed ore." He put down the tongs, leaving his handiwork to cool. Reaching over to a rack, he handed me a long-handled hammer. "Here, can 'ee wield this?" He pointed to the anvil. I hefted the tool and swung it, the jolt of iron on iron ringing up my arm. The corners of his mouth turned down, he nodded grudgingly,

"Not bad. Y'can at least lift it. As I said, there's money to be earned if you'm not too proud. I merely mention it." He turned back to his fire.

Pride was not one of my vices. I had a child to keep and we had a household to support, so the next morning, I climbed the pack horse trail onto a moor covered white with frost, and for the wage of tuppence-farthing a day I was set to the task of smashing lumps of tin ore into small bits. It was all-weather work. The cold was never a problem for the labour was strenuous, but on wet days - and there are many wet days on Dartmoor - I returned to our hearth bedraggled and exhausted, with barely enough time to dry my skirts before the next morning. My many blisters soon became calloused; my ring would not fit my fingers now, whether I wanted to wear it or no.

Hester still tended you, and she kept a compassionate watch on Grand'mer Toms. Alongside seeing to the routine of a home, her work continued much as we had done in the church-house. The vicarage still required her services but Reverend Smyth now paid her a few farthings. When two women joined me at the dressing floor, both with babes under three, they arranged that Hester would mind their infants for tuppence a week, if she would include some broth at dinnertime. In addition, there was the promise of whatever produce they could spare from their cottage gardens come growing season. More than happy with children at her skirts, Hester said it felt like the best days at Pendennis, when the little ones would run to her for stories. With the parish relief still being paid to support Grand'mer Toms, though nobody could say we were safe from destitution, we were able to avoid starvation and just about make ends meet.

I do not know exactly when the notion came to me, but one evening, I pulled the old doublet and breeches from the bag hanging by the door. I sniffed the fabric, checking for mildew then I held them against me. Once I had been made to wear a boy's clothes under duress by Fenwick but later, out of necessity, I had worn these garments for nigh on two weeks and had found them passably comfortable. It was unorthodox, for certain, and against the King's laws, and probably Parliament's laws too, since now they held sway. Yet, I thought, neither the King nor Cromwell had ever had to toil on backbreaking labour weighed down and chilled to the bone by wringing wet, heavy garments. I considered my soaked overskirt steaming before the fire. The dripping clothes would not be fit to wear the next day. There was no doubt the man's garb would be far more practical in my present employment.

So it was that the next morning, woollen hat pulled down over my coif, I stepped forth dressed as a boy.

XVII Hester: To Totnes at last

With Grace up at the mine from dawn to dusk and infants round my hearth all day, time passed quick enough and, before we knew it, the sun had a little more warmth in its rays. Even the three hens that had been scratching round the wasteland of Goody Toms' garden had started to lay. That came as a surprise a'cause the birds were so scrawny we'd expected nothing. If they'd had meat enough on them to eat, they'd have been in the pot weeks ago. The old cockerel must have done his work, a'cause one chook had gone broody and now had chicks, but at least the other birds were giving us eggs.

Spring also meant that the reverend might have news about my venture at the church court in Totnes and 'twasn't just me that had business to attend to. From what I heard of the vicar's mutterings around his house, there seemed to be another official for this or the other as every week passed and they were causing a stir all over. Prices were high, and there was all'us grousing over taxes where folk gathered, at churchyard gate or pump. They who had enough to pay tax were being asked to pay more than ever, and more than once I heard men-folk grumbling that the King had never pressed folks so hard.

I didn't care to pay much heed to politicking, but there was no help for it. We might not get the newsbooks too often, only if a carrier happened through, and even then it might be weeks old, but folk had a knack of gathering gossip one way or another. My luck weren't the best, but the King's fortunes hadn't improved a jot. The Scots had got tired of giving him bed and board with little in the way of returns so had handed him back to Parliament in exchange for a grand sum of money. The King, by no means free, nonetheless was now lodged at some fine house. To top it all, it seemed that

Parliament and the gentlemen of the Army were beginning to find each other very trying indeed. But, truly it mattered little to the likes of we, for we had nothing to begin with, and so had naught to be troubled by. I had summ'at to look forward to but, for the time being, Grace, Hal, Grand'mer Toms and me made the best from day to day and, if we got no worse than a spiteful glance or gobbit of spittle from my in-laws in a week, on a Sunday we would thank the Lord for his goodness.

With the time nearing for the Archbishop's sessions, I'd often looked at my latchets and wondered how they would get me to Totnes and back, thinking they would need more than a few hobnails to mend them.

"The Lord have mercy on my soles," I said, as my finger poked through a crack in the leather by my big toe. We were sitting at the back door, keeping a quiet Sabbath, watching Hal who was finding the cluck of testy hens very funny as he toddled after a scurry of yellow chicks.

"Hester! Hush yon blasphemy!" came a token scolding from Grandma Toms.

"D'you think some thread could stitch up this slit? The tanner might find me a slip of hide for a patch for the hole in the bottom if I take his wife some eggs. If I put it inside under my foot, then maybe I wouldn't feel each and every pebble," I sighed, "though the wet will still seep in."

The idea of new shoes was hopeless. There wasn't enough money coming in to afford them and our pile of coins was already melting away, even though Grace worked long and hard and I did what I could. 'Twas the way things were. We didn't want to be beggars, so we had little choice.

"A bit of grease might clean them up a bit, ease the leather a little to stop it splitting more," Grace suggested, hopefully. I nodded ruefully adding,

"And as long as I don't need to kneel then nobody will see the hole." I would use the old lady's splintered pattens, strap them over my battered footwear and make do as best I could but I wasn't looking forward to it one bit.

Though Grand'mer Toms had looked as though she was sleeping, she'd been listening to every word. From under the cloth there was a grunt then,

"Y'should get 'ee a new husband to put new shoon on yon feet!"

Now, 'twas strange but those words really riled me. I let out a bellow which gave Hal a fright. He toppled over into the chicken's water bowl, and Grace needed to pick him up to still his crying.

"And where would I find a man to wed? They don't lie under every rock or tree stump! Nor ten a penny. This bloody war's seen to that!" I glared at the old woman, and Grace put her hand on my arm and gave a gentle squeeze. My ill-temper faded as fast as it had flared. There was no point in being angry with anyone for in truth, I was bitter, sad and missing William all rolled together and Grand'mer Toms had meant no harm by her remark. Women did remarry, it was common enough.

A thought struck me, and before I could stop myself I turned to Grace, with the words tumbling out,

"And you? Would you ... wed again? Well, you d'know ...I mean ... if Sark ... well, would you?" I knew Grace well enough to know when she was avoiding a subject; she had no idea if the man she truly loved was alive or no. So I wasn't surprised when she simply shrugged then said,

"I cannot. It is a simple fact. Until there is good evidence that Fenwick is dead, I am not free to remarry. The church and state, whatever the new regime, will sanction separation but neither he nor I can take another spouse." I should have changed the subject completely, but instead I said,

"That is plain enough then. And anyways, what benefit is there to a widow remarrying? I wed William Mattock for love. I ha' yet to meet a man to match him." I was relieved that Grace hadn't been offended, as she quipped back,

"Match Will? You want another Goliath then? Two such giants would be impossible and you said yourself, there are few prospective candidates anyway! And love? What of it?"

On winter's nights a-front the fire, Grace had told me some of the stories from her father's book, of Romeo and Juliet and such so I was having none of that,

"Well," I mused, as if I was a-thinking "let us make up a tale of a man who, loving at first sight, pledges secretly to protect a beautiful girl too far above him for them to wed. He keeps his distance, endures a fearsome foe to be at hand when his woman needs rescuing, but still he does not force his suit, for she is properly wed and he will not impugn her honour!" Grace's face was a picture as she realised what I was saying was a version of her life.

"Hester Mattock! Write your whimsical notion into a manuscript and we shall take it to Stationer's Hall. 'Tis a good fiction worthy of ..." I could see Grace was really trying not to laugh, even though she sounded huffy.

"Grace, I should really like to know. If you could, would you?" Perhaps I shouldn't have asked, a'cause Grace was suddenly very serious,

"Remarry? And who would take me? Widows with a child must make poor bedfellows without their husband's goods. I have nothing except my willingness to work and what little learning I have."

Grace looked so sad at that, that I could think of nothing to say except,

"You've still got your looks ..."

Now, for some strange reason, Grace thought that was very funny, and she began to laugh, with me and Grand'mer Toms joining in until tears ran down our faces.

Luckily for me, the first trip to town was on the pillion of the reverend's old mare. I think he felt sorry for me but, not being proud, I wasn't going to refuse. There was a deal of waiting, and eventually some official came back with a lot of long words that told me very little except that I was to return in three weeks time when the Archbishop might see fit to attend to probate matters. I was sure I heard 'billious' but it might have been some lawyer's Latin phrase.

Three weeks later, and this time there was no choice for it but to walk. Being the best of June weather, I didn't hardly mind, though there were grumbles from the women whose babes I would normally be tending. There was little to be done a'cause I had been bidden to go, so go I must. Grace had packed up some food in a cloth, a chunk of oaty cake and a small pot of curd cheese. We had worked out that we could afford two nights at most in one of the poorer sorts of inns. That would have to be without food, only paying for small beer. If the sessions took longer, I wasn't sure what I would do.

Still, I set out a first light, the better to be first at the Archdeacon's feet at the start of business. The place was thronged and Totnes town-folk looked to be thriving, war or no. Some official came, took my papers, then returned and gave them back with not a word. I asked another black clad fellow but he said summ'at about due course and such. With the church chimes at each hour, I grew more and more desperd-fearful while the line of folk, glum and sullen, got longer. Nobody complained; there was barely any talk. I supposed that, if all were like me, here on the business of the dead, 'tweren't no chattering matter. My belly would only take so much waiting though, so eventually I broke off a little oat cake and scooped some cheese to nibble at. Mind, a'cause of where I was sitting it felt as if it might be terrible bad manners. 'Still, Hester' I thought to myself, 'even the high clergy have to eat, and so must you.'

The shadows had started getting long, and I needed to relieve myself, but I didn't want to move and forsake my place in the line. Just when I thought I could stay no longer, a man we had not seen during the day, not a cleric this time, but looking summ'at official, swept round the corner. He brandished a sheaf of papers at the waiting crowd. Every head craned hopefully, necks all stretched up to see, like a gaggle of geese watching a fox. But there was a girt groan as they realised what he was saying, that the day's examinations were ended a'cause, he said, His Grace the Archbishop had succumbed to a sudden malady. There were more long words, with judges, summ'at-stration, cravings and letters amidst them. The woman opposite me called out to the fellow to say plainly what he meant.

It seemed that whatever illness had overtaken His Grace, it was likely spread by committees and commissioners. In its wisdom and for the greater good of the commonwealth, Parliament had decreed that Probate was no longer a church matter but one for the judges. These pillars of the law would serve nowhere but in London. For the likes of me, London might as well have been the moon.

I picked up my small bundle and set off on the road home. I would sleep in a hedge if needs be, for there was no point in wasting good coin on lodging. My husband's last wishes would not matter one jot. He had left no legacy. There would be no will proved here, nor in London; not now nor ever. Ma Mattock had won.

XVIII Mary: A Cornish exile no more

Written this day 17th April 1647
At St Helier
Jersey

Dearest Papa,
My dutiful love you must find in every stroke of my pen, for
this is necessarily a short missive. I write to tell you that I am
coming home, and hope to be at Penwarne by May Day.
My journey is necessitated by the duties now undertaken by
Lewis. ~~He is gone to seek out Sir Richard Grenvile~~.
He will be much away from Paris in the next months though I
must give you few details, wary should our correspondence
go astray. There is much talk, nay, constant news of shipping
intercepted. Any letters that are captured will surely be
opened and even such dull and domestic dialogue as mine is
read and sifted to seek out secrets and information. As if my
poor wits could form anything so clever!
If it has ever been anything else, my mind is now gone soft
with sleepless nights and tending babes-in-arms, teething and
infant colic being the most complex issues I can fathom. I
shall be a sorry companion for your parlour of an evening
for I am asleep as soon as I sit down. Perhaps Penwarne will
give solace to both my mind and to my matronly frame for I
do long to be home in Cornwall and to see my daughters
dandled on both their grandsire, Carew's and Tremayne's,
knees. Let us hope for good weather and a safe crossing for
us all.
I would be pleased if you would give my due respects to John
Tremayne at Heligan.
And keep me in your prayers,
As I am your loving daughter,
Mary

To John Carew,
The Manor of Penwarne
By Mevagissey, in the county of Cornwall.

Written this day 17th April 1647
At St Helier
Jersey

Dearest Agnes,
Thank you for yours of March 26th.
No doubt Papa will have told everyone in Mevagissey the
news, so you know that I am to return home. I wished to write
to you for I am filled with happiness that I would share with
someone, my favourite sister being the very best person of
all. Though I am almost certain and Lewis says we should
remain a little circumspect - perhaps he is a little
superstitious - I think that I shall again bear a child this year,
perhaps in late September. I have been a little sick but
nothing to compare with my first childbearing and I am so
much more at ease. Perhaps it is because this time I hope to
be at home? Of course I am also the old and experienced
matron now too! If God wills that the King's fortunes mend,
Lewis may be once more a gentleman upon his land and at
peace.

Honor has again been poorly. She does not thrive as Mary
does. I told you, I think, that I had success in finding a good
wet-nurse. The fashion here is for ladies not to nurse their
infants, and though that notion sat ill with me, I had no
choice as I had not sufficient milk to satisfy both babes. I still
wish that I had Hester at my side, not for her to feed the girls,
but for her sound common-sense and lightness of heart. I can
little think that any here would have news of them since she
and Grace were shipped from the Fal. But I do often think of
them both.

How are things in Cornwall? ~~Nay, you have~~ *No need to reply for I shall be there soon enough.*

We must hope that this year brings better fortunes for the farms and I shall be glad to be there, instead of imagining all manner of horrors, which Lewis assures me are much worse than the reality. Such are the fanciful workings in the mind of an exhausted mother!

My wits desert me too. Sometimes I can barely bring myself to read. I was never the most studious of children, I admit, but I think that all my wit and learning is fled, seen off by napkins and puke. Do you recall the time when we were children when Diccon refused to talk, only communicating in secret? It infuriated Master Cobb, the tutor, and it earned Diccon a beating. It must have been disappointing to him to only have sisters to play with but do you remember his codes? I never was able to impress Master Cobb but much to our brother's dismay I could work out his cyphers almost instantly. I cannot imagine being able to do that now! I am addle-pated at the age of twenty-three!

I will try to think of any light-hearted news that I can offer of the life at court here.

The Queen's attempts to set His Highness the Prince of Wales together with la Duchesse de Montpensier continue to stumble along, with the Prince speaking not a word, claiming he knows nothing of the French language, and la mademoiselle magnifique left to wonder why he seems to be able to understand everyone else so perfectly well.

The Queen has again had a bout of bad toothache. His Majesty of France was yesterday to accompany Cardinal Mazarin on an inspection of the newest horses in the Royal Stables. There was to be a presentation of a new suite of gilded saddles more suited to the King's age, his equipage becoming outgrown. The Prince of Wales was given the honour of riding at His Majesty's right hand side, but I have not heard any report of the event and as it was a foul day cannot think that much splendour was found in the occasion.

Your news of the locality was welcome but disturbing. I can only hope that the Committee for Sequestration acts circumspectly if they come to examine Penwarne though I cannot believe that they will, given the Coryton's experience. It seems so unjust that even despite Fairfax' indemnity they are still burdened with such a fine. Though I do not count Philippa Coryton a bosom friend, to act as intermediary as she did was a courageous thing, and you would think, since it was to favour the Parliament's cause, it would be acknowledged at least in the Coryton's assessment.

I feel sorry for the Scawens as they will find their penalty too harsh with Alice bearing again, though they are not alone in that. I know too well that imprisonment in St Mawes or Pendennis is a cruel threat to so many gentlemen of quality. Did we hear aright that it has been proposed that Cornwall be disallowed any members for Parliament? None at all was what is reported in our circles. It is said that it would be as retribution for their former enmity and rancour. If such a thing should happen, I think that it would go ill against any Parliament that says it represents the commonwealth against tyranny. ~~*They should beware, for Cornishmen have never been reticent to take action when they are offended by government*~~

I shall be glad to be at home and at papa's side and with Lewis' father too, for at least whatever befalls, I shall see the reality rather than my nightmares. To that end I ask you to pray for our smooth sailing and safe deliverance.
Your loving sister,
Mary
To Agnes Carew
Penwarne Manor by Mevagissey
Cornwall

XIX Grace: A new acquaintance with news

A chronicle such as this has all the advantage of hindsight, yet in those months and years the events just unfolded around us. Looking back, perhaps what I believed was pragmatism in my choice of clothes was a mistake, though the consequences took time to become evident.

Hester returned from Totnes in the lowest spirits I had ever seen her for even when William died it was as if she was detached, there had been no howling or wailing. Coming back to Cornwood that evening she had lingered on the road until there was little chance of an encounter with the Mattock women then slipped through the shadows to collapse, exhausted and sobbing beside our hearth. I could only imagine her despair for I had never had any illusions about my situation, or held out any hope. Though she did not expect wealth or riches, idleness or ease, still Hester had been buoyed by her natural optimism, holding to a vision of a future which was now destroyed. How precarious our situation truly was we were yet to discover.

What we were realising week by week was that the hardships we endured were being felt everywhere and that the new order was anything but stable. Though the battles were over, the war continued to impact upon poor and rich alike, although in differing degrees. A few of the gentry in the manors around Cornwood had been Royalist and, in an area which had largely favoured Parliament's cause, had been fortunate not to be sequestrated. Compounding was bad enough; fines of two years' income on estates which, before the war, had yielded good crops and fat livestock. Now they could only produce a fraction of their former harvests, ruined by ransack or neglect. No farm had anywhere near their full flocks or a whole herd, requisitioned by one army or the other. For many there was little income to hand over to commissioners, but still the officials made their demands and more besides. I wondered what had happened to the Tremaynes and whether it was any better in the west.

An answer came quite unexpectedly late in September when a careworn figure riding into the village on a piebald mare created a flurry of excitement. Captain Benjamin Burrell, late of His Majesty's dragoons, was returning home. In the following days all the villager talk was of his unexpected arrival. Burrell had been among the Cornwood recruits who had answered the call of the Commission of Array, recruiting in the autumn of '42, a young man of nineteen years, who his parents had hoped would make much of his education, complete his studies at law and become a gentleman. Instead he had ridden off to fight for his king taking numerous Cornwood men with him, William Mattock included, though they had gone their separate ways to serve in different units

Before long he heard that a local comrade-in-arms had left a widow, now resident in the village and he came to pay his respects. Hester was embarrassed at the attention, barely recovered from her setback at the courts. Clean-shaven, he wore plain countryman's clothes and looked older than his twenty-six years, his dark hair greying with a distinctive flash of silver at the temples. Only a puckered scar, a finger's length, above his right eye marked him as a military man. Captain Burrell was attentive, respectful of two women who, he said, had endured with the most loyal of the monarch's supporters rather than, like himself, abandon the cause. Captain Burrell gave us to understand that his last clash with the enemy was at Dartmouth and after Fairfax stormed the town, rather than agree to fight for Parliament he had fled abroad. When the Prince of Wales left Cornwall two months later the captain had made his way to offer his services to the regrouping royal force. He remained in awe of - and, he said, shamed by - those brothers-in-arms who had fought on at Torrington and held out in the last siege in England.

He had been in Jersey when the last futile missive from Pendennis had reached the Prince of Wales, tragically too late, and after the surrender he had mingled with the steadfast exiles, as their numbers swelled the prince's court near Paris. Burrell did not explain why he had returned, though by the look of him I suspected penury might have been a factor.

When he realised the implication for Hester, that William Mattock might not have died had relief come to the beleaguered fort, he went down on one knee before her, took her hand and begged her forgiveness, as if the failing had been personal. My mind was racing, preoccupied by what I was hearing, so it was Hester who falteringly asked,

"Sir, did you meet a Colonel Tremayne, he was William's commanding officer - a right good man too. He may have had his wife, Mary, at his side ..." The Captain was effusive,

"Aye, faith, madam! I certainly did, and an honour it is to know him. A man of integrity, a fine soldier and well respected," he replied, "Heligan, Cornish, that's the right chap, eh?" Hester nodded. "Well, we can't all be from God's own country!" he chuckled. I was jolted from my thoughts by the levity and Hester and I chorused,

"What of his wife?"

Captain Burrell looked a little taken-aback by our outburst; he might have been a little embarrassed by our female inquisitiveness. He was a soldier after all.

"Erm ... well ... I know that Colonel Tremayne is a father, for I heard someone once ask after his daughters. I did not meet his lady. I believe she was to return to their home though, since the Colonel's duties increasingly were taking him away from St Germain." Hester looked at me, the tears in her eyes mirroring my own. Our friend was now a mother, her dearest wish fulfilled, though I knew how hard she would take being apart from her husband, no matter the politics of the situation. Hester asked the question I could not,

"And, sir, if I may beg your pardon, what of the message that came from the siege? What of the messenger?"

"Mistress Mattock, I recall little. I only heard tell of his mission. He left soon after his assignment had been discharged, perhaps for home, for his name resonated from the islands; where was it, Alderney?" I could barely whisper, for my throat was tight.

"Sark." Our visitor looked surprised,

"Aha! Your geographical knowledge does you credit ma'am! Yes, indeed. Sark; that was him! Never met him myself, but we all heard his damned dog! He had a hound that followed him like a black shadow and it howled like a demon if they were separated, so much so that they had to allow the wretched cur in when they interviewed the chap or they'd not have been able to hear themselves think!"

I excused myself at that point, leaving Hester to interrogate the Captain if she wanted to. I needed some time to myself, to think about the implications, to compose myself for I knew that howl, had heard it last from a castle's battlements on that sultry summer night, and the memories that flooded back were too uncomfortable to share. Burrell had gone by the time I returned. Hester made as if to speak, but I forestalled her,

"Hester, let us be glad of this day's tidings and be grateful for this stranger crossing our path. But please, speak no more of Sark. I have done my mourning, have buried hope. Anything else will be an eternal torture. So, if you care for me at all, say nothing." Hester was as good as her word and despite his promise to call we did not see Burrell at our door again.

Times were hard, attitudes harsher as folk protected what they had from threats, real or imagined. There was widespread harassment that became real enough for as '47 wore on, where the bureaucrats of Parliament pounded the populace with their ordinances, the militia came with ordnance, or to be accurate pistols and swords. Jet Beale had returned from Plymouth with stories of a destitute and desperate garrison, the Governor of Plymouth reduced to taking out loans in his own name to keep body and soul of his soldiers together - and to prevent outright mutiny when the Army magnates in London suggested that troops would be better used in Ireland, or disbanded completely. Decrees that the arrears in pay would be paid from Devon's tax missed the point entirely; Devon had no resources with which to pay. As autumn wore on and the meagre harvests failed again, an increasingly belligerent military had started taking matters into their own hands and were ransacking the countryside for supplies, funds, and plunder. Cornwood was not exempt.

It was October, just before the Quarter Day, which we could no longer call 'Michaelmas'. It was a Monday, for Hester was at her weekly duties at the vicarage. On these days the small children, including the two she minded for the village women, were accommodated by lessons of a sort, delivered with mixed efficacy by the vicar and his eldest daughter, Tabitha. Hester's charges were old enough to sit, overawed by the clergyman, but you would toddle round after Hester, brandishing a goose feather in imitation of her dusting, and it was not unknown for you to curl up to sleep in a basket of laundering.

Hester told me the morning began peacefully enough, given that the house was always a shambles, with a tide of domestic chaos that one morning a week was never going to stem. It was perhaps a little before midday that she first heard the rumble of hoof-beats, heavy and reverberating. She was in the front parlour and looking out onto the square watched as, within moments the shouting of men joined the noise of horses. A platoon of heavily armed troopers thundered into the centre of the village. There were two score or more. It was evident that they knew exactly where they were going, though the officers barely seemed to have control as the horsemen barged arrogantly into the small-holdings and kitchen gardens, casually trampling through precious herbs and vegetables.

When a shot rang out, the echo bouncing round the valley, Reverend Smyth, with a gaggle of alarmed children around his knees, staggered out into the street. His wife, tremulous at the best of times, stood at his back, her clenched fists thrust to her lips, looking so near to fainting that their daughter took the initiative, rounding up the brood, and hustling them back inside where Hester met her.

Even then you were fascinated by horses and oblivious to any danger, proved hard to contain, protesting with increasing volume at being denied access to such a feast of equine excitement and Hester had to hold you tight while grabbing the ties that doubled as reins at the shoulders of the smocks of her two charges, bundling you all through the house, and out of the kitchen door. Instinct telling her to keep a distance, Hester watched the drama unfold from some way off.

The constable had come running, and a growing number of villagers were gathered, their protests completely inaudible above the noise of the soldiers. The local gentry, who might have commanded a modicum of respect, were noticeable by their absence. Parochial authority had no control over this militia and they were so unlike the soldiers we had met at Yealmpton. Hester said they looked as if they had become a law unto themselves. She noted the constable directing two boys who took off at a run past her towards the church, thinking perhaps they had been sent to Fardel House to fetch at least one 'gentleman' but it transpired that the lads had been dispatched to hide as much of the church plate as possible, which they had resourcefully done, burying it in the pile of earth from a freshly opened grave.

The crowd was growing and Hester could see Ma Mattock and the girls, puffed from running up from their lair, elbowing their way through the increasingly noisy throng. The captain stood up in his stirrups and fired into the air, sidling his horse menacingly near to the vicar wretchedly stammering at his own front door.

"By order of the Governor of Plymouth, and with the power invested me by Parliament, I have powers to arrest and detain one Henry Smyth, zealot and traitor to Parliament and preacher of doctrines contrary to the laws of the land!" boomed the officer, who had put away the gun and now brandished a sword. Reverend Smyth staggered forward,

"I am the vicar of this p-p-parish, if t-that's what you m-m-mean but I do not unders-s-stand …" There was a ripple of mocking laughter from the soldiers closest to the house, who had heard the poor man's halting admission, and smiling menacingly, one trooper dismounted and throwing the reins to a comrade, pushed Smyth, kicking behind his legs and knocking him to his knees.

"G-g-got some b-b-balls, Captain, this 'un, I'll say that for 'en," he said, cruelly mocking our vicar's stutter. His men laughed again. "Most of the misbegotten king's lickspittle preachers would hide themselves in the crap-house rather than introduce the'self, all polite like! On ye' knees and we'll have some respect for the captain!"

He pushed Smyth's forehead to the ground and put his filthy boot on his back. Mistress Smyth sagged to the floor and, just at the same moment, the old man Cled teetered through the door, stopping dead in his tracks. The folk who could see him watched a dark stain spread down the legs of his threadbare breeches as his feeble frame tottered then slowly toppled over. This was greeted with even more ribald laughter and the captain, having subdued such a reprehensible threat to the good governance of the nation, gave a wave of his sword and ordered the soldiers to search the premises for each and every item contravening the laws of Parliament.

Dismounting, they callously stepped over the prostrate form of the old man and, ignoring his cowering mistress, pushed into every room, every nook and cranny of the vicarage. The sergeant had now tied Reverend Smyth's hands behind him but remained 'guarding' the prisoner and, doubled up as he was, the reverend could be heard sobbing, pleading his innocence, begging for someone to help his wife and family. The officer, remaining mounted, his heavy-footed horse skittering and jumpy, made a great show of reloading his pistol, resting it prominently on the pommel in front of him. It was a blatant threat to his horrified audience. A buzz of resentment, like a skep of angry bees, hissed round the crowd but the villagers were powerless against so many heavily armed, mounted men.

Eventually, Tabitha emerged, evidently shaken but firmly in control of her siblings. Running to her mother's side, she helped her to her feet. Neither the sergeant nor the officer even looked at them as they stumbled into the crowd, sympathetic arms clasping them as they watched as their

106

home was ransacked. Nobody dared go to the aid of the old man. Books and household wares were being brought out, bundled in bed-sheets; pillow cases of provender from Mistress Smyth's larder and store-room were loaded onto the horses, and even a small stool with a padded cushion was slung across the pommel of a saddle. When the 'investigation' had been completed to the captain's apparent satisfaction, his soldiers were ordered to find timber to bar the doors and nail the premises tight shut. Once their task was completed they mounted once more, and the officer again stood in his stirrups to address his appalled audience,

"By the powers vested in me by Parliament ..." There was a murmur of resentment at that, but he glared and brandished his weapon again. "This malefactor has been thwarted and the evil plucked out for the good of the community of God and of this land." A voice rang out from the back of the crowd,

"Aye, and for the benefit of the bellies of thieving Roundhead bastards like you ..." The reaction was as immediate as it was terrible. The captain swiftly and without warning raised his pistol, aimed it just above the heads of the crowd, and fired. The shot ricocheted off a granite wall running beside the road, shattering shards of stone. Screams began at the back of the crowd which fragmented, and swirled round prostrate figures whose blood was beginning to seep onto sleeves, caps or aprons.

Amidst the disarray an order was given and the raiding party headed out down the lane towards Lutton, their prisoner, our vicar, slung across a saddle like another bundle of plunder. Behind them, the villagers of Cornwood were left to comfort the stunned family and pick up their maimed and their dead. The former included Goodwife Mattock, and the latter was the deaf servant who had only ever been known as Cled.

XX Hester: Trial by fire

What had England come to, that a good man such as our vicar would be most cruelly treated, and his wife and children put on the streets to fend for themselves? Fardel Manor took them in, but we never saw Henry Smyth in Cornwood again. 'Twas said he was taken to gaol in Exeter like a common criminal and Mistress Smyth went back to her family, somewhere up Crediton way. The parish was sent a new vicar, a thumping girt lump of a man called Shute with no hint of meekness or mildness in him, and a manner in his preaching that offended every one of his flock. 'Twas as if he was able to rub each and every person with a scouring stone, setting teeth and nerves on edge.

Even our mild-mannered constable, the cooper Triggs, was discomforted a'cause, though he hated the sight of the man, he was obliged to attend at vestry meetings and do his bidding. The word was that if he could have stepped down from his sworn duties, he would have but there was no remedy, a-cause he'd two strapping sons to run the cooperage while he was on parish duties and he'd taken an oath to serve. The new vicar seemed to know just how to vex him, calling for his attendance for this and that, whether it was the constable's place to be there or not. The clergyman had it in his head that his most God-given task was to search out evil in every form, weed out sin, purify by sermon or scourge - and he seemed certain sure that the only person in Cornwood who was sure of the Lord's grace was Walter Shute.

His very first sermon was full of warnings of God's wrath over disobedience, un-cleanness and all wrong-going affections and he preached of works of the flesh and sin at every door, missing out all the kind bits about charity and forbearance that I remembered from Old Ezekiel Judd's readings back in his Bideford cottage. Soon the whole village was a-bivver, all uppity and no person at ease with themselves let alone their neighbour.

It weren't too long before the reverend's beady eye lighted on three women, living together cheek-by-jowl, in a plain little hovel on glebe land. The first I knew that summ'at wasn't right was when Martha Hamack said she'd not be bringing her lad to my hearth again, scurrying away with the bairn as if Lucifer was at her heels. She left the payment due, which was more than Goody Rugg did, who just never came to my door again and who cold-shouldered Grace when she asked her how we had offended. 'Twasn't long before we found out and it befell like this.

Everyone d'know about the 'bawdy courts'. Of course, properly they're the Church Courts, same as the one in Totnes, only not always such important clerics as archdeacons. But a'cause of the notices on Sundays that all'us spice up a dull service, they'd got a name that folk thought better suited their business. There'd be whatever banns might need reading, and other such matters, then came the bawdy court notices. That was what woke folks up in their pews. There'd be charges laid against somebody or another, probably someone sitting t'other side of the nave. Maybe they'd be a-brawling in the churchyard or begotten a child out of wedlock, even done bigamy if it was a particularly good week. My business with my husband's will had been read out for all and sundry to know a'cause 'twas all the same, though the whole parish already kenned it well enough for Ma Mattock had seen to that.

Then again, that was in the old days. I'd already found out that those matters the church courts used to manage some regular judges would rule on now, if they found time to set their minds to it. 'Twas strange enough, that when all I wanted was my rightful inheritance the route was longer than Methuselah's beard, but when it came to accusing two luckless women of scandalous doings the venture could be undertook at the blinking of an eye. Anyways, now we had a clergyman whose God-given mission was to fill those courts with the blackest and most sinful souls and see them get the proper reckoning.

Shute was a man who worked like ice. Oh, he was hot enough in the pulpit and smooth to your face, but like ice he was freezing the cracks in Cornwood circles, splitting us apart like a rock riven by a hard winter. Little by little, he wormed his way into villagers' lives, 'getting to know his new flock', he said, and all the whiles he was listening for any little shred of spite or any hint of malice. He cajoled, wheedled, flattered any poor sod who even hinted they might know something about a neighbour until the 'facts' were plain him and before long Thomas, Richard or Henry were putting their mark to a sworn statement they didn't even remember making.

At the end of that year there was no cheer; no Advent, nor Christmas service, no marking of that day at all. Our vicar's long Sunday sermons battered our ears with warnings of thunderbolts from the heavens if we had even so much as thought about the papist superstition that was Christ's birthday. Then we were told that anybody who allowed even a smile to cross their lips on Twelfth Night, let alone a song, was damned to hell's fires. Two hours into that sermon, by the time he got to the subject of Mummers, Shute was spitting and frothing at the mouth. He cried them as 'pagan players, clothed in the stinking robes of Beelzebub', practicing their riotousness and lasciviousness, the temptations of the devil and all his works.

Well, I knew the old crate of rags the villagers used for guises smelled a bit, a'cause it used to be kept in the corner of the vicarage parlour and I'd looked in once then shut the lid quick for the head of St George's dragon had leered up at me and given me a bit of a start. But 'twas only fusty and not how I reckoned Satan would stink at all. Needless to say, Twelfth Night passed without so much as a nut shared between neighbours - not that we could afford more than a bean anyway and that would have had to be carved up betwixt us - all a'cause nobody wanted a visitation from the vicar, never mind the hosts of hell.

Another year beginning, sixteen-hundred and forty-eight, and 'twas the coldest January I could remember with Dartmoor about as bleak as it could be. It was hard keeping the hearth warm enough to comfort Grand'mer Toms who'd got quite frail. I warmed stones, wrapping them in sackcloth and putting them about her feet, but often she said she couldn't feel them, wouldn't even eat her broth. 'Twas a worry for we were fond of the old lady.

A greater chill had come between the Parliament and the King too, a'cause we heard that the great men in Parliament had decided to stop all dealings with His Majesty, Shute in his pulpit roaring on about tyrants and reprisals and all. As we left church on the last Sunday of January, ankle deep in snow, I had passed the time of day with the Beales. Sarah hadn't been to see Grand'mer Toms, as she'd all'us done on a Sabbath morn and I nearly asked if all was well but something made me hold my tongue. Jet was formal, as he often was outside his four walls, but Sarah was shifting like a hen on hot coals, her face flicket, eyes looking anywhere but at me. Grace didn't seem to notice ought wrong, but that Sunday I came home from church not uplifted as in the old days, nor comforted or even chastened like sometimes I'd felt after Judd's homely preaching, but instead I was rattled, affeard of summ'at, but what it was I couldn't say.

The next day I found out. We were sent a message, one even I could read now. Nobody but a blind man could have missed it, for it was there, smeared in blood-red mud across the render of our front wall: 'unnatural whores'. Grace tried to scrub it off before she set off up to her work, but the stain was frozen into the lime-wash. Then, when she got to the mine workings the other women had all turned away from her, holding back any tools, so she was left standing, she said, like a leper, until the mine master strode across and told her she was no longer wanted. There weren't any wages to collect, it being Monday, so there was naught to be done except come home. And then it was no time at all before the awful sight of Reverend Shute filled our doorway, with the constable Triggs on his heels as well as the parish clerk hiding behind him, a wiry little man with ink-stained hands that fluttered and flapped. Shute loomed at us, thundering,

"In the name of God, by the powers vested in me by Parliament, and with these men as my witness, I hereby assert that you, Hester Mattock and you, Grace Sark, stand guilty of….." I stopped hearing after that, until the last word came, 'accused'. The parish clerk was trying to say summ'at about courts, us being not yet guilty and due course, while Triggs just muttered into his beard,

"Keep within your doors, and we'll not have any trouble now, will we?"

No matter that there might be the small matter of a fair hearing, Shute was certain sure that he had found sinners, and for the time being, Cornwood could rest, all prim and decent, and in righteous outrage turn its back on the likes of we.

On the first Sunday in February '48, the third banns were read of one Rose Mattock, spinster of the parish and one Thomas Triggs, bachelor of the same parish. Even though her ma wasn't there, seemingly still being pained summ'at bad from the wound got when the soldiers came, there was a rustle of approval for the match of the cooper's lad and the alewife's maid. Then it went quiet. You could have heard a brass pin drop as every ear was cocked for the next notices.

All formal, the vicar read out the summons for two Cornwood residents to appear before sundry properly appointed judiciary that they might answer a number of charges,

"Charge the first: that the said individuals do live as a man with a woman, though both be women, which is contrary to the laws of God and of Parliament. Charge the second: that they are guilty of the detestable crime of lewd living, to wit, the making of a house on glebe land into a place of sin and fornication. Furthermore, they also stand accused of the corruption of innocents, namely one child, Henry Charles Sark and one adult woman, Eleanor Toms, she being of feeble body and mind, to the scandalisation of her family. Further to this, those heretofore named have, to the certain and sure knowledge of persons of good character, appropriated monies given by the people of Cornwood for the compassionate relief of the needy of this parish, to which they are not, were not and have never been entitled. As they shall answer to God, so shall they answer to the court."

The names that thundered from the pulpit into the frozen silence were ours.

Now, I knew a witch-hunt when I saw one and I'd seen the inside of the wrong type of a court too, so I'd have packed up our pans and run away the very same day, but Grace would have none of it. We'd paid the quarter rent, she said, so we should stay for we'd done naught to be ashamed of. And Grand'mer Toms needed us, no matter what the tattle-mongers said. So we stayed, kept ourselves to ourselves, and hoped for better times.

Then on a clear February morning three days later, birds singing in the crisp early sun, we woke to find Eleanor Toms had slipped from this world to the next, with nothing so much as a sigh to say farewell. Little Hal didn't know why the bony hands tucked beneath the blankets would not reach out to catch and tickle him, as they had done every morn he could remember. When she didn't answer his lisp-y call, his lip began to wobble, fat tears rolling down his face and once he began to cry, neither Grace nor I could not stem our tears.

Yet, our grief was hedged about with matter-of-fact concerns. We had not gone abroad since the notices in church and Sarah Beale would need to be told. Grand'mer Toms was Sarah's family yet it felt as if the blacksmith and his wife had turned their faces away and I was certain they'd would not thank us for going with the sad tidings. Grace and me would lay out the dear woman and, though I could hardly spare it, perhaps my old shift would serve as her winding sheet. Then there would be a funeral to see to - and God knew we had no money to arrange that. The fact that, of late, the poor rate had helped keep Grand'mer Toms meant that she might have had a pauper's burial, but a'cause of our shaming, those funds had stopped. Would the parish abandon her mortal remains in death too? We didn't know.

In the end, as I was standing at our door trying to catch my breath, still weeping, one of our problems was solved. Jack Triggs - honest, sensible and kind Triggs - was passing with a cart-load of wood, for once being a simple cooper not the constable and a'cause he saw me crying he stopped. When I told him of Goody Tom's passing he came in, paid his respects then, quite unexpected, said that he would break the news to Goodwife Beale. In that moment the constable and the Good Samaritan were one and the same in my eyes and that set me to burbling all over again.

"Should we use some of the coin? Would that be our Christian duty?" Grace whispered, as we gently washed the fragile body. "Though there is less left of the twelve shillings that Jet got for my ring than I would like, I could not bear for her to not have the proper rites." I didn't know what to say, for 'twasn't my coin. But I reckoned even combining every penny we had, it would not be enough to do the right thing anyway.

We had just placed my battered Bible beneath Eleanor Toms' head, 'so that she would rest knowing God's word' I said, when Jet and Sarah came to pay their respects. Grace and me stepped outside into the yard, we being too angsty to offer more than a few words of sympathy. At least that seemed to be accepted. Jet said some words of prayer over the body, and as they left he nodded by way of thanks, saying that 'the laying out was well done'. At any rate, they chose to leave Eleanor Toms with the folk who'd cared for her to the last.

Which was why, at the end, all our fretting over a decent burial didn't matter one jot.

Through the night we decided that each would take turns to watch over the body. I took my turn first, Grace coming to sit at midnight. It felt as if I'd not long drifted off to sleep, when she was shaking me, her voice croaky, her eyes wide with fear,

"Hester, wake up! Wake up … but quietly … shhh …" she hissed, "There are folk around the house, two maybe more! I can hear their feet! I can hear …!" A horrible thud shuddered first at the thin timber of our door then the shutter of the little window overlooking the street rattled, clamped tight into its frame. Someone was hammering in nails. I was wide awake now, but 'twas strange a'cause I was quite cold and clear in my mind. Shaking her by the shoulders I remember saying,

"Grace, listen to me. Listen well! Take Hal, take whatever you can to wrap around you both, and then you must get out, get out through the back window. I will gather what I can, I'll come after ..." I pushed her through to the little room where she and the bairn had slept.

The hammering started again, properly waking Hal and starting him howling, his little fists clutching round Grace's neck. If he stopped to gulp a breath we could hear them outside, three men querking and growling, a'cause now they were careless of the noise they were making. And by the gutter of the rush-light, I could see there was a slinking coil of silver grey coming beneath the door. I tried to shout, but the words just stuck in my throat. Grace came back though with the little one, wrapped and held fast to her by a snap-sack slung across her shoulders, its strap across her chest.

"They have barred the back too! May God have mercy on us for we've no way to get out!"

It was daft, but I couldn't help myself. In all the dinder, I still carried on struggling to gather up things into a basket - a leather jug, clay jars of this and that, my good knife, the hard boiled eggs and oatcakes I had cooked for breakfast, my prized skillet, three onions on a string, the bag of small coins we kept hidden in a hollow below the salt-pot beside the fireplace. Suddenly the feeble flame of our light went out, and the hearth blew back a puff of bitter smoke and then I could hear it, an eerie crackle; a bonfire at our door. 'Twas odd for all I could think was is this how Beelzebub's world will be, sour peat smoke and pitch black? No demons nor brimstone just no air.

I dragged the basket across the floor, but forgot about the form set up in the middle of the room, and it came crashing down. The last of the peat-glow lit Grand'mer Toms, a grey-white blur splayed over the toppled frame. Grace screamed at that, but I grabbed the Bible and the only other blanket we owned that had lain over the corpse and shuddering, pushed Grace through to the back room, fumbling along where the wattle wall met the cold earth floor. It was barely two arms' length before we were in the corner, nowhere to go.

I wanted to laugh. Me, Hester Phipps, who became Mistress Mattock, the very same that had survived shipwreck and dodged the gallows and Grace, a woman who'd endured every villainy man could think of, and here we were going to hell in a hovel. I'd stopped screaming a'cause it made my throat hurt more. Grace reached for my hand. By the glisten on her cheeks I could see she was weeping. Hal had gone quiet now which somehow seemed worse. Just loud enough for me to hear Grace said,

"May God forgive us for all our sins, forgive us our trespasses, and may be He with us all at our ending!" and I said 'Amen'. Those few honest words meant more than every sermon I had ever heard. Then we prayed together, the Lord's Prayer, soft and fervent, with the horrible sound of the fire growing louder minute by minute. There were no voices outside now. They'd no need to stay to see their work done a'cause the morning would show Cornwood how God punished evil sinners.

I tried to shift, so that my body was between Grace and the flames coming from the front of the house, but standing was worse. There was naught to breathe and I came over all zaundy. Wrapped in a rug, with that stubborn bit of me still clutching the basket, I had no hand free to stop myself falling.

When the weight of the basket, the skillet and me all crashed against the daub wall it must have been where it was the thinnest. My elbow went clear and sheer through the hazel frame, splinters cawtching in the woolly cloth.

"Thanks be to God! Oh, praise be to God!" I whispered over and over to myself as I wriggled and kicked my way out. I might have added, 'And thank the Lord for badly-made clobb walls!' I dropped my basket and took a deep breath, then turned back to haul Grace and the bundled infant out by the strap across her back. Then, keeping low a'cause we were affeard to be seen, we crawled to beyond the midden. You'd not think anyone could ever be glad to smell dung but I was that night

By the light of Eleanor Toms' pyre, we could see a few figures struggling with pails of water but they soon gave up. Our home was burning too hard to quench it now.

We huddled in the dark until dawn then set off towards the moor, keeping in the deepest rimy shadows of the hedges. I wanted to get as far from the good people of Cornwood as possible, just in case they realised that where they had believed there were the bodies of three women and a child, in truth there was only one skeleton in the stinking, smouldering remains of Toms Hall.

XXI Mary: A wife writes

Written this day 23rd of June 1647
At Kestle Wartha
Heligan

My dearest heart,
I pray that this finds you safe and well and in the company of
good men and in comfort. Here at Kestle we are as content
as may be without your presence, and praise be, I am now
restored to good health. The sickness did not last long and
Agnes says she thinks I ate too many gooseberries which
were not ripe, and that I should have been concentrating on
the task in hand of making the vinegar not consuming the
ingredients.
I am, I think, a little smaller than at this stage when I was
bearing the girls for my bodice still laces up reasonably well
but there is no disguising my condition. I feel different and so
perhaps we shall have a boy?
The flock of local gossips have already taken me under their
wings. My lying in will be so different here with
Mevagissey's women to superintend the birth. They think that
Kestle will have its new infant perhaps in the last week of
September. I have been told, in no uncertain terms, by Goody
Symons and Mistress Richards that I must on no account eat
this season's raspberries for they say that fruit brings on a
birth. You know more than most how perverse is this female,
she who would not stay at home even when her husband bid
her do so. So it will not surprise you to know then that the
thing I crave most is a bowl of ripe raspberries and the
cream off the new milk.
I forgot to tell you that I did as you said and took on Margery
Butland's granddaughter, Jane to be housemaid. She works
hard, though is very meek.

Your daughters are the delight of everyone here. Mary managed to roll herself over on the grass yesterday. It being the best weather we have had so far this week Bridget, Agnes and I took our needlework and the babes out and sat in the shade in the orchard. The twins lay on a blanket. Mary was on her front and reaching for a ball of knitting wool. Though she has taken some time to discover that one plump little arm keeps getting in the way if she wants to turn, the expression of surprise on her face when she found herself in a different place was very funny. Now I shall have to have a care where I put her down.

Honor is not yet so strong, and does not care to lie on her stomach as Mary does, but her smile is compensation. She still has one tooth more than Mary which makes for a pair of lopsided but captivating grins.

Both grandsires are besotted with the babes, which is no more or less than I would have expected. I must have told you of the swing papa had the stable-hand make for us down at Portmellon Cove when we were small - he has already commissioned its replacement for our children. They are barely six months old, and last Sunday your father spoke of the ponies he will choose for them, as if the estate has any spare cash for such frivolities.

It is bad here. There is want of wheat for flour, and the price of wood for the hearth has risen again. The charge on the parish for sick and injured is a burden which weighs heavy, for all it is our Christian duty. Our duty to Parliament you well know. We are more fortunate than many for papa's business remains steady, if not as abundant as of years past. However, since the gospels tell us that sufficient unto the day is the evil thereof, then we must be content to live each day in the knowledge that the Lord will provide. ~~So long as such as He provides is not what the county committee would fetch away.~~

The machinery of the Committee for Compounding with Delinquents - Oh! But that word has such an awful sound - has not troubled Heligan or Penwarne yet. I think perhaps

*we have cousin John Carew to thank for that? His loyalty to
Parliament and even his promotion of a republican cause is
well known.*

*But the final demand that Richard Edgecumbe will have to
pay has been set at nigh on £600, and we are told he is to be
grateful as he is another reprobate who has been given
leniency, thanks to Fairfax's generous intervention. If that is
so, then the great estates like Trelowarren will quake. There
is now talk of amounts the equal to near three year's income
for each property brought to the committee's bench. These
are assessed at the values of '42, and not now, when fields
are ruined. ~~How are estates to replace a whole herd or flock
taken to spit-roast for roundheads' suppers? The demands
upon those who have so little bring such hardship and it is
the lawyers are the men who rub their hands no matter who
prevails.~~*

*Your father says he will send you a copy of the accounting,
though the better part of it seems to be tax upon tax, with
more duties to be paid on that tax too. The latest demand was
a reconstruction levy, the sooner to rebuild decayed bridges.
~~How more can be squeezed from fish, farm or failing tin
mine?~~*

*I should not allow myself to be so vexed, it makes the infant
kick the more when I get anxious. But I cannot help but
worry. How will Heligan fare if they come demanding? What
should we do? Your father says that his time incarcerated by
Fortesque will be his lever, for if they had no proof of
malignancy here then they will have none now. I hope that he
is right. As the terms of Exeter's Articles of Surrender did not
help Sir Richard Vyvyan, who rightly should have had benefit
of the same, I do fear that Pendennis' terms will not serve to
help us. I do not understand all the legal matters, and simply
worry that the girls and I shall have no roof above our head
for you to come home to, delinquent, surrender articles or
no.*

It is no secret and you will already know I am sure, that the King is not now in Northamptonshire but at Hampton Court, the which is, Uncle Arundel says, a proper palace and so much more appropriate for His Majesty's dignity even if it is the Army who control his existence now.

I have forgotten to say, we received a visit from our Arundel cousin from Trerice, Gertrude and their eldest two. She obtained a pass to travel with no demur from the authorities. There was little news to impart but the company was pleasant nonetheless.

It seems that there is much agitation between the army generals and men of Parliament, so now they do argue between themselves. How has England come to this? Did you hear that ~~everywhere in many places across~~ *men wore the Prince of Wales emblem, three feathers, on his birthday? I did not know the date otherwise I might have sought out a chook to pluck a plume or three.*

Papa had heard something of the matter of the privateers that you talk of. There is always some flurry of seafarers' news about here and he likes to keep abreast of it, as you know. He is right then that French ports do not now tolerate ships operating on letters of Marque from the King or the Prince of Wales, and that this is a political gambit by Cardinal Mazarin? There will be more than a few folk out of pocket as well as beset by the law in that case, if what I heard and saw at St. Malo is anything to judge by. I am sure Monsieur and Madame Condeleu ran more than just their tavern business. It strikes me though, will this affect our friends aboard the Dolphin?

Resumed this day 25th June
I was called away from my pen by the nurse and I am sorry to have taken too long to return to my epistle. Honor has a fever and slept but fitfully again last night. I stayed with her. Today my eyes droop closed each time I sit down, but she is a little better. More teeth perhaps? Time will tell.

Forgive me but I shall close this letter with nothing more
newsworthy than the fact that your favourite sister-in-law
Candacia no longer rails against the monotony and boredom
of Penwarne compared to the glories of Antony House. I
remain suspicious of her unnatural affability.
I will close with apologies for the deplorable hand writing
and regrettable errata. My excuse is motherhood, which
turns my wits to curds. And that I write as I would talk if you
were here, correcting myself as if I can hear you chide me
which I hope gives you some comfort.
I pray God keep you safe.
As ever, I remain she who loves you,
Your dutiful and affectionate wife,
Mary

To Lewis Tremayne
Rue des Abbeyes
St Germain-en-Laye

XXII Grace: A moorland encounter

Perhaps when you are grown, after reading this, if you are ever curious to see the western counties, you will cross the strange landscape of Dartmoor. Maybe you will not sense it, but in that place I think it is not difficult to believe in a faerie realm among the many granite tors where it feels that there are matters that are unfathomable to man, things that we cannot explain. Often we tell tales of ghosts, to scare ourselves by winter firelight, and you have always enjoyed the story of the prince of Denmark who met the shade of his dead father on the battlements. Even without the lesson of King Saul and Samuel, Ann Fanshawe's insistence on her own mother's encounter with spirits has always been enough to persuade me of an 'otherworld'. Only, when I write of such things, they do seem incredible, yet I know that it all befell as I shall give account. The reality or otherwise I will leave to you to determine.

When Hester and I escaped with our lives we had few options as to where we could go. Our only concern was to find some shelter. By the time the sun was up, and anyone who knew us might be abroad at Stall Mine, we were far enough away to avoid being recognised. Working up on the moor's edge I had learned a little of the land from listening to the legends bandied about. There were tales of caves and ancient burial sites, places that might offer us a chance to shelter and gather our wits about us, although Hester said she'd much prefer a taittie-store.

Using the small knowledge I had gleaned at sea, I chose a route as near to north-by-east as I could manage. We skirted some tors and climbed others, giving us a view of the landscape ahead. In some woodland, as night fell, we came across a hollow, the opening of an underground chamber.

Creeping under the stone lintel we discovered that a nearby farm was using it to lay up their meagre crop of potatoes so Hester was keen enough to bide here, until she realised we had the company of bats flitting in and out. There was perhaps half of the cave empty and so we crawled in to curl up as best we could. It was a poor sort of shelter. The night was lightless, the waning moon yet to appear over the tops of the trees.

We were both close to the limit of our endurance, for nothing at Pendennis had tested us as Cornwood had done and our nerves were ragged. Hungry by midday, we had long eaten the eggs Hester had snatched from the cottage, and were keeping the oaty cake for you. Her intuitive salvage of a small pot of honey proved a god-send for your sucking on sticky fingers soothed you to a fitful sleep.

"Reckon they'd not begrudge us one taittie each, eh?" she whispered. I didn't care, and said so but perhaps was more waspish than I should have been.

"Do you think they count them?" I said, striking flint and steel to light a stem of bracken as a taper. We let it burn just long enough to pick out two vegetables, swiftly peeling and paring slips of raw potato before the light went out. It was vile. What little water we had collected from springs on our route was all we had to wash the taste out.

In the inky-black of the cave and in the absence of sleep there was plenty of time to consider what to do next. I could see nothing but a bleak future and said as much, adding,

"I wonder how I would go about seeking a passage to the New World?" There was a sharp intake of breath from the gloom. "What is there here for me?" I had sighed. "Perhaps some pioneer requires a hard-working wife?"

"Aye, 'tis a plan." The voice was a little hesitant at first, and I feared she would break our rule of silence on my past, but Hester only set her mind on practicalities. It seemed to restore a vestige of equanimity and her sense of humour. She nudged me in the dark, "You'm not too old yet, and hard working. You d'know a pen from a ploughshare - just - and a'cause you *do* still have your looks you might do passably

124

well." I could hear the smile in her words. Despite all our tribulations Hester could usually find something to be cheery about. In this case it was teasing me. It did no harm though, and prevented me from becoming any more maudlin. In the dark her tone became earnest,

"If you were to go, where would you find a ship? Plymouth?" she probed, hastily adding, "I only know it for being the nearest place, and Will said it was a common enough for pilgrims to set off to the Americk lands from there when he was a lad."

"Where else do you suggest?" I responded, "It is near. Or Dartmouth?" She was quiet for a little.

"There is somewhere else, Grace. There is a place us both d'know, one where I believe we would find a friendly face." Her words rang with optimism. "'Tis a godly place, and one where you and Hal could take ship, if you must. Think of a parrot ..." My mind went back almost three years, to a walled garden in high summer and the start of our uncommon friendship.

"Barnstaple? Your wits must have flown with the bats, Hester! How do you propose we cross the whole of Devon, in February, with the militia checking every traveller? And if we get there, why should Mistress Palmer even give us 'good day' let alone a welcome?"

"A'cause she is a virtuous woman. She and Master Palmer are proper Christian folk. And they'm on the winning side after all, for 'twas a town all'us for the Parliament, even when the King's troops sat within the walls. I'd wager Barum will be back to thriving by now!" She paused a moment, then added, "That is, if I were a gambling sort, which as a good God-fearing woman, I am not."

"So, first; we have to cross the moor on foot. If we can find the lych path to Lydford it would be a shorter route ..." I had no need to see Hester, for I could feel her go rigid at that proposal.

"Odds figgins! I b'aint walking the Way of the Dead, and I don't care if we have to go all round by way of Launceston or Exeter, I won't set foot on that track, nor any other that they take coffins to church by! You'd have seen the corpse-candles on their way along the church path to haunt Cornwood last night, foretelling of our deaths. Will used to tell me all sorts of tales, about hell's hounds and such and unhappy spirits finding their way to haunt their earthly homes along the moorland church ways a'cause they'd not been carried right." Her teeth were chattering.

A little moonlight now glimmered through the undergrowth around the entrance to the cave. It might not have dispersed Hester's demons and spectres but I did not think I was afraid of ghosts and could not resist asking,

"What way is the right way for Dartmoor folk to carry their dead?" Hester reply was whispered into the gloom,

"Feet first, so they point away, then the spirit can't find its way home. And they *all'us* carry them across running water. They d'say spirits hate running water ..." I tried some levity,

"Well, three of the corpse candles, whatever they are, will have had a fruitless journey!"

"Grace, will you hold your tongue! If the piskies hear us ..." Hester's hand reached out to clutch mine, her skin clammy. I could feel her quivering.

It was kindest to change the subject and within minutes we were planning an alternative route. We would to make our way east towards Tavistock. I insisted that, using some of the ring-money, we would buy ourselves at least one night's cheap lodging and some food, before setting off on the pack route around the north of the moor to Okehampton. With no papers in our possession except the old documents Hester had kept folded in the back of her Bible, I had no idea what to expect once we reached a town that had regularly held a large garrison.

Eventually, getting fewer responses from the shadows I leaned forward. By what little light there was, I could see that Hester had fallen asleep. I let myself doze, lulled by your infant snores. It was not a night I would care to re-live. My dreams were muddled, welling up from locked chambers of memories that in waking hours I could suppress. And, despite my cynicism, I could never swear that we and the bats were

126

the only other beings in that space. The events of the next day were not destined to settle my nerves either.

One of the benefits of our new strategy was that very quickly we would be able to join a well-worn route which we knew crossed the moor. One hundred years ago it would have been the route between the south Devon abbeys. Now it was secular trade that trod the way. Even at this time of year there would be packhorse-men, tinkers - and probably soldiers too - but as far as Hester was concerned it was a far better option, ancient popish feet being better than possible ghoulish ones. So, stiff, damp, cold and hungry we set off at first light. When we came across a stream too wide to jump over, edged with boggy grass, we had to struggle in what seemed the wrong direction for quite a distance. It was, I think, by a piece of good luck that we came upon the track for which we were seeking near to a cross of rough granite, a way marker. From there we were able to strike out more or less westwards again.

We had not gone two miles, grateful for the weak sun on our backs, when a figure, a woman, appeared to rise up from the furze. Walking a few steps revealed that it was only a trick of the landscape, for she was, like us, on foot. The track dipped, rose and dipped again which is what had created the illusion. Hester released the bunched cloth where she had grasped hold of my sleeve, and shrugged herself back into her shawl. She sniffed nonchalantly. I wasn't fooled. She had been alarmed and if I am honest, so had I. You, on the other hand, merely waggled dirty fingers in the direction of the traveller and with the self self-assurance of the very young squirmed from my grasp to trot in her direction squealing,

"Herrow, lady! Mama! Lady gots chuddeebuns. See bassikt? Pwease, nicely ..." The woman reached into the creel on her back to produce a napkin which, unfolded, did indeed contain a sweet bread roll which she handed to you. You plopped yourself down at her feet to enjoy the feast, squirming happily in your stinking breech-clout and by the time we reached you, she was smiling, quietly chattering to you while you pulled the soft middle from the bun. As she

127

began to refold the napkin the thought crossed my mind that, with that cloth, I could up-end and clean you there and then.

As the distance between us closed, her gaze met mine and there was a sudden jolt of recognition. I felt that she knew me though I was sure we were complete strangers. She turned her gaze on Hester and again, I caught the flicker of her eyes. This time there was an almost imperceptible nod, perhaps of satisfaction, I could not tell. I began to pull my purse from my pocket, but the woman put up her hand to stop me,

"It is a gift," she said, "and this." And she handed me the neatly folded linen cloth. I think my mouth must have dropped open; Hester's already was.

"God give 'e good-day, ladies, and a fine one for the time of year. We are well-met, I think, for 'e have the look of women who are on a mistaken road." The stranger smiled at us, her eyes glinting. "Here stands the Claziwell Pool, and if I might be so bold, it is not wise to make light of the legends of these parts," she admonished, quiet but firm, tilting her head to glance at me, "for there are folk hereabouts whose advice is seldom in the recipient's best interest." I was remembering my night-time ridicule of the other-world. Hester shifted very slightly closer to my side. The woman went on,

"But, nare 'e bother about that for I'll see 'e right. You'll be bound for Tavistock, I would say," I felt a tug at my skirt, heard the tiny, sharp intake of breath from Hester before, "though it is no witchcraft to know it, not when you go west along this road." The smile that followed these common-sense words seemed genuine enough.

"My name is Goody Yendacott. You may call me Loveday if you prefer. I would be pleased to have your company as I travel - if you would be so kind." And she smiled again, warm and reassuring. Hester looked a little awkward, but now more embarrassed than afraid. When Mistress Yendacott offered us both a roll, any reluctance to extend our acquaintance vanished.

We stepped out as best we could, though it required patience to walk any distance with a small child, for every pebble on the way seemed to be a novelty. Hester or I would resort to letting you ride pick-a-back in order to make up some distance. When you became tetchy through tiredness, our companion suggested that, since she had little in the way of produce, we should carry her basket between us. You rode inside it like an eastern potentate before you fell asleep, curled up in the bottom. The miles passed a little quicker after that and conversation was less erratic. Although I felt easy enough, my sense of 'otherworldliness' returned as Loveday began to talk of brewing; the unreliability of maltsters, poor hop seasons and the efficacy of willow-bark beer. The conversation had the feel of a lesson rather than a debate. A rather arbitrary pronouncement changed the tone,

"Bad beer will make a good man vicious." What followed set my spine tingling, "but the evil in a man will taint liquor, though he keep his evil hidden." She was looking directly at me. How could she know of Fenwick, the matter of his poisoning bottles of wine? I blinked, unsure that I had heard right, stammering through a reply,

"As you say, Mistress, as perhaps when a maid keeps an unclean dairy, she spoils the butter." It was a vacant response but I could think of nothing better to say. To my relief, the subject appeared closed. We asked if she knew anything of the King's fortunes, though Mistress Yendacott was remarkably reticent, saying that she was sure it would all come to a head soon enough. I remember Hester and I saying that we thought it had already done so, at Edgehill fight. Her remark had merely seemed an offhand one at the time.

By late-afternoon, on common land that rolled off the edge of the moor, we came to another cross. Here Loveday stopped. From a snapsack I hadn't noticed beneath her thick mantle she brought out a stoppered leather bottle, handing it first to me then to Hester.

"Drink! It is last summer's best!" Your squeals of delight and Hester's clapping proclaimed more bounty, this time a handful of jumbles, the biscuits still smelling of caraway. Eyes closed, I was savouring the strong drink, a smoky and fruity balm warming my core, when I was jolted awake by Loveday's announcement,

"And now, our paths divide." Hester's disbelief was palpable,

"You aren't coming to Tavvy?" The woman slowly shook her head. It occurred to me that we had assumed her destination to be the same as ours. She, however, had never been specific. The hairs on my neck prickled.

"Nay, but don't 'e fear," she took Hester's left hand, and running her fingers gently across her palm, said,

"Return to Cornwood. Will matters and things will change." At least, when we discussed the strange events of our day by the hearth of an unassuming inn later that evening that is what we decided she must have said.

As I bent to pick up our basket, Mistress Yendacott knelt down beside me, holding both my wrists so that I was forced to look into her deep-set, slate grey eyes. She met my gaze, then murmured,

"For a woman twice dead ..." There was a pause, those grey fathomless pools momentarily closed, "life to come crosses water."

Her hands slipped down to clasp mine, but as she did so she flinched, withdrawing as if she had been burned. Warily she picked up my rigid fingers again, and examined my palms. To my horror her eyes were glistening with unshed tears.

"You have given life; yet will take a life," she whispered, "for a life believed lost." Swiftly, and before I could move, she cupped my face in her hands, kissed my forehead and stood up. As she walked away, she ruffled your hair, such an ordinary gesture, and so incongruous in the light of the statement she had just made. In the fading light of a February dusk she was already becoming indistinct against the heath, but from the shadows came the words which stopped the breath in my lungs,

"You do not hear yet, but she that was a Carew and now is a Tremayne has called you both. She will call again, and one of you will answer."

XXIII Hester: William's Will

Burned home b'aint a very good scent and once we got indoors the smell of bitter smoke on my clathers really began to bother me. There wasn't much to be done about it. I just hoped it might blow away once we were out on the road again. Mind, the smell of the apple-wood logs that the Tavistock inn was burning that night was fine, different from the peatiness of our own hearth. We'd not burned such good wood in Toms Hall.

We expected there to be plenty of soldiers but we didn't see any. There hardly seemed to be anyone about even though 'twas late on market day - mind it had started to rain. Hal was getting teasy by then so we had to look for an inn sharp-ish. What we found wasn't fancy and when Grace asked about a room, the landlord shrugged and said that he'd but one and 'twas small, but I didn't think it overpriced, for all the town was a garrison. We expected him to want see our papers, which would have caused a stir, but when Grace offered he seemed surprised saying,

"Nomye, Mistress Zumm-body! Papers? Nomye! 's long as ye do have the coin, and I'll see that now if ye please, you'm as welcome as any," adding glumly, "and more than some who expect free quarter!"

So, that was that. Grace paid, and we were settled in and toasting-cosy before dark. The apple-round serving girl seemed fair smitten by Hal's bright blue eyes and his baby-boy ways, so he charmed his way to the kitchen, to apple-cake and warmed milk, while she brought us mutton broth, decent bread to mop it up and some cheese on the side, with small-beer that my throat thought was made by angels. This was costing good coin so I was determined to make the most of it, from fireside to bed-bolster. I sat as close as I could to the flames and took deep sniffs of the sweet smoke. Our little room was at the back of the place with just the one saggy-roped bed, and Hal was soon sound asleep in the middle of that, so once he was settled, we went back to the hearth, relishing the quiet and the warmth, both trying to dry out our shoes.

After what that woman said on the moor I was still all of a dudder. 'Twas a wonder I'd been able to walk the way down to the town a'cause my knees were so weak. If you ask me, 'tis certain sure that there are some things, unnatural matters, that are unfathomable. Grace and me couldn't help talk about it though. How had the very same woman that Mary Tremayne had told us of, the one who, back in '44, had read that lady's fortune at her granny's farm, how come she was in the middle of nowhere just when we were in the same nowhere too, and us there more by luck than judgment as well? No matter how we looked at it, 'twas summ'at very odd and no getting away from it.

With no others in the inn, we sat making our drink last as long as we were able, talking over the strange things Loveday had said. The only thing we could agree on was that she'd told me, for sure, to go back to Cornwood.

"I think she said that it matters that I go back, and the will may change," I said, but Grace thought she'd heard different replying,

"How can it? It is written in black and white. I am sure the message was more that the matters around the will may change. Perhaps the courts will be sympathetic?"

"Aye, but they'm not on my doorstep, and there's the rub." A little while passed while we each kept our own thoughts. My mind wandered where it probably shouldn't. I could never keep my thoughts close, so out it came,

"Grace, when does a soul make a ghost?" She didn't answer straight away, a'cause she'd got her eyes shut, resting her bones like me, but when I spoke she pursed her lips, the way she does when she's pondering.

"Why do you ask? I have never seen a ghost. I hope never to see one either." I remembered the story in her pa's book,

132

"But they'm real, for your pa's book has them. I do remember me the tale of Hoglet…"

"Hamlet," she put me right. "But those are for players to pretend them, Hester." She was looking at me, sort of sideaways. "I know that often we tell tales of ghosts, to scare ourselves by winter firelight. What is it that the playwright wrote, 'There are more things in heaven and earth', Hester, than are dreamt of in our philosophy." She looked at me, knowingly, "What ails thee, my friend?"

I didn't rightly know how to carry on, for I wasn't altogether sure what was troubling me but I was certain sure it had become worse with the day's events.

"I can't say really, only," then it came tumbling out, "Oh, Grace, 'tis silly I know, only they do say that a ghost is an unquiet spirit, them who died in unhappy circumstances. If anyone did then my William died when times were unhappy." My breath caught in my throat. I sagged, slumped like a badly stuffed bolster, then whispered,

"Grace, I do not think I would mind seeing William's ghost. I am so affeard that I will forget his looks. I can hardly picture him now, even when I shut my eyes tight. And I did love him so …" She slid up to my side and clept me close, and even though there was nobody to see, hid me in her arms while I cried.

The tears helped. All the unknowns, all the fears, and that terrible knowledge that someone hated us so much that they would do what had been done, had taken their toll. I felt better for the weeping though. Will did matter; Goody Yendacott was right.

Grace decided we should have summ'at to settle us for sleep and after a while the innkeeper, right deferential, bought us both bowls of caudle, the wine headily scented with spices, thick with egg and sugar. His opinion of us must have risen with Grace's spending. As I asked the cost Grace put her finger to my lips, saying that it mattered not, and that it would restore us both. It did.

I felt so much better that I was about to open the vexed subject of our future when a figure, bescummered with mire, thrust in through the low doorway from the street. His hat drooped over his brow, so at first his face was hidden. I glanced at him, thinking to myself 'Hester, no more of your yowling. We've got company,' but then had to look again, a'cause the chap, now bare-headed, had the very daps of Captain Burrell, scar an' all. I was just about to nudge Grace to point out the likeness when he whirled around, and seeing us gave a holler that wasn't quite a manly sound, I'd say, more a cross between a yelp and a squeak. But then, when all's said and done, he thought he was looking at two spectres sitting cosy by the fireside, grey with weariness and me with my eyes all red as well. 'T would be enough to make anyone swimey.

He emptied the cloam of ale that was handed through the servery hatch as if he'd got the devil after him, downing it almost in one go and signing for another, so he was either all of a bivver or summ'at thirsty. But like the gentleman he was, he gathered himself swiftly enough, and coming over, made a bow to us both.

"I hardly know how to say it, but may God give you a very good' een, ladies, and … Gad's my life! How the hell are you here? All Cornwood is croaking about the tragic irony of it all, you being cruelly ta'en into God's care just when …" The girl had bought the second jug of brew, and shuddering as if someone had just crossed his grave, Burrell took another long swig. He looked so like a badger, with the white stripes in his hair and the clay cup like a long snout that the sight of him made me smile. He might have taken that the wrong way so I turned my face, pretending a yawn behind my hand.

"Mistress Mattock, You look - ah, I cannot find the words … so, so …" Grace finished for him,

"Well?" and she smiled politely.

"Thank you, mistress! Yes, well! I suspect the disciples were at a loss for words at first … Oh, hell's teeth!" The innkeeper, rattling some pots, leaned through and glared.

"I beg your pardon, I meant no blasphemy …" He tried again,

"Look, I am heartily glad to see you." Grace took pity on him at that point replying,

"And we to see you too, Captain. There is no biblical resurrection here, simply a lot of good luck."

"And a lot of poor building," I added. I wasn't certain that I was so happy to see Burrell. Me and Grace had been contented enough with our own company at the fire.

Still, he was there and it was plain he wanted to ask how we came to be alive in the 'Drake and Hind' in Tavvy instead of dead in cinders. He pulled up a stool opposite the settle and me and Grace explained what had happened. Burrell looked truly shocked. He scratched his chin, which looked badly in need of a shave, and narrowed his eyes, considering the matter.

"So, if I understand aright, ladies, pre judicata and in the absence of a ruling on the charges presented by the officers of the parish to a properly convened court, whether that panel be ecclesiastical or lay, a person or persons did maliciously ..." I was a bit vexed, a'cause he sounded as though he hadn't got the facts aright at all,

"Oh, 'twas certain sure persons, sir, for 'twas were more than one voice we heard ..."

"Hush, Hester, the Captain merely uses the legal phrases to have the matter clear in his mind." Even though I glowered at him he went on, all lawyer-like,

"These persons, finding you within doors at Toms Hall, did barricade you into that dwelling and without care for life or property, deliberately did set a fire around the premises?" That was about the size of it, only much longer worded than it needed to be. We nodded.

"Ergo, your parish summons notwithstanding, those persons have committed a tort, in that they have trespassed upon property, have willfully damaged said property, and in addendum, with malice aforethought, did intend to commit wrongful death. That said," The corners of Burrell's mouth turned down, just like a proper judge's did, and he leaned forward, all forbidding, finishing with, "murder is de facto a criminal offence, ladies, and a hanging one at that."

Murder. When he put that name to it my blood ran cold. I whispered,

"Murder? Hang? As in an eye for an eye?" Our gentleman at law, clutching his pot of beer, leaned even further towards Grace and me, and said, low and deep,

"Aye, an eye for an eye …" I let out a little squeak. Burrell, sat back on the stool, cocked his head on one side, now more like a beady-eyed cockerel than a lawyer, and most unexpectedly chuckled,

"To use a phrase I have, on occasion heard applied to cases such as this, it seems there are some nasty bastards about." So then I couldn't help but smile even though I still thought Benjamin Burrell liked the sound of his own voice too much.

Some time was spent discussing how we might deal with our sorry plight, Grace talking of 'new beginings'. I hoped she would not speak of our encounter with the witch of Claziwell pool a'cause I thought he would think us mad and have us carried off to Lydford gaol. The inn did see two more customers while we talked, but neither stayed long. While Captain Burrell asked about accommodation, ordered more drink and some supper, Grace went to check that her boy was sleeping soundly. I was feeling quite at ease, almost dozing and wondering if I could hear the church chimes to tell the hour, when Burrell slipped onto the bench beside me. I edged into my corner, a tad wary. He backed away, just enough for me to see he'd noticed.

"Hester, I know how hard these months, these years must have been for you. And there may be nothing I can do. I never did complete my legal training, and probably never shall. But I do know a little of the law, and shall have to go to Exeter and possibly London on … business. Perhaps I can help? For William's sake?"

"You weren't his officer. What happened weren't your fault …" I was discomforted but didn't want to show it. "But thank you for your kind offer, Captain." Grace came in, Burrell quickly going back to the stool. He sat looking at his feet. She took my hand, raised an eyebrow, a silent question but I gave a little nod to reassure her. Clearing his throat our soldier-lawyer looked me in the eye, though he was still very ill at ease. I felt sorry for being surly.

"I have no right to ask, and yet I must. Would you do me the honour of letting me see the papers? I did at least learn a little of the mystery of trusts and estates. If I am honest, I was a young Jack-Bragger, thinking it all very dull ..." I gave a quick glance at Grace, and she squeezed my hand as he finished,

"There may be nothing to be said or done, and if I overstep the boundaries of good manners you must say so, but I would not rest easy if I did not make this simple offer." He sat quite still, hands clasped between his knees and in the firelight he looked only like a lad not a grown man who'd fought on English battlefields. I sighed. What harm could it do? So I fetched the Bible with all my bits of paper, but I was dog-tired and said so. Burrell promised to look over the will and return it in the morning and with that Grace and I retired to our room, curled ourselves round a softly snoring Hal and slept the sleep of the dead.

In the cold tap-room in the gloom of a rainy Saturday in February, with the fire barely smouldering, a breakfast of cold bacon and yesterday's bread wasn't going to raise anyone's spirits. The kitchen maid was surly and Hal was sulking, thumb in mouth, a'cause there was no apple-cake on offer. I wished we'd made some plans in the warm glow of the night before. Today didn't seem too cheerful. I asked the girl if she'd seen ought of the gentleman with the greying hair but her sullen reply was that he'd left, early, horse and all, saying nothing, not a word.

'Well, Hester' I thought to myself, 'you sawney wench. That will teach you to fall for honeyed words from a clever fellow. Now what's to do?' The answer came with Grace, bearing a piece of paper, neatly folded, and with my name on it.

"Ben Burrell left this when he rode out at first light. That contrary baggage meant only that there was no spoken message ..." I took the letter, then handed it back,

"You do it, Grace, a'cause I doubt I can manage all those words." Walking to the window for more light, she began slowly,

Mistress Mattock,

Forgive me for my untimely departure. As I do not know your plans, should you depart from Tavistock I would urge you to leave details of your destination that I might send word.

On reading your husband's deposition I discovered something which appears to have

heretofore gone unremarked.

I must have been looking blank. Grace came back to stand beside me, a warm hand on my shoulder. Hal climbed into my lap as she read on,

I plan to go to Exeter on your behalf, but first ride to Cornwood to establish in fact what I currently have in my mind as hearsay. I will say no more at this time, but trust that when we meet again I will have the means to provide clarification. BB

"Well, now what's to do?" This time I had spoken aloud. Smiling, Grace drew out her purse and counted out coins for another night's lodging.

"I think we should not be too hasty to set off on our journey, Hester. The weather in February can be so unpredictable," and, giving Hal the money to hold as he trotted after her, she left to find the landlord.

Burrell's words were buzzing about in my head. He had said little, promised less. But he seemed certain sure that matters were not how I believed them to be. If I'd learned ought from life, it was not to pin hopes too high, for disappointment lay round each curve in the road, but like a drowning soul who would clutch at a straw, I couldn't help myself. And there was nothing to do but wait.

XXIV Mary: The untimely arrival

Written this ~~Tuesday~~ Wednesday 15th September 1647
At Kestle Wartha
Heligan

Dearest Heart,
I received yours of late August by the carrier today - I do not
this minute remember how it is dated. I have had scant time
to read it, but for all that, I am glad to have your hand in
mine, even if it is to touch the ink your fingers penned. Your
missive had not, this time, been opened, the seal being
unbroken.
When I did offer my apologies for the tardiness of my
correspondence yesterday, I little thought that I should have
to put pen to paper again so urgently. You wished to hear
more often of home even though there was little enough
except infant matters and poor news. Now you may un-wish
your request and I write with extreme haste, so you must
forgive all errors.
There has been such turmoil here that I know not where to
begin almost fearing to tell you.
Here we had thought to ~~keep a quiet place and with and stay~~
be safe but now it seems past misery can find us ~~out~~ for I
have this morning had a visitation from a very demon,
Bartholomew Fenwick. ~~He was here~~ He was first ~~came to~~ at
Heligan and came then to Penwarne.
Your father thought to send a man to me, which was a boon,
for Rob Tubb is a size to be reckoned with. Though he do just
stand and look fearsome I was glad to have him there where
he stood across the yard but I do not think he could have
stopped Fenwick.
I must begin at the start for I can imagine you saying 'Be
calm, speak slower' but my heart races so.

Grace has said little enough of the man and I do not wonder at that now, for if I were Grace I would never wish to see or think of him and I cannot fathom how she has born the notion that this man is her wedded husband.

I can hardly believe that if it had not been for Sark he would have killed you. Now he has found us, my very soul is in fear.

How it fell out was thus: I am near enough my time to be confined here at home so visitors are few, except for your sisters and Bridget and Agnes, and they do come by the proper door. But there was a commotion in the kitchen some time before dinner as Rob came and the new maid took his message. He would not come into the house, saying he was bidden to remain outside and act as watchman. Jane brought to me a note from your father, very short, saying that a captain by a name he had cause to recognise had been at Heligan after breakfast and had two armed men with him, though no proper authority that your father could determine. He added that Rob was instructed to stay at Kestle and run for aid if trouble arose.

I was in two minds as to whether to take the girls to Penwarne. Your dear father did not write the man's name. I suppose he feared that it would make my nerves worse. I would not have recognised Fenwick, would I? I have never met him, yet the very name strikes ice into my heart.

However the babies were in their cribs and I was reluctant to waken them, and so we were still at home when there was a hubbub and, without waiting to be announced, he strode into the parlour with poor Jane running behind before he dismissed her.

It was the man's eyes that struck terror in me for they are cold, a translucent grey and quite without life.

He used the manners of a gentleman, for all he did not wait for the proper introductions, and seemed courteous, but in the way that steel is smooth but cold within.

I pretended confusion, which if I am blunt, was not so very far from the truth. But he was not to be gain-said. His words made me feel sick. I still quake but I will give account of what he said as best I may. Fenwick gave his name then continued,

"I had cause to become acquainted with your husband, madam, some years ago, during the recent unpleasantness of the war. He is unlikely to have mentioned me, for our association was but brief. Naturally, it is to my eternal regret that our politics were at odds. However, I believe that he has unwittingly become entangled in matters which are not his concern."

This was the very man who would have seen you and Grace drown. I am sure he realised that I was aware of it. He has a smile that plays about his mouth more like a sneer, and it made my skin crawl. He continued without regard to anything or anyone,

"Madam," he spoke, with such icy politeness, "let us play no games. Parliament's agents know your husband's movements. Your regular correspondence does you credit, madam, though the style is too mawkish for my taste. If you were my wife ..."

I shuddered at the malevolence in that statement. Then he picked up Mary's teething ring - the coral one that your sister gave her at the christening - and twirled it between his fingers, kissing it before laying it down again. He might as well have been holding a knife to our babies' throats.

Then he became obsequious though his tone was cold.

"But I digress. Perhaps after all, it is not your husband I seek, Mistress Tremayne, but you. It is evident that you are well recovered from your debilitating stay within the walls of Pendennis fort."

His eyes slid across me, an insulting look, and vile. There was little point to contradict him so he continued, and used my name as if I were a servant and not the mistress of the house,

"Mary, your compassionate nature found such a fortuitous outlet in the infirmaries, did it not? You are aware I suppose that your reputation extends beyond these shore?" My thoughts went to poor surgeon Wiseman who had unwittingly

*fallen prey to this devil and as if he read my mind Fenwick
said,*

*"Richard Wiseman spoke so very highly of you, indeed of
all those who showed courage above that expected of the
weaker sex. He spoke of many women..." He made a weighty
pause. But the worst was yet to come.*

*"I have a close association with the castle authorities,
being with the fleet of the Western Guard. From my earliest
connection with Colonel Fortesque, during the blockade of
that very castle and the obstinate few who were too stupid to
acknowledge that they were beaten, I have enjoyed a
gratifying degree of familiarity with the governor and his
officers." He was wandering the room, picking up my
sewing, tossing it away, turning things over and around as he
spoke.*

*"They were most accommodating when I wished to
substantiate a report that a certain senior officer who had
been given the benefit of the Articles of the Terms of
Surrender was in fact a miscreant Royalist, an associate of
Skellum Grenvile. Of course, such a one would lose all such
benefits, obtained as they were by deception." He stood close
to me, hot breath in my face,*

"Do you understand me, madam?"
*I did, only too well. How are we to contend with this, for I
swear Fenwick is in league with the devil.*
*Even without the malice of any single individual, the
authorities have ridden roughshod over the explicit
protection which the provisions of the Exeter surrender were
supposed to give Sir Richard Vyvyan. Yet the Vyvyans merely
deal with a committee of men.*
Fenwick is inhuman.
*I wished that you were here, but then rejoiced that you were
not, for he threatened you more than any of us.*
*He perched upon the arm of your chair; he even stroked my
hand. I will find no salve to stop the sense of that contact, no
electuary to take away the taste of the bile in my mouth.*

*"Mistress Tremayne, Mary ...I may now call you Mary,
may I not, for I am sure we understand each other well*

*enough. I have had access to the register and record of all
the proceedings at Pendennis. I have even been given a copy
of the remarkably detailed lists of the - ah how many? - one
thousand senseless individuals at that ignominious
surrender. But I regret some papers were already dispatched
to London before I was able to establish all of the facts I
required."*

*My tormentor, our persecutor, sat like a carrion crow in my
parlour. I had said not one word in all this time. His black
voice filled the air so that it felt as if there was none for me to
breathe.*

*"Mary, I want you to be quite certain that, unless you tell
me the information I require, I shall be the means by which
the lives of your husband, your family and all those you care
for are wrecked."*

*He had the audacity to smile at me, a frozen grimace. Then
like cat with mouse he continued,*

*"However, my dear Mary, your co-operation will secure
my highest regard, and my total discretion. You will hear no
more of the matter. But, Mistress Tremayne, be sure I <u>will</u>
have the intelligence I seek."*

*I prayed all the while that God would give me strength to
stay on my feet for my head was swimming, and I began to
feel cramping in my stomach.*

*Then this monster told me that he had watched as the few
who could do so had marched out that day. With a horrid
imitation of intimacy he confided in me that he had been
quite shocked to see a woman who looked remarkably like his
drowned wife in that pathetic phalanx of camp followers.
He called her a wretched creature wearing the poor vestiges
of woman's clothes. He said that she was 'a distinctive ghost'
and, he said, an ungrateful ghoul for she had discarded the
garments he had so thoughtfully provided when last they
were together.*

*"She had a bundle in her arms, madam, a child, a pitiable
brat."*

*I was now very close to being sick, but he grabbed my throat,
hissing and spitting like a serpent,*

"Yet, Mistress, why should I be so surprised since a drowned man appeared very much alive amidst those officers of the King who negotiated the final capitulation of the castle: phantoms cannot put their signature to a surrender document."

He laughed in my face, but he did not let go.

"Your husband should have died that day. If nothing else it would have spared me this trip!" I had to shut my eyes. His voice was like poison.

"My bitch of a wife has something that belongs to me, Madam and I will have it back ..."

As God is my witness, he shook me by the neck and with the breath going from me, he demanded,

"Who were the other women who left the fort that day? I will have names, lady!"

May the Lord in heaven forgive me and preserve us all, for though I feared for my life and that of our unborn child, I could not give him what he wanted. I did not know who left through those gates that day. I could not give him what he wanted but instead gave him what he needed. I gave him Hester's name and with her name the wherewithal to ~

Added by the hand of Agnes Carew
This day 16th September
To my well-beloved brother-by-law, Lewis Tremayne

Lewis,

I pen this at the bydding of my syster your wyfe who was taken early into labour yesterday after the visitation of the straynger.

I came from Penwarne with our people, though we did arryve too layte and found her fallen beside her table. He was gone.

I have not read her words, but only do as she wyshed, as I promised on her life and that of the babe, to seal and send this letter with all hayste.

You have a son, small but with a payre of good lungs. Mary names him John, for she says this is how you wished your firstborn son to be called. He is to be baptysed this afternoon. The birth was lengthy. Mary is recovering but her women fear to leave her yet, she being overwrought. A wet nurse has been found for the boy. I will write more as soon as may be and when we are at church this noontide. will ~~say~~ speak to ask Master Tremayne your father to pen word to you. Keep yr wife in yr prayers. In good faith, I remain your respectful syster, Agnes Carew

To Colonel Lewis Tremayne
With the Prince of Wales
Rue dis Abbyees
St Germay de lays
Nearby Paris
In France
With every possible hayste

XXV Grace: Fortune's wheel turning

Perspective, insight: these you might use to reflect upon this narrative. Yet you must remember when judging my actions that I had no such tools. One might, of course, wish for a scrying dish in which to read the future. Who has not thought, 'If only I had known'?

After a day spent with a woman who seemed, at the very least, ambiguous, Burrell had seemed a reassuringly solid presence. His note was something tangible even if the man had made himself scarce. Hester looked surprised when I decided that we would wait for his return. Yet I reasoned that in the middle of a wet February we had nowhere else to go. There was little comfort to be had between Tavistock and Barnstaple that would cost less than the cost of our present lodging. If his promise held true, then one more night at the inn might prove a worthwhile investment. If not - well, then we would have to shift for ourselves as usual. We could afford no more indulgence in spiced wines though.

Our would-be lawyer had not returned by dinner time, but there were a few patrons in the tavern. Hester had taken you to see ducks on the river while I had decided to tackle some mending. Just as I had sat down to my task a loud clanging and shouting began, coming from the kitchen across the tavern yard. A cracked bell was effectively if discordantly warning of fire.

As I hurried out of doors there was a choked scream followed by more shouting. Smoke was billowing from the door and windows, though there appeared to be no flames. The innkeeper with two other fellows dragged a woman's body out onto the cobbles, left it and ran back into the building, snatching buckets of water from customers who had formed a haphazard chain from the pump at the water trough. Nobody was attending to the casualty. It soon became evident why. I knelt down beside the girl who had served us the previous evening. She was barely recognisable. The shock was like a physical blow, and I reeled away, sick and trembling. I pulled off the shabby neck-cloth I was wearing and went back to place it over her poor face. I prayed a moment, and then withdrew from the mayhem to cry in private. I returned to my sewing, shaking so much that to thread a needle was impossible and I was still shaking when Hester carried you in from the street.

Eventually, filthy with soot and with his hair and brows singed, the landlord fetched jugs of beer for the crowd of people who had helped save his premises. As it started to rain again, the weather served to reassure all concerned that the fire was truly beaten, and the company drifted back into the tap-room. I did not see who carried the serving girl's body away, but when I suggested that Hester and I could attend to her the innkeeper shook his head,

"Nomye, Mistress Zumm-body, Bessie's been ta'en. She is …" he cleared his throat, "She *was* my niece and so I've seen to it that she'll be laid out a'right, but I thank ye."

Then with what seemed a hardhearted pragmatism he said,

"I doubt ye can serve? Or brew? There's word that Sir Hard-heart Waller and a might of his soldiery are to be quartered at Tavvy a'cause Plymouth won't 'av 'en. And Roddy Rawle here has no staff!" He glowered - at the world in general, I thought, rather than at us - then added with a snort,

"Mind, mayhap the Colonel will bring the cash for to pay the last bill! Pah! That'll be when the river Tavy runs back into the Colley brook!" His complexion was going ruddy under the soot, and exasperation was in every syllable,

"A tavern-keeper cannot keep his roof over his head with promissory notes and never any hard coin in his hand. Waller or Grenvile, it never made no odds, a'cause none of 'en had ready money." He slammed a jug on the servery, to emphasise his point.

"I'm for joining my cousin in the colonies just as soon as the sailing season begins, and King, Parliament, Crown or

Commons can all ..." Remembering his audience he took a deep breath and turned back to us,

"So, I'll ask again, do ye serve? Last night, yon gentleman and you, I overheard ... and sorry I am for your loss." He had the decency to look slightly awkward. "But 'tis an ill wind they say, that blows no good. I need a serving wench; ye had to pay me for lodging. Thereby we've a common cause."

He must have taken our stunned silence for reluctance. Pulling up a stool he sat between us, with his thick arms resting on the table. You had been sitting on Hester's lap, and slid down, attempting to clamber onto our host's knee. Momentarily flustered he settled you astride, resuming his proposal with a 'harrumph'. I couldn't help notice though, that he was gently jiggling you up and down as he spoke,

"If ye will take the work between ye, a'cause of the boy mind, and only a'cause Bessie did take to the little fellow, then I'll see ye right with bed and board ..." He paused, obviously weighing his offer,

"With £2 for the year." Hester was gawping at me. I cleared my throat,

"Sir, the wage is ..." I was about to say 'unexpected' but our would-be employer thought he needed to drive a hard bargain. He set you down on the flagstones again,

"I'll pay no more! That's a'cause of the lad. A growing boy? He'll be eating all my profits. Ye'd have more if 'tweren't for the lad! Nomye! £2 all found is my final offer!"

Hester had already nudged my foot, though she could hardly have expected me to turn down such an astonishing stroke of luck. There was little more to be said.

Whilst Roddy Rawle owned the inn, we would be engaged as serving women. Our few belongings were moved to a room above the kitchen, a space half the size of Toms Hall. And the only drawback either of us could see was that it would take some time and a deal of elbow-grease to cleanse the place of the clinging grime and stench of cinders and smoke.

We were set straight to work, the arrangement for sharing duties meaning that Hester was behind the bar when Burrell reappeared. The threatened troops had not arrived, but the place was now busy for all that, the fire bringing a local notoriety and extra custom to the 'Drake and Hind.' In a brief lull in business Master Rawle signed that Hester could take a few minutes to speak privately with our visitor. With you asleep on my lap we settled in the last quiet corner furthest from the glow of the hearth. There was no doubt he looked in good spirits.

"Mistress Mattock, Mistress Sark, forgive the delay in returning to you. It took longer than I hoped, despite my not needing to travel to Exeter, for which I am pleased as obtaining a travel permit would have been most awkward." He smiled diffidently,

"However, I am delighted to say that my legal acumen has not deserted me. It was in part a matter of establishing some unhappy facts but also, as they say, the devil may be found in the detail." He took a deep breath, becoming formal and solemn,

"Firstly then, let us look at the specifics." Unfolding the paper which I knew contained William Mattock's dying wishes, Burrell pointed out several sentences quite a way down the page. I had never read the will. Hester's literacy was limited so she could make out little more than the basics. Now it transpired that the parish worthies at Cornwood had either not read the whole document, or assumed that the particular details were already understood.

What our acquaintance was indicating showed that Will had made provision for his sisters to have a share of the brewhouse, but only until their marriage. We had heard Rose Mattock's banns read and now Benjamin was confirming that, as he had suspected, she had that very morning been wedded to Tom Triggs, journeyman cooper. Sibling Daisy was another matter, and Ma Mattock was the biggest challenge of all. I do not think Benjamin Burrell was being facetious, for he genuinely seemed to care for Hester's feelings.

"The other matter is more delicate and one I had not anticipated having to broach. Mistress, I regret being the bearer of sad tidings" he continued quietly, respectfully.

"Hester ..." he paused, wordlessly asking for permission to speak on less formal terms. Hester simply nodded for him to resume.

"Hester, I am sorry and offer my deepest condolences for your loss, but William's mother, Margaret Mattock, known in the parish as Peg, went to her maker on Friday last, the 11th day of this month." Hester and I reacted in the same instant.

"What?" we both cried, making other customers turn to stare and Roddy Rawle thrust his head through the hatch to the servery.

"I am afraid it is so. I took some time to investigate. She departed this life in the early hours of the morning. The village is in some uproar after the incident at your cottage, so it took a little longer to establish the facts." A fleeting expression on Benjamin's face was unreadable, but he continued courteously,

"The injury she took from that soldier's misplaced shot festered and there seems to have been a general sepsis. Nobody saw fit to send for a barber-surgeon although in my experience such wounds, which I have seen many times on battlefields, rarely, if ever, respond to an apothecary's ministrations." Burrell placed a comforting hand on Hester's, patted gently, then respectfully withdrew. Perhaps he did not see Hester blush.

"Mistress Mattock did, however, see fit to clear her conscience before leaving this world for the next; Reverend Shute seemed a little perplexed by her revelations. And she did leave her mark on a will." Hester faltered over a response,

"Oh, my! Oh, I am right sorry to hear of her passing. Though she was not the woman I would have chosen for a mother by marriage, she was Will's ma for all that, and she must ha' loved him. It cannot have been easy to see the man march off and not return, do you think?" Hester, forever

150

kindhearted, had no idea what Burrell was going to say, but the next words drained the colour from her cheeks.

"Goodwife Mattock left her interests in the brewing business in Cornwood to her daughter-in-law. Hester, she left it all to you."

What Burrell was saying made no sense and I said so. Hester managed to stammer a weak 'why?' and he proceeded to explain, clearly having established all the facts before coming back to report his findings. Burrell, though he appeared to have chosen otherwise, would have made an excellent lawyer.

"I took some time to speak with Reverend Shute, who, as I said, was somewhat out of sorts. I would not be deterred and finally established that when she realised that her end was nigh, the late Mistress Mattock had asked to see the vicar to 'set things straight a'fore I see the Holy Spirit, and meet my son again.' Jet Beale was there in his role as the new parish clerk, along with Constable Triggs and told me her words verbatim."

Roddy Rawle had brought a jug of beer, and lingered to pour for Burrell. He was obviously curious, but waiting for him to move away, Benjamin took a mouthful before he continued,

"Reverend Shute heard something that day which probably gave him cause to regret that he had witnesses. The lady concerned made a formal confession as a prerequisite to making her will." Burrell held my gaze, as if to give his words more weight. "With Beale and Triggs there Shute could not suppress it: she confessed to spite, to malicious intent towards her daughter-in-law, and to inflaming hateful actions towards two innocent women. Distraught at the knowledge that her ill-will had caused the death of an innocent child she wished to clear her conscience."

Hester began to weep silently as Burrell detailed the facts as he had extracted them from Shute, from Jet Beale and Jack Triggs. There had been customers, whom Ma Mattock would not name, who, fired by the sermons in church and egged on by the alewife, had been encouraged to give us a fright. The matter had gone so much further than Peg had anticipated. Burrell gently added,

"The matter of your indictment has been dropped, the defamation cleared. Your reputations are restored."

"But they think us dead ..." I whispered. This transformation of our fortunes was hard to take in.

"Ah, there I have to confess to an intervention" said our friend. It seemed that the fact that Shute had also acted on the malicious words of a woman known by her neighbours to be cantankerous had not gone un-noticed by the other men. Burrell's expression was one of wry amusement.

"Well, Jack Triggs resigned as constable at that point and walked out. Master Beale was ready to do physical harm to the man who, he said, had inflamed the whole dirty business. He deemed Shute just as responsible as the pathetic old woman for the death of good Christians who had cared for his wife's kin as if she had been their own." He spread his hands in a gesture of apology,

"In order to prevent an assault I had to reveal the true facts. The news was received with great joy. I believe the reverend to be chastened by the turn of events. He was certainly much shaken when I spoke to him, as was your sister-in-law, Daisy. She seems ... how can I put this delicately? Let me say, a little simple and very forlorn. I think she is at a total loss as to what to do." Hester's inherent kindness and generous spirit was indomitable.

"Then us'll have to go back and show her, won't us? 'Tis all'us best to let bygones be gone."

Drying her tear-streaked cheeks she puffed,

"Still, for now I has work to do!" and she bustled off to resume attending to the taproom.

"Can you be happy in Cornwood, Mistress?" Burrell asked me, with a perceptiveness that I found unnerving.

"It has for some time been in my mind to think further afield, to consider a new start perhaps in the colonies. My prospects are very different to my companion's," I replied, cautiously, "and although I am sure of her love and care, there may come a time when I will need to make a life for myself and my son." Burrell nodded slowly.

"May I offer some advice, Mistress Sark?" I nodded and he continued,

"I have been to the northern colonies of Massachusetts and know men who have sailed to the Indies, the Barbadoes and the like. The voyage is not one I would recommend for a woman with a small child. Nor are the destinations for the faint-hearted. Consider your options with care; take advice where you can. And most importantly, check the credentials of the ship's master."

I thanked Master Burrell for his kindness and promised to take his advice to heart. Although the irony of his last piece of advice did not escape me, try as I might, I could only hear the words of Loveday Yendacott ringing in my head: 'Life to come crosses water'.

XXVI Hester: To sow a seed

'**T**is summ'at strange how our fortunes do twist and turn.
Where once I was condemned now I was a propertied
woman. 'Twas as if all had been redeemed, and for the life of
me I couldn't tell what to think of it all, it being so sudden. I
b'aint used to such quick reverses. Still, they do say you
should nary look too closely at the teeth of the mare you've
been gifted, and so spring saw me back at Cornwood, to the
brew-house at the bottom of the hill, and to the life my Will
had wanted. Only I did sorely wish that he were there too, but
I did say naught of that to anyone, not even Grace.

There wasn't much need to explain matters to Roddy
Rawle, for he had made sure he'd heard most of what
Captain Burrell said, though he seemed none too happy to
discover that his new serving women were about to leave him
short-handed. I said to Grace that I didn't think there was
such a hurry to get back to Cornwood. A few days at the
'Drake and Hind', bed and board for free, couldn't hurt, just
until Rawle could find hands to take our place. He seemed a
tad relieved a'cause the town was now seething with men of
Waller's regiment. 'Twas not long before the pronouncement
that townsfolk should pay cheerfully for the soldiers' billets
and count it as part of what was owed in the general
assessment had Rawle raging about free quarter again and
quite back to his usual self, with the tavern full to the rafters.
The only good thing was that these soldiers were well
mannered and disciplined - even if their quartermaster had no
cash.

'Badger' Burrell rode off home to let the good folk of
Cornwood know their new alewife would be brewing before
very long and in the meantime, he said, he would ensure that
Mistress Triggs and her sister kept things as they should be
until he came to fetch us back again.

154

It was on the third day in our job, while Grace and me were scouring the pots with an eye on little Hal as he tottered about trying to catch the kitchen cat, that what I thought was certain all went to pieces. I was just saying how Rose Mattock, now Triggs, might mend her rude ways a'cause she had become the constable's daughter-in-law. Grace replied,

"I think you have little to fear now, Hester."

"*We* have nothing to fear, you mean. 'Tis good for *all* of us, Grace." It was her quietness that made me look up.

Since the night in the cave, when Grace had spoken in the dark of her plan to leave England, I had tried to forget what I'd heard. I knew well enough that Grace believed she had nothing in this world to bind her to her old life a'cause she was already dead to her husband.

As for Sark, well, he might not have died in the waters off Pendennis but where he was now, the Lord only knew.

I'd keep my promise to not speak of him for it did seem the kindest thing to do.

Maybe Grace was being matter-of-fact, adventuresome even, with her ideas about taking ship to the plantations. But she'd not had a sentence pronounced against her that doomed her to an existence out there, and try as I might, I could not fathom what good there was in taking herself and Hal off to a place full of felons. 'Twas hardly a fitty place for a well bred merchant's daughter to my mind. I rushed on to fill the stillness,

"After all our travails, I d'think it a wonderment that we will have a proper home. 'Twill be a safe place for me and you and little Hal. And Daisy too." Grace turned to me and her sigh was deep, heavy with misery,

"Oh, Hester! Though I love you as the sister I never had, I cannot bide in Cornwood with you. It is your place, not mine."

It felt as if someone had knocked the breath from me. Grace looked grim. I watched her hands, turning a gritty rag round and round her fingers as she went on,

"This land is uncomfortable to me; there are so many memories which I believe I might leave behind if I can begin a new life. They say the settlers have built a place where honesty and hard work earns respect, where women's words are valued. I am not afraid of hard work; I can ..."

I blurted out words, anything to prevent the cold, sinking feeling that was creeping into my gut at the thought of Grace and Hal leaving.

"You cannot. Not by yourself. 'Tis the reality. Surely there is no need for you to cross to continents full of wildness and dangers to find ..." Grace cut me short, her tone suddenly hard,

"Hah! The dangers we have faced in these last days make the tales of savages and monstrous beasts seem bland!"

"Grace, don't try me! You d'know what I mean," I cried. I began again, "And what about getting justice? What about Fenwick's book?" Grace put down her cloth and put her hands on my shoulders.

"There can be no justice, Hester. Even the Prince of Wales' own secretary told me that. Sir Richard Fanshawe said it would be my word against that of all the Parliamentarian officers. I have no witnesses."

"You'm wrong! There's Colonel Tremayne! And Sark!" His name was out before I could stop myself and it pained me to see the shadow that flitted across her face, giving her away. She was even graver now.

"Where are they? Dead, or at best scattered, defeated and in exile!" I remembered Mary, and her dread at leaving Cornwall. Grace changed her tack,

"Hester, you now have a new start, with the proper entitlement of the widow of William Mattock. You are an independent woman by law, by right. You can make your own choices; you might marry again or no. In either case you have a future here. But I do not."

I made to interrupt, tell her that I would sell the brewery, that we could go together, but she put her finger to my lips and quietly, firmly went on,

"I know what you will say and I cannot let you make that promise, to throw away everything William gave you. And if I stayed, how long would it be before the village, once more looked for a convenient door at which to lay the blame for all their ills? It would happen again, Hester, for gossip and horrid rumour are rife in an uncomfortable land such as this."

There was no disputing that, for 'twas true. Folk were edgy. We heard men talk, the rumbling of rebellion and war again. Some said the king had not learned his lesson, escaping then stirring up more trouble; others muttered that the army and parliament were about to come to blows once more; everyone begrudged the taxes. Grace gently shook me to make sure I was listening.

"Hester, I will not risk your future. You have given me so much more than I could ever have hoped but I have to make my own way. Besides, Goody Yendacott has proved right for you, so why should her words not be a guide for me too?" My skin prickled at the memory. Over Grace's shoulder I saw the bobbing baby curls of Henry Charles and my eyes filled with tears.

That was when the innkeeper clattered through the doorway, and catching us idle, glowered. I quickly wiped my face with the back of my hand and turned back to the task. Grace hurried off to draw water for rinsing. I worked on, all my thoughts churning round in my head. If only Grace would try, perhaps there'd be a way to get a message to Colonel Tremayne; Kestle Wartha wasn't so far. Cornwall was no foreign land for all it was over the Tamar. As I rubbed and polished, an idea began to grow. If Grace was not to leave until the sailing season began, maybe I yet had time to change her way of thinking. I'd a notion to speak to our would-not-be lawyer, Master Burrell.

In the meantime, I could hear Rawle's deep tones rumbling away across the yard. I supposed that he was berating Grace for our laggardly working a'cause when she came back to the kitchen, she was shaking and her face was scarlet. Grace shut the door and leaned against it, lips pursed tight together. She stuffed her apron to her mouth but 'twas no use. She burst like a girt bubble, bent over and started to laugh like I'd never heard her do before.

'Twas a catching thing and first I smiled, then could hardly help but join in though I'd no idea why. Hal looked summ'at worried, and that made us both laugh all the more. It took an age, but in due course Grace got her breath back enough to tell me what had brought on such mirth. Her red cheeks were not from any shame but rather had been blushes. Roddy Rawle had only gone and asked her to marry him, to become his good-wife and helpmeet and to go with him to the New World.

The days passed summ'at strange, with Grace courted by her new suitor and him swithering between tongue-tied and tongue-run-away-with-'en and all'us harassed by the busy nature of the tavern. In the end Grace did promise to think on his proposal but, making him mindful of our recent troubles, she begged Master Rawle let her go home with me if only to see me settled in safe. He was all of a bivver, angsty to make it right and I almost felt sorry for the man. He agreed in the end, with Grace promising to send word, before the Leap Day, whether she would wed him or no. Even if she answered 'aye' to him, I was sure that Grace and Hal would bide with me a-while. They would not wed yet. And Master Rawle would need to set his business in order and made ready his plans before any move to the new Plymouth, to the plantation on the far side of the ocean. I prayed that it would be months away.

On the twenty-first day of February, on a mild and dry morn, Captain Burrell rode into the yard of the 'Drake and Hind', bringing two mules saddled for Grace and me. Hal, squealing with excitement, was put up on the saddle in front of Burrell, and so it was that Grace and I, with the few belongings we had, rode back to Cornwood. We plodded on, two animals side-by-side, with Grace's lazy mount ambling along some way behind us. The captain spoke to me of Will, about soldiering and where he'd been. I listened and once in a while I had summ'at to say too.

We had a right warm welcome at the home of the Beale family, and after a good meal and endless embraces we went on to the scruffy courtelage of the Mattock brew house.

Daisy met us, biting her lip and gawping like some diddlecome loon but when I held open my arms, she ran to me and hugged me tight. She clutched my hand then, and grasped it all the whiles as she showed me around the place. There was much to be done, I could see that. The place was desperd musty, cobwebs and mire in every corner but it was naught that a few hours with broom, brush and lime-wash couldn't mend, and a little hard work hurt nobody. There was even an old sign, lying cracked and faded in a corner. Daisy said her ma had never bothered with any sign, and 'twas brother William's notion. Just as soon as I saw it I knew that we must have it hang outside the door. I told Daisy to fetch any good ale that there might be in the place, and Grace and Burrell and me drank a toast to William Mattock and to all absent friends.

When he rode for home in the dimsy light of the evening Benjamin Burrell had agreed to an undertaking. He had also agreed to keep it secret, for in such a way nobody could take any hurt if nothing came of my scheming. For on our journey I had asked the good Captain to think on whether he might write for me, a message to Heligan Manor, in the parish of St Ewe, Cornwall. He'd taken thought and he was ready to help. While Grace was fetching milk the next morning, Burrell stopped by, with his pen and ink and I told him what to write. I said he was to direct the letter to Mistress Mary Tremayne on behalf of her obedient servant, Hester Mattock.

If the message I sent was put into the hand of the woman who had been our friend in adversity, then Roderick Rawle, ex-tavern keeper of Tavistock, might just find himself jilted and on a ship to Massachusetts Bay colony on his own.

XXVII Mary: Corresponding with old friends

Written this 23rd day of February 1648
At the sign of the Clasped Hands
Cornwood
In the County of Devon

This message written as a true notation of Hester Mattock's
spoken word,

Mistress Mary Tremayne,
I hope that as you read my letter finds you are in the best
health. I hope that it finds you. I cannot write well yet so
have had this put down for me. If I make mistakes I beg you
to forgive them.
Grace and me are here at Cornwood and there has been
some more ferment, as if the war had not been enough. ~~And~~
~~as I am now a~~ *It would take a book to tell you of it all. But in*
the end, all ~~does~~ *has come well. The papers yet have to be*
seen by which ever court men do think fit, but in the mean
time I do have the running of the brew-house that William
left to me. With William's sister to help in the work we may
manage well enough. Grace and Henry Charles bide with
me.
~~Cornwood is hilly and~~
~~I~~
~~We~~
I would not write ~~but have a matter which~~ *but that I need*
your help and the help of ~~Master~~ *Colonel Tremayne.*
Grace has set her mind to going to the colonies. She will not
hark to me and thinks that there is nothing for her in England
and that all the wrong-doing of the man she is wedded to
must go unpunished ~~because~~ *since there are none who can*
stand as witness to what he did.

*I am greatly affeard for her and for Hal who is handsome
with curling locks the colour of straw but I do think he is
getting darker. He has the blue eyes of his father. He speaks
a little saying 'go to,' and 'thank you' only cannot say it well
and sounds like fankoo, and even if we cannot tell the words
he will jabber in his own way. He likes horses.*

*I will get to my point.
Colonel Tremayne does know well all the trials and troubles
that Grace had and particularly that Grace would have been
drowned at her husband's direction. He and ~~Master~~ Sark are
the men who could give their word that Grace does tell no lie
and bring justice to what happened. Grace does not believe
that anyone can do this and that the law would judge the
fault to be hers and there be no case.*

*I beg you, for the love of God and the ~~friend~~ hardships we
shared if there is ~~naught more~~ little to be done, do what you
may to ~~make show Grace that~~ help put matters right.
We have no more news here and so I will take no more of
your time, but pray ever for your health and happiness.
I remain your loving and faithful friend, and always obedient
servant,*

Hester Mattock

*To Mistress Mary Tremayne
At Heligan or Kestle Wartha or Penwarne
In the county of Cornwall
Or wheresoever she may be if not at these places*

Written this day 29th February 1648
At Kestle Wartha
In the parish of St Ewe
In the county of Cornwall

My friend, my dear Hester,
Let there be no formality betwixt us two and I would include
Grace besides, for there is nothing except true and honest
friendship here, for we have lived through too much together
and I cannot tell you how much I have missed your company.
You have been in my thoughts and prayers so often, and there
is much to tell you. I know not where to begin. The days have
often dragged slowly, time is laggardly here, and yet it is
unbelievable that it is nigh on two years since you were first
brought to this house, bedraggled and so weary, being with
child. The memory must still be painful so I am sorry to
cause hurt, for the sadness of baby William's loss will not
have been easy to bear. I know this now for I am a mother.

I am happy beyond words to know that little Hal thrives. You
will not know ought of my children so in haste I will tell a
little of the newest of the Tremayne family, for I have two
girls, twins born on the last day of '46 and a boy, now nearly
six months old. Mary and Honor, being twins and my first
birth were a trial and it is nothing less than a miracle, if I
might be allowed to say it, that both survive, born exiled and
in a French garret and not with my own folk about me.
Honor is not so strong and some days I am anxious for her
well-being.
John came a little early, last September, but now thrives. I
was at home, for which I thank God.

Lewis still bides abroad. I never thought to say it but I am
glad of that for there is much unease here in the western
parts, ~~and I wish Lewis not to be part of it.~~ Too much of our
correspondence is opened, <u>but if the Committees wish to</u>

_know of babes and infant colic and teething, then they may
read on._

Yet this I must say, and regret that it is so.

I know that, given the freedom to do so, Lewis would attend
on every court of law if they were to be proceedings against
Bartholomew Fenwick and I personally would ~~have that
devil's servant hanged, drawn and quartered~~ ~~dispatched~~ see
justice done.

I write ~~with~~ to Lewis as often as I might, and he has been
sometime in Jersey where I was with him, and France with
the Prince of Wales, and to a place on Holland's coast which
has an infernal spelling so that my pen will not command it.
The name begins with Hel, it is where ~~there have been ships
readying for His Highness~~ Prince Rupert has been.

I think my husband to be perhaps now returned in to France
but if it is so I cannot say. What matters is that I will write to
him, most urgently, Hester, and press for his assistance in
any way he can devise. Surely Parliament would not deny
this?

Excepting this, there is no thing that he can do, for he is
bound by the Articles of Surrender and may not return home
except that the Committee for this-or-that - I know not who -
needs to pardon him first. Parliament I think must allow his
return. But I will write this very hour, and see what may be
achieved.

It seems most curious that your letter has arrived for I have
recently wished so hard to know that you are safe and your
whereabouts. I have often spoken of you to my sisters I long
that we three were here in my parlour for there is so much to
tell you and so much I wish to ask, that mere letters cannot
carry it all for I often will forget news in my haste to send. To
sit with honey cake and something warming to drink, to talk
as we used to would be a joy.

 There has been a matter troubling me since John's birth,
and even now that I have the wherewithal to do so, I know
not quite how best to tell you and then you will know how to

inform Grace. I think, however, that there can be no need for
alam. ~~I am sure that~~ ~~it that he can~~ *But perhaps it is well*
to be advised.
Did you know that one of the ships in the blockade of
Pendennis point in '46 was that of Grace's husband? It was
our ill-fortune to sail upon that very vessel when we went
into exile, to Jersey. I am sure now that he recognised Lewis
even though we mainly kept to the cabin we were given,
because of my being sick. However, do you recall the
surgeon, Wiseman, at the fortress? It matters not how but he
was ~~accosted~~ ~~interrogated~~ *questioned about his patients at*
the castle by Bartholomew Fenwick. Perhaps he should not,
but I think that surgeon must have unwittingly given that
menace some information. And last September, Fenwick
came here asking after my acquaintances among the women
at Pendennis. He seemed to know much and yet still had
questions.
He knows Grace is alive, though how he discovered her I do
not know. He believes her to have something he wants back,
which I take to be that perplexing book?
It compounds your quest, does it not, for if Fenwick seeks this
document then it must signify some great import.
I do not think he can find you. How could he? ~~He threatened~~
~~us all.~~ *But I am much relieved to be able to warn you both for*
the incident has troubled me.

Perhaps in the very worst of cases, the colonies might be a
refuge for Grace, though as God will be my witness, I cannot
think that any lone woman and her child ought willingly to
go without desperate matters driving them.

Your new venture will keep you a busy woman and I long to
hear all your deeds. Is it too inconvenient or can you write
often, for I should be most happy for correspondence.

Yet to have you here would be what I have longed for so
most.
Kestle Wartha will always hold out the warmest welcome,

164

And I will ever remain,
Your loving friend,
Mary

To Mistress Mattock,
At the sign of the Clasped Hands
In Cornwood
County of Devon

XXVIII Grace: To woo, perhaps to win

Even with a crystal ball at hand, few women can expect to determine their own destiny. I am no exception though my circumstances were no worse, nor better, than thousands of others. My means were slender, my options few. But there were still choices to be made.

In my life I have made a few decisions on impulse, and these you already know. You know too that I am sorry for none of them. Others have hardly been informed judgments, for there was nobody that I could ask for advice. Inevitably I listened and learned from those around me, reacting to situations as best I could. Nevertheless, although it was not a reckless act, to make a decision based on the words of a soothsayer was perhaps irresponsible.

Of course, I could not accept the proposal of marriage from Master Rawle though he courted most gently and winningly. I wrote to him saying that I must clarify matters pertaining to my marriage; my husband was a seafarer. So far, no lie. I admitted that I had been made homeless in the troubles, and had not seen my man in years, as he had been long absent through the war: also, no lie. He might be dead yet I did not know for certain that I was truly a widow and so could not go to church or state and, under oath, swear that I was free to marry again. That was a half-truth at least, and kinder than an outright refusal. I could not say I had loved another, lost to me now but who could never be replaced in my affections.

My would-be suitor would not be daunted. Some fortnight later he rode to Cornwood early one morning, to speak to me in person. I welcomed him, indicating that anything we said would be shared with Hester, now not only my dear friend but the proprietor of the premises in which he stood. He looked very different outside his own neighbourhood. Even though his greying head practically touched the bowing ceiling of Hester's taproom, he seemed very reserved, vulnerable even. Hester was bristling, obviously uncomfortable with Rawle's presence, though I doubted that it was due to any conflict of business interests. She pretended to be busy, furiously rubbing each tiny pane in the mis-shapen windows. There was no offer of refreshment.

Taking a deep breath Rawle responded to my rejection with a speech that he had obviously rehearsed,

"Mistress Grace, I do thank ye for the gentle words in yon letter. I am right sorry for the predicament. However, I am here to beg that ye will harken to a few more words before there is an end to the matter completely." He waited for me to nod, and I sat down on a settle, it being only courtesy to give him my full attention. Though I gestured that he should take a seat he refused, preferring to stand.

"Well. Ye have heard forebye, that it be my firm inclination to make a new life in a land unsullied by the godless and profane, by strife and tribulations. To that end, I intend to follow the business I have known all my days, but in a new land of opportunity. Now, this is not built on a fanciful notion! Nomye!"

He then argued most convincingly that as the colonists grew their territory, then wayfarers would be in need of accommodation. He was ardent in his belief that a good tavern, an inn, ought to lie at the heart of every new settlement.

"Good ale be most essential for the health of every man, woman and child," he declared. "I ha' made enquiry, and I d'know that the ingredients required for good brewing will grow in that foreign wilderness. There may e'en be more, new hops or the like perhaps, that a master brewer like m'self might employ for the good of all."

I was impressed by his thoroughness. This was not an impulsive man, so what was spoken next was the more surprising for that. Clearing his throat Master Rawle puffed out his chest and, hands clasped behind his back, made his revelation, his formal tone beginning to slip back his familiar dialect,

167

"Nomye, well, then, hark ye just a tad more, before ye turn Roddy Rawle off completely. Now then, what I mean is this …if ye be not a wife, then would ye set forth as an associate in this venture?"

I heard Hester slap the cloth into the bucket of water she was carrying as she stopped work, now unashamedly listening. I could barely keep up with his words, his single-mindedness all too evident. Faced with the legality of matters on this side of the Atlantic, Roddy had clearly set aside the notion that it would be more satisfactory if we were wed. However, he was equally prepared to establish the enterprise without matrimonial ties. To my amazement, he said that he needed no financial commitment and even extended the same terms of employment as at the 'Drake and Hind' to me, solely, if I would take ship with him over the seas to the New World. My passage would be paid; he was prepared to guarantee my well-being with food and good quarters once we reached our destination. We would work as if we were indeed wed but would, he insisted, maintain all proprieties. In addition, I was to have four guineas in order that I should obtain some necessaries for the voyage and for my future as colonist.

"And should ye ever discover ye be free to wed …" The sentence was left hanging, the man's embarrassment finally taking its toll.

The offer was certainly a very unconventional one but unquestionably generous. It offered me the means to escape and leave my past with Fenwick behind, with the potential to bury the desolation of loss beneath the hard work and endeavor of Rawle's venture. It gave me serious cause for thought. Such an offer was not to be refused lightly for all that there were emotional and physical ties to bind me to England.

With him there in person, as well he knew, it was much more difficult to decline and Roddy Rawle was not a man to be gainsaid when he had set his mind to a matter.

All the while, Loveday haunted my thoughts but so did Burrell's words.

"Master Rawle …" I began.

"Call me Roddy … Roderick if you prefer …" he waved expansively then regained control of himself, his hands clasped firmly behind him again.

"Roderick, I am deeply mindful of the extreme honour you do me in making this offer. But I have a son whose security is paramount." Roderick had evidently expected this objection.

"He will grow up learning my trade; he could inherit … I can keep ye both safe!"

Hester let out a whimper and turning, I saw her face crumple, tears falling unchecked. However, before I could reach her to offer comfort, the door thumped back against its hinges and Captain Burrell swirled in, his cloak spattering muddy droplets across the floor. The door to beyond the taproom opened at just the same moment, revealing Daisy, carrying you.

For a few minutes the place descended into infant-driven pandemonium, your delight at discovering your favourite cavalier noisily evident, as if the man had been absent for weeks rather than days.

Burrell had been brandishing a letter which he rapidly tucked back into his doublet as you launched yourself at him. However, the man must have sensed the atmosphere and as soon as he was able, greeted everyone present in a most gentlemanly manner and offered his apologies for intruding.

Hester was quick to reassure him,

"Nay, Captain Burrell, think naught of it, for you'm welcome here as any and more than some." I glanced at her, hoping that the barb was not aimed at Rawle, but her expression was quite without malice. I spoke to cover the awkwardness,

"Captain, what brings you to us in this filthy weather?" He looked a little stunned at first, but gathering his wits, shrugged slightly and withdrew the packet. There was a raised eyebrow, an unspoken query and a slight nod in response: Burrell handed the letter to Hester. What I heard next was a revelation.

"Mistress Mattock, this comes from St Ewe parish. It is regrettable that under the present circumstances I was unable to take the message myself and that the route by which this missive has made its way to you has been necessarily obscure, and hence slow. But I can at least vouch that your correspondence is unopened."

None the wiser, the statement nevertheless struck me as unusual; why not simply apologise for the delay? Hester paid no heed, and had ripped open the seal. She glanced at no more than the first line on the page then, grinning, thrust the sheet into my hand saying,

"You read it to us!" Rawle frowned, looking as if he would rather absent himself, but Hester would have none of it.

"Master Rawle, this matter affects 'ee so if you would be so pleased as to stay." Rawle lowered himself onto a stool, frowning so hard that his bushy eyebrows made a hirsute stripe across his brow.

"You'm making some plans, Grace," said Hester, speaking with assurance, "and who am Hester Mattock to be gainsaying them. But 'tidn't all'us easy to see the tor ahead of 'ee, and mayhap your friends ... oh, fie Grace! Mary and me, we've been tossing words to and fro. Captain Burrell here has made use of pen and ink and seen that the right words have been passing and, well ... see!"

I read aloud. Mary's familiar and reassuring tone was in every word. At the end of the commonplace, if delightful, exchange of nursery news was something that set my heart pounding. It seemed that Mary Tremayne had written to her husband to ask if he would provide written evidence against Bartholomew Fenwick which, once presented to the proper authorities, might at least start the process of bringing the villain to account. In his reply Lewis had agreed wholeheartedly and the matter was now in hand.

Burrell spoke, politely deferring to Hester,

"Mistress, if I may?" I must be frank with you. While Colonel Tremayne remains in exile your cause is unlikely to prosper. However, there is a significant chance that such a matter, if brought to the attention of the right individuals, could result in the recall, and possibly the pardon of Lewis Tremayne as well as the pursuit of ..." Hester could not contain herself,

"Grace, it would bring him home to Mary! Two birds and one stone to slay them both!" She was triumphant. Nevertheless, the cold sinking feeling that any mention of Fenwick's name gave me remained.

"Who is this Fenwick? What is he to you?" Rawle was getting to his feet. I gently placed my hand on his shoulder, and he meekly subsided.

"Master Rawle, Roderick. This man was my husband. I ..." Hester took up where I faltered.

"Grace took a different name so as that godforsaken embodiment of evil would not be able to find her. 'Twas just a name, a sark, like a night-shift." She held my gaze. Hester knew I would not want your father's identity to enter into this conversation. I let her continue.

"He tried to kill her and Mary Tremayne's husband was a witness." Then Hester's nervousness got the better of her. She rushed on,

"And he knows that she lives and is seeking her out!"

A black pall seemed to fall behind my eyes and I became unsteady on my feet. Hester ran to my side,

"Oh Grace! I feared to tell you, and I was going to, but 'tis true. Fenwick has been to Kestle, he questioned Mary about the women she knew at Pendennis, a'cause he had found something out. Oh 'tis a long matter ... but yet, there is no cause for alarm, for he cannot know where you are, can he? Mary said so."

As the faint passed I lifted my head to look around the room: Rawle looked dubious; Daisy completely overawed; only Burrell seemed unmoved. Hester held me tight, buried her face in my shoulder, mumbling over and over,

"Fenwick should hang!"

Burrell, cut through the emotion with his lawyer's tone,

"It may not be that simple. The English legal system has become a little ... disordered these last years. However, the new regime will be keen to establish the Rule of Law so I fail to see why the perpetrator should not be pursued. It will take time, of course." Rawle stood up, interrupting brusquely,

"Aye, sir! But I do not have time. The sailing season will wait for no man. Mistress Sark … or Fennel … or whosoever thou are, wilt thou come with me to the colony or no?"

With the spectre of the man who abused me at my back and the echo of a strange prediction in my head, the words were spoken almost before I was conscious of the thought that directed them,

"Aye, I will. Yes, Master Rawle, I shall. If you will undertake to provide a living, then I will, for one year and with the stipend on which we agreed at Tavistock, as well as four pounds and four shillings in advance, I will work with you on your venture. I reserve the right then to choose to return to England or stay, if it is agreeable to you." The words hung in the air. I turned to Hester,

"My dear friend, I cannot wait for the justice that might never come, though I would wish it otherwise. I must go. If you do think me wrong or mad or both, then I risk losing your affection and regard." I took her hand, "I have no right to ask. Yet I will. Hester, would you take on the nurture and raising of Henry Charles for me? As God is my witness, you have been a mother to him in all but birthing, as much if not more than I. We both know that Hal is the light of both our lives and, if I can, I wish to make a new life for him and me." I looked at Burrell, and back to my friend whose hands both now clasped mine as if they would crush the very bones.

"But Hester, he is not yet two, and very small, I think, to manage the voyage. Thus I would leave him sheltered by your love, where he will be safe, and when the year is up, then …" The future was best left unsaid.

In Hester's eyes I saw the very reflection of my own emotions; the wordless fears, the unknown hazards, the anguish of love and the blackness of despair. Yet now there was also hope.

Momentarily the room around us seemed like a tableaux, a painted scene from an old church mural, then the illusion shattered and a cacophony of contradictory noise began, seeming to rattle the very jugs and tankards standing on the shelves. A sobbing Hester hugged me; a bawling Daisy hugged Hester; Rawle was whooping with what I assumed was delight and I could do nothing but laugh.

A bellow brought the havoc to a standstill as Jet Beale stepped through the doorway. Within seconds and with the new authority of his role as constable very evident, he took charge of a situation which had threatened to descend into an emotional chaos. Ben Burrell, his expression still unreadable, slipped away as plans were made, options discussed, prospects explored.

In the following days and weeks, there came no more letters from Kestle Wartha, nothing more to disrupt the preparations, and when Roderick Rawle sent word that he had secured passage on the *Four Sisters* under the command of ship's master Roger Harman, sailing from Plymouth's Mill Bay anchorage on the spring tide of the new moon, 12th April 1648, everything augured well: Goody Yendacott, it seemed, had been right.

XXIX Hester: Hidden depths

When spring finally arrived in '48 it came with all manner of storms with late snow, hail and rain that stripped the buds off the trees. I missed Grace as I would miss a limb and couldn't bear to think of her at sea in those tempests. I imagined all manner of monsters rearing their heads to snap a ship in twain and devour all of them on board. I knew of the hazards right enough, being wrecked myself and I'd seen the sea maps on Grace's pa's table, all those years ago, when I should have been about my household tasks, but was instead looking at the figures of girt fish with gnashing teeth bigger even than the boats pictured with all their sails set.

But 'twas not only the weather. The growing disquiet amongst folks was worsening, with our customers seeming uneasy. I'd never had much cause to consider it before, but now I was a woman of means it looked as though I was to be hard-pressed for tax like everyone else who had two pennies to rub together. No wonder Roddy Rawle got so angsty. With a commissioner for everything you could name looking over our shoulders into everyone's concerns, it was a wonder we were allowed to breathe freely without Parliament's say-so, and I do reckon they'd have taxed the air too if they could, so 'twas more than enough to make men uppity.

When Tinker Luccombe came into our yard, crying his clanking-clattery trade of mending pots and what-you-will, he brought all the latest news from across the moor and beyond. Folk gathered at the 'Hands' to listen and Ben Burrell, with most of the men of the district, took a jug of our ale in the fug of 'baccy smoke in the taproom, to hear as much of the traveller's tales as possible.

And troubling it was too, for the story was that across the Bristol Sea, Wales was in uproar with the army in revolt over pay - or lack of it - and now the countrymen were joining them as they marched. Rumour said that the King had escaped, yet again, and there was to be a girt rising of Royalists. He had supposedly summoned massed armies from Scotland and all the troops in revolt were to join him. 'Twas said that French ships had for certain sure sunk every one of the Parliament's fleet and were about to land armies all along the south coast, paid for by the Queen's jewels, and all would march on London so that His Majesty could come into his own again.

Rumour never could be trusted.

Yet it had a seed of truth a'cause it was common knowledge that Plymouth troops had refused to disband when they'd been ordered to. As men went back to their hearths and tables, no doubt to report rumour as solid fact, all were of one mind: the country would soon be at war again.

'Twasn't only when Luccumbe passed through that Ben Burrell - for now he asked to be called that and not 'Captain' or 'Master' - was at my door. He'd begun to call more often before Grace sailed, and afterwards I began to look for him. He was ever courteous and respectful and all'us ready with pen and paper to send whatever I wished to Mary. In the main it was ordinary matters that he wrote on my behalf, day-to-day prattle of progress at the brew-house, with more of Hal's latest antics or the like.

One day I remarked to Benjamin that I was sure Mistress Tremayne would find my letters dull as ditchwater, but he said that she could not or else why would she reply in the same manner? That seemed right enough, but I did think he all'us seemed more keen to set words down than me.

My reading, though not up to much, had improved no end with Grace helping me the whiles. I might not be very good at putting words onto a page, but I was better at making sense of them than my inky-fingered friend realised. A few days after Grace left, while we sat down together, he wrote summ'at that was not at all what I had said, so I pointed to a word, quite clear in Burrell's plain script, and took him to task on the matter.

Well, you'd have thought I had called him the devil's own, for in an instant he looked as raged as a rutting buck and indignant to boot. I held up my hands and cried 'whoa!' and after a pause for breath, Burrell eyed me, then locking the door to the road and making sure that Daisy was not within hearing, he drew his seat so close to the table that our heads were touching. I could barely hear his voice a'cause he began to talk, fast and low.

"Hester, you have me at a great disadvantage. It is true that I have taken liberties with your correspondence and for that I owe you an apology and yet, if I explain myself, I must insist upon your total discretion. When I account for my actions, I believe that, nay, I pray that you will not think ill of me. The truth is that I place my life in your hands from this moment on." Pishh! thought I, and that's how I answered, though a little more lady-like,

"Fiddle-faddle! Captain! I'll have none of that talk! Be straight or else!" and I sat back, piqued at such a silly to-do. He took my hand and drew me towards him again, hushing me then whispering,

"I will be so, mistress! You have my word, on my life and that of Colonel Tremayne, Sir Richard Grenvile, Sir John Arundel and many other great gentlemen in Cornwall and beyond."

Now, I recognized the names, for wasn't my William under Sir Richard Grenvile's command in '45? And I knew that old Jack-for-the-King Sir John Arundel, who'd been governor of Pendennis fort, was Mary Tremayne's uncle. He went on,

"The King's men are rising, and I have for some time now been a messenger." He looked right furtive, knotted brow, scar and all. But I wasn't having him be-twitting me as if I was born yesterday.

"Oh aye, do pull the other leg for there's bells on't! You? A messenger? Pray tell me then, how have you been about that, with every road with sentry posts upon it and every traveller needing papers just to pass water? Go'rn!" Burrell looked odd at that and thrust away from the table. When it came, his reply made me sit up sharp-ish for his tone was quite different, gone stony-cold,

"I have not needed to travel, Hester, for your letters with Mary Tremayne have carried secrets hidden in the lines, secrets that, in the wrong hands, put your life at risk as well as mine."

There was a shift about the man sitting opposite me. No more was he that modest, bookish lawyer or Hal's jolly playmate. Here was a dangerous man of secrets, a hardnosed man of steel.

It struck me then that he had probably been that all along and that this must be the skill of the acting-men that Grace spoke of, the fellows that pretend and speak the lines from that book of stories that her pa kept. Mind, now wasn't the moment to tell the soldier he'd do well on stage. Still, Hester Mattock b'aint no delicate Lenten rose and I'd faced worse than him. I wasn't afraid of Ben Burrell, nice or nasty, or his veiled threats for that matter.

"Hmm, and there was I thinking you were all bashful, coming courting on the sly, under the guise of being my pen-man. Oh well. I was never one for a love-sick loon. So, what's afoot?"

From the expression on his face, I doubt that was the retort that he'd expected, and there was almost a twitch of a smile before he kicked the stool back to the table and sat down,

"I am beginning to see why William Mattock wed thee, mistress!" If he thought to get round me with flattery he'd have to think again, and I shrugged off his words.

"Well, rare looks, quick wits and good housekeeping do rarely come together, but then Will did all'us have good taste in women." I decided if I was to have an explanation, then it might as well be in comfort.

"Speaking of housekeeping, I've yet to dine so you'll take something with me?" I didn't give him chance to object. Once I'd fetched in bread and cheese and a pot of small-beer, as we ate I asked questions and he answered.

It was no great surprise that there were still secret cavaliers who would rally to the King, nor that in Cornwall there were some prepared to take action. William all'us did say they were independent thinking across the Tamar and quick for an uprising. With an unhappy army with its own axe to grind, it sounded as if there'd been goings-on much longer than my packets had been passing to Kestle Wartha. When Burrell - I hardly felt like calling this charlatan by his Christian name - came to answer my question, 'Why Mary Tremayne?' I could not take it in for it sounded so unlikely and he had to tell me twice over.

For the whole scheme of burying secrets beneath a good-wife's prattle had been Mary's own. She had taken a nursery game, played to liven up the dull lessons of a tutor, and turned it into sport of a deadlier kind with naught less than a kingdom at stake. As Burrell talked, I could sense a female's wiles at work.

Though her husband was known to be a Royalist to the last drop of his blood, she was only his lady wife. Her family had married into almost every great household in the Duchy - and many in Devon, for that matter. Her cousin John Carew, well connected in London circles and a thorough Parliamentarian if ever there was one, could be called upon to ensure that Lewis' awkward politics should not in any way impugn her honour, and he might well speak up for her, believing that, like any good woman, she would do as she was bidden. 'Twas all very likely, unless you knew Mary Tremayne as I did.

Once the bare bones of the matter had been laid out it took no time for me to make up my mind. 'Twouldn't be the first time I'd been party to penmanship that was not all it seemed. I might not write but I could prattle with the best, and where Mary Tremayne led there would I follow.

"So, Captain Benjamin Burrell. Let you and me set to our task then!" I declared. He looked at me hard, eyes narrowed,

"Very well. You do understand the risks?" While he was speaking, he ran his hands through his brock-ish locks so that white wisps stood up like horns. That, thought I, said summ'at about Captain Burrell's nerves for all his stern outside. At my nod he laid out paper, inkhorn, and slipping out a slim dagger, swiftly sharpened up a quill, and we set to work.

"Each piece of correspondence is different," he explained, "which makes the system all the more secure, for there is no cypher as such, no code to be broken. The message might be but a few words, rarely more than a dozen. Few people know the key. Mistress Tremayne signifies it thus, by adding the hour to the date. If it is three of the clock, then in the third sentence, and every third one after, each third word will be relevant. Do you see?" I did, for 'twas simple enough. He said that was what made this so clever, the very plainness of it.

"But 'tis just a jumble of words. How do 'ee make sense of it?!" If you asked me, reading was a mystery enough without making it harder. But Burrell showed me how writing in onion juice could only be seen if the paper was held across a flame. 'Twas like something magical.

"If we truly need to separate parts of the message, then we put a line between," he said, "but most of the recipients rarely need it."

Still, once we began to make up my letter I found it much harder to hide the words he wanted amongst my own. It read as if a dolt had composed it. That was when he showed me that it mattered not if there were words scored out, as if I had made a mistake or wished a word unsaid. The finished message sounded so ordinary that I doubted even Mary would want to read it.

"I do not mean to insult you, but the letter is perhaps what would be expected of an alewife untaught in her letters, which, should it fall into the wrong hands, will not raise any suspicions."

"Aside from an alewife having aught to do with a gentry lady!" I scoffed.

"Hmm, perhaps we should make reference to the 'olden days' and your shared history under siege, do a little reminiscing. That would offer some cover." I could see the sense in that so we agreed to use the ruse in future.

I wondered then how the letter would make its way, and Burrell wryly told me that, against his inclination, he was acting upon some minor legal matters for a friend of his father. It had restored paternal pride but also gave him good reason to occasionally go to Plymouth, Tavistock or Ashburton. There the right contact could speed the passage of a letter when needs pressed, but more often a plain and simple carrier might be paid to do the task. Though there was a watch upon known 'delinquents', it seemed the authorities often times missed what went on under their very noses.

As he began to tell me how an ex-Royalist trooper squared his war service for the King with the local commissioners I put up my hands to my ears,

"Nay, sir! I've heard quite enough. Let us leave it at that! What I don't know can't hurt me. Set some wax upon that sheet and send it forth." I cocked my head at a noise, "Then brace yourself, and fasten the lid upon your ink-pot, for I can hear Henry Charles, fresh from his crib, and if I know the signs, he's seen your mare and is right folshid that you've not yet said hello!"

So there it was. Matters of state all wrapped in the day-to-day and I, Hester Mattock, finding myself with yet another string to add to my bow: servant, wife, widow, brewster, spy.

XXX Mary: Reading between the lines

At 3 o'clock on this day 10th April 1648
Written at Rue des Abbeyes
St Germain-en-Laye

Dearest heart,
I thank you for your letter. A most welcome sight on my
return from a dull duty. You describe Portmellon Cove, and I
dream too. Spring in Cornwall is always so lovely. Trees in
Paris are in leaf already. Perhaps the land is warmer this far
south? We have not had the storms which sweep the western
seas though. I suppose that might account for the foliage.
Tulips are full out. My father asked me to buy bulbs if I was
to go to the Dutch again. They are very dear but I will buy
some if I can and if I send them, you must make sure that he
plants according to the experts if they are to be worth my
investment. At full moon the bulbs will thrive, but only if they
be planted deep. For myself I cannot understand the fashion
in costly foreign flowers. I prefer those with which I am
familiar. Now, at Kestle, the season's brief, their flowers
more precious like silver, yet roses for ever will cause my
heart to burst. The scent fills the gardens. Here the Queen
has roses grown for cutting and has them placed in great
bowls set on tables in her rooms.
I remember Trerice! The roses there are the envy of all
Cornish gentlemen gardeners. I remember my mother
wanting a garden in the same design. She asked Arundel the
secret to the even dispersal of blooms. He told her his
gardener used horse dung, rotted down and spread between
the bushes. Mother used seaweed instead. She saw problems
in her getting enough rotted horses' dung in time. Kelp
seemed quicker. Mother was ever eccentric. Her temper's

*very hot and short, like a Grenvile in how anxious she
became.*

*Here there has been little of real import though the numbers
of courtiers are swelled by the arrival of another Irish lord,
Inchiquin, who the ladies all say is most handsome and when
he is stood by the Earl of Ormond, they look for all like two
chess pieces for Inchiquin is as dark as Ormond is pale!
Ireland may yet come to the King's cause.*

I will attempt to ~~draw planned~~ *sketch my Prince, Rufus,
Rebel, James and Pug. As hounds for hunting they leave
much to be desired. Hardly worth their keep, in truth. Pug
did escape from the garden, a great game with many a fine
courtier lady seeking him. Perhaps the twins will draw me
pictures? I would like that.*

*Always to end every lonely month, my heart masquerading,
never to join my very Queen of Hearth and Home! I do
nightly wish that I could be in Kestle's parlour, my children
on my knee and you at my side. Ah, what dreams.*

*Greet my brother and father for me. I hope they keep good
health.*

*I remain your loving and sorrowing husband,
Lewis*

*To my lady, Mistress Tremayne
At Kestle Wartha
In the parish of St Ewe
In the county of Cornwall*

*Given to the hand of R Harman, Master of the **Four Sisters**,
to Plymouth*

Written this 14th day of April 1648

At the sign of clasp'd hands
Cornwood in the county of Devon

To my friend Mary,
I write just after the chimes of 4 o' the clock by the church
here for it is a quiet time of the day. Hal is usually napping at
this time and customers are few yet.
You know I think that Grace planned to go to the new
Plymouth? I held out no hope that any news would make an
about-face. So with Master Roderick Rawle she did take ship
from the old Plymouth just two days gone. The last hours
were the worst. Saying goodbye was so hard though she says
one year which she is bounden to do is not so long. And
Rawle pays court to Grace still.
 The boy asks when mama will return. If I say in a few days
he does not seem afraid and I think this is because he has
been so long close with us both. I worry that the last hours
have seen bad storms here again and pray that at sea there
be no wreck.
With out Grace what ever is ~~doing~~ *happening here makes our*
Pendennis time as friends really the most very important time
for me. I do miss us talking together. Though we be very
different it is a joy and honour to me to know that you do
rejoice in that time also. It seems so long ago. 'T'was the
common risk that bound us of that strange women's
regiment, though we were coming south, north or west. Or
east I suppose. Though less from west Cornwall than Devon.
I often wonder about other women like Jenny the armourer's
wife and if they are safe after all our hardships. It seems the
fort and friends are not forgotten.
But anon. Of my news. You did ask how is business and what
of customers.
There was a file of folk who must have been curious, hold
good hard coin out to buy beer. It may be that since Ma
Mattock was ill the brewing lapsed. That did not go well with
the people around here. There is no other tapster nearby.
They were all desperate for good ale, the smell of rising of
bread does make them thirsty, and so haste in the kitchen to

provide vitals is ~~west~~ *haste well spent. Ham if I have it will sell. There is little profit in wine. I must pay dear for it. Only an old Exeter vintner will readily still consider my custom, refusing to receive any orders from anyone new, from old Master Wall who he says errs in his accounting officers. As the vintner charges too high as well then my customers will have no burgundy nor rheinish and will needs make do with comes from my vats, and the local cider.*

I hear Hal waking so must close now.
I remain your friend in deed.
Hester

To Mistress Mary Tremayne
At Kestle Wartha
In the parish of St Ewe
In the county of Cornwall

Written this the 25th day of April 1648
At Kestle Wartha
St Ewe in the county of Cornwall

Dear Hester,
I cannot sleep so thought to take up my pen. The chimes rang 3 of the clock, and I have just heard the cockerel, which makes me think that mayhap the spring and better weather and warmer days will soon be with us if old Chanticleer is crowing so much before dawn. I have received your letter, welcome and newsy. Hal is yet young. He may forget Grace is his mother though I think you will not let that happen.

184

*How is money for you? Does the tavern have credit with men
like your vintner? Did your mother-in-law leave capital? I
am ready to lend. Do not fear to ask. Or be ashamed. There
are men with coin in coffers in Penzance who lend, also near
in Helston, but they gather high interest. Do not go near
these usurers, though they be against the law, they prey upon
unwary folk. Ask me. My dear Husband, I'm sure, joins me in
agreeing. We will lend you on the strength of getting a barrel
of your first best winter ale for our cellar.*

*What have I been doing with my time? A new sark for Honor,
at last ~~she latter~~ lately she may be growing eighteen inches:
she's leading twin Mary at talking however. Mary is the
taller still. So new sark, new gown because she broke her
leading bands and both need new caps.*

*Now Mary mounts the little bay pony well. That is the one I
told you of, the one my father got for the girls but Honor is
too small.*

*Baby John thrives. He likes boats. He is yet but seven months
but will roll and push himself up, and will play happily in a
bath where he has a toy boat with real sails. My father waits
for him to grow for he would take him fishing. To go offshore
is his plan. There he will teach John all he knows. For a man
who was struck by an apoplexy eight years ago and has had
but one hand forty-and-some years since, papa is a marvel.
On our landing there are many woodworm holes. Lewis will
be annoyed I think. You do not have a remedy I suppose? To
do re-enforcement of boards must we truly make haste. I once
saw worm such as this weaken the floor of a place so badly
that you could place a finger through the plank. My house
might fall down if the worm eats all the wood. That would
signal disaster and burning timber, like bonfires, is
impractical, smoking my furnishings. Especially indoors. So
any remedy you can discover I would be grateful for.*

*Light is now coming from behind the morning clouds so I will
close my silly gossip, but hope that when you read it you
remember that I am ever your loving friend,
Mary*

To Mistress Hester Mattock
At the sign of the clasped hands
In Cornwood in the county of Devon

*Messages read thus:
From Lewis: Portmellon I land this full moon/ will only be Kestle
brief /more silver for cause to Trerice Arundel to distribution/
problems horses/ time getting short Grenvile anxious
Attempt planned Prince James escape garden game/ a lady end
month masquerading / join Queen and brother

From Hester: No news about court/ what happening Pendennis
really important/ Risk of regiment coming west / Fortesque must
hold out/ desperate await rising/ make haste to west/ Exeter still
refusing orders from Wallers officers

From Mary: Received welcome money/ ready men in Penzance also
Helston gather/ Husband joins sark at latter May eighteen leads
Mount's Bay boats offshore/ plan landing many reinforcements/
must make signal /burning bonfires smoky

XXXI Grace: A voyage into the unknown

If I have taken anything from my experiences of life which I can offer you as a maxim it is that, prepare as you will, matters rarely follow the pattern you design. The events of spring 1648 were a case in point. Roderick Rawle laid out a strategy, meticulous in every detail and admirable in its thoroughness. Yet even he could never have anticipated the events which overtook us as we sailed westwards.

I suppressed all the troubling misgivings I suffered at leaving you, reminding myself that I was doing so in order to make a new life in which you would inevitably join me. I had nobody to whom I could voice my concerns now. I had made my decision as objectively as I could, but a familiar way of life, no matter how arduous it might be, was hard to leave behind. Unless the alternative was Bartholomew Fenwick.

Roger Harman was a ship's master who inspired confidence. The vessel was immaculate. To me the ship was a delight, reminding me very much of the *Ann of Bristol*. Even the most nervous traveller, seeing the disposition of a professional commander directing the efficient working of an evidently competent crew would have had their qualms reduced to a minimum.

Our voyage began cheerfully enough, a brisk north-westerly wind on the beam filling the sails and setting us on a comfortable south-westerly course. The weather was as perfect as any novice seafarer could wish for, though I was no novice. Rawle, on the other hand, had discovered that his constitution was better suited to the land than the sea. He kept to the tiny private cabin for which he had paid an exorbitant supplement but which now proved worth the price. Consequently I was left to my own devices. On deck, wrapped in my new, serviceable cloak, I was generally ignored.

As the second day of our voyage dawned we were already beyond the last landfall on the Cornish coast. Some way due south of the Isles of Scilly, a vessel appeared on our port quarter. It looked ominous. Piracy in these waters was a hazard that Parliament had been able to do little to alleviate. The privateers had simply based themselves in Ireland. I had encountered pirates before and knew that if our ship was facing a challenge this was likely to be a rapid and ruthless engagement.

Nonetheless, as the ship bearing down on us came closer, I had to pinch myself to ensure that I was not in some cruelly ironic dream. It was the *Dolphin*. As she drew within the range of her bow-chaser guns, I spotted the scandalously hirsute man commanding the poop-deck, Pasco Jago. When I caught a glimpse of the man directing the guns aimed across our bows it is no lie to state that my heart seemed to miss a beat.

The beard was an innovation, an effective disguise if it were not for his stance. I knew it so well; that long back, broad shoulders; the confident stride, the unconscious shrug of the shoulders as he settled to concentrate: Sark. As I took an involuntary step back, a hard bump against the mast making me gasp, I realised that I had been holding my breath.

Making an untimely attempt to get some fresh air, Rawle came to stand at my side, peering shortsightedly at the developing drama.

"Though I be no seafarer, it do seem to me that there vessel is a tad too close for comfort and has mischief in mind." My response came out as an unladylike snort. "There may be danger here," he added, feebly, "I think ye should seek some shelter." I shook my head,

"No, Roderick, though I thank you for your concern. I would prefer to remain on deck, if you please." He looked ready to take the matter in hand, so I added,

"You must, of course, go below but I fear that if I do I shall be ..." I sought an excuse, "I shall be ... most awfully sick." The words turned Rawle's own pallor from sallow to grey-green. He turned on his heel and stumbled back towards his accommodation.

At Harman's direction our guns had been run out and men were adjusting the sails. The crew was completely engaged with the preparations to defend the *Four Sisters,* so I crouched into a corner on the quarterdeck, hard by the starboard rail. This afforded me a view but kept me hidden from most of the maindeck. I watched as a puff of smoke anticipated the thump-crack of a small cannon firing. A ball whistled through the rigging, a splash to starboard proving this was no blank shot just for show. The *Dolphin* was intent on a prize.

The vessels manoeuvred, though it was plain that we were at a disadvantage. A second warning shot, taking splinters off our bowsprit, was persuasion enough. Our sailing master thought better of putting up a fight, allowing the boarding party to clamber up from their skiff unopposed, though two marksmen with muskets at the *Dolphin's* rail, their weapons trained on Harman, were Jago's insurance.

Steeling myself for what was to come, I persuaded myself that our separation would have changed everything. Sark was a man of war, with a life on the sea. I should expect nothing from him; I could expect nothing from him. I would be strong. Yet despite my resolve, as Sark swung onto the deck my knees gave way and I folded into an anonymous bundle of woman's garments. I could not stop shaking. Peering from below my hood, I prayed in one moment that nobody would notice me and in the next heartbeat wanted nothing more than to rush forward and announce my presence.

In the event, I did nothing. Harman swiftly volunteered the details of the *Four Sister's* voyage, handing over the cargo and passenger manifest to Jago who scanned the papers. I saw his brow furrow, his beard jut ominously, and while I could not hear their discourse, I saw Jago beckon to Sark who took the documents. After glancing briefly down the details, his gaze came unerringly to where I was hiding. I heard him stride across the deck, taking the companionway steps two at a time.

"How do you, pretty lady?"

Blue eyes twinkled into mine, though tension was evident in his face, even through the beard. "I think you know me, do you not?" Without hesitation I quoted words which I knew he would recognise from the only two books we shared.

"Those eyes are not the same you wore in Rome." His mouth twitched. Remarkably, amazingly, he was trying not to smile. My spirits lifting with each second, I impertinently added,

"And by that white beard I'd fight with thee tomorrow!"

"Oho, so musical a discord, such sweet thunder!" was his instant retort.

"Thou hast seen nothing yet." He followed my lead from Shakespeare to Cervantes,

"What man can pretend to know the riddle of a woman's mind?"

It was so easy to slip back into an intuitive rapport. Though our dialogue would make little sense to anyone else, Sark cryptically reminded me of another instance, another deck where danger loomed.

"As in a theatre, the eyes of men are idly bent on him that enters next." Sark was sending me an instruction. We were to play-act, though I did not yet know the plot. I hoped that this time perhaps Sark would not feel compelled to forcibly subdue me.

"Travellers must be content." I conceded, raising an inquiring eyebrow.

"Have patience, and endure," he responded. Turning towards the deck he shouted down to Jago, faking an accent not his own,

"I think this is the lady, Cap'n, in disguise an' all. Parliament will be happy to make her acquaintance and we can pocket the reward!" He grabbed my cloak and hauled me to my feet. I kicked and squirmed, making contact with a bone or two in the process. At first I was just making a show of protest, but something in me found a satisfaction in landing those blows.

Until that moment, I had not realised how much anger I had suppressed beneath the carapace of misery I had born since that July night in '46 when this man had left us to our fate in that western fort. He had thought to do his heroic duty for the greater good, but it seemed to me that we had not featured in his plans.

Something inside me snapped. A crimson haze filled my vision and I thrashed out, no longer pretending; each scratch, bite or punch that made its target truly heartfelt. I was feigning nothing and I was not quiet.

Once down on the main deck, Sark bundled me across to two sailors I did not recognise, who gripped me so tightly it was impossible to move. He was frowning hard, distractedly rubbing the back of his head where I must have made a particularly effective contact. The red mist faded as fast as it had come, leaving me shaky.

His booming Devon mannerisms ringing round the deck, Jago addressed Captain Harman with respect,

"Zur, I must apologise for insistin' that we come aboard your ship this day, but my offizur here do 'ave some matter of significance to raise." He gestured to Sark to take over negotiations. Briefly nodding in acknowledgement of Harman, Sark took up the thread, still disguising his voice beneath pseudo-formal overtones,

"Our vessel, being independent of political affiliations," - a lie, but Harman was not to know that - "must make what it can of opportunities in these uncertain times." One way of couching it, I thought cynically. "Parliament has pronounced a reward for the capture of Ann Murray, known accomplice to one Colonel Bamfylde, who has conspired against Parliament's wishes, to contrive the escape of the boy, James, Duke of York. They say he dressed as a girl and made away from the gardens with a lady and this woman fits the description!" My mouth dropped open at the audacity of the tale. But Sark continued,

"Captain Harman, though she d'sail under an assumed name, we must insist that this woman is handed over so that we might do our duty and return her to justice." I gave an ineffectual wriggle. Sark did not look at me as he stepped back, letting Jago resume negotiations.

"'Tis evident to I that zum of yon passengers have had 'ee hoodwinked, Zur!" Jago chuckled, "Zo, let us speak plain. You'm has a voyage to complete and no doubt there be many other paying passengers who expect nothing less. I'd not have them inconvenienced but I has a crew to pay and a ship to run. Still, let no man to say of the *Dolphin* that she takes more than is fair. Zo, let us come to an arrangement, Cap'n." Jago paused, for dramatic effect.

"I find uz in want of black powder and lookin' about, 'tis certain you have … sufficient. So, my offizur here will arrange for … let us say … three barrels, to be transferred." He nodded at Sark.

"As for a balancing of shipboard accounts, then, the reward for *her*," - Jago pointed rudely at me - "will serve nicely." He did not wait for Harman to agree but directed the sailors to their task of requisitioning the gunpowder supplies. Reasserting his grip on my wrists, Sark bent to mutter in my ear,

"Madam, I trust you'll do nothing rash. With that proviso, go below and gather what necessaries you may need … but know that I am behind you." He drew his knife, and glaring, manhandled me towards the accommodation.

Any conviviality was gone. I had no idea if he was acting for the benefit of onlookers. It never occurred to me to object. I was trembling as I clambered through into the tiny space I shared with the only other woman émigré on the voyage. She was curled in the corner, weeping silently as I picked up what few belongings I had unpacked and stuffed them into my canvas bag. Sark's guard never wavered. With feeble indignation, Rawle emerged from another doorway, queasily protesting. Sark put his stiletto to Rawle's cheek, drawing a small bead of blood. When he spoke the drawl was again false,

"Silence, old 'un! You'd do well to mind your own business. Now, get out of my way and forget you ever saw me!" Roddy Rawle needed little persuading.

Once back on the main deck I was pushed to the ship's side, then man-handled into the bow of the waiting skiff. As he clambered down the rope ladder, Jago bade Harman a sardonic farewell,

"Our business concluded, Cap'n, you may go on your way, and I thank 'ee for yon kind co-operation!"

Keen to make an escape, relieved no doubt that the ship had got off lightly, the *Four Sisters* swiftly made sail and pulled away. Jago was at the tiller and was affable enough, but now was not the time for polite conversation. Sark sat pulling one of the oars, his back to me, so the crossing to the Dolphin gave me no chance to gauge his mood. The gunpowder and I were unloaded, the small boat was secured and from then on each man set to his task, all hands following a familiar routine with the minimum of orders.

There was no atmosphere of elation on the deck of the *Dolphin*, rather a sense of impassive efficiency. Sark had gone below, carrying one of the barrels of the captured gunpowder, the two men who had guarded me following with the remainder. For all the drama of my 'capture', I might as well have been invisible. I could feel a great lethargy creeping over me, and I wished I could curl up to sleep. Nevertheless I was well aware that where I stood I was in the way of the ship's operation so I dragged my pack into a corner, perching on the saggy baggage to await developments.

It was already late afternoon. By my reckoning the wind had shifted slightly but the *Dolphin* was still making good way, I guessed heading for the Channel Islands. I marked a few sails, most were vessels smaller than ours, but nothing to indicate any of the Parliamentarian fleet patrolling the Western Sea.

Mouth-watering aromas occasionally wafted from the galley, reminding me how long it had been since my breakfast of porridge on the *Four Sisters*. I prayed that one person in particular was still on board, Goody Jago, the indomitable and extraordinary wife of the master. It would guarantee a thick fresh broth and lumps of warm bread for supper. She took the welfare of her men very seriously. Because Pasco Jago, a dedicated trencherman, had always deferred to his spouse in every aspect of the ship's victualling the crew of the *Dolphin* were probably some of the best fed men who ever sailed. At the very least there would be a pottage of fresh fish, the ingredients of which I knew she would have caught herself. Not only that but I was sure in Mistress Jago I would at least find one sympathetic individual, no matter what else happened.

Suddenly there was a bellow, a thunderous sound from below deck followed by a furious barking. Up the steps of the companionway onto the maindeck came a mop of grizzled greying curls, only marginally controlled beneath a head-wrap of faded red-striped linen. A weather-beaten face was scowling down at a squirming sailor, the collar of his shirt grasped in a tightening twist in the massive left hand of this emerging giantess, broad-hipped and burly. Her skirts were hitched forward between her legs, tucked into a broad belt, making the resulting 'breeches' enormous but enabling her to stride purposefully, dragging her captive. The lad was going from scarlet to blue around the lips by the time she tumbled him at the feet of her husband.

Scampering at her heels was a slender hound, glossy-black except for the white stripe down his chest. When she stopped, the dog crouched low, paws splayed, and began to bark at the offending crewman who curled himself into a ball and covered his ears. It was all I could do not to cry out, for not only was the angry woman in the tableau Goody Jago, but the ship's dog was none other than my own beloved Patch. If he was now devoted to a new mistress I did not care for I had presumed him dead, a doomed companion on Sark's reckless mission. Someone clicked their fingers, the barking promptly ceased. Patch sat neat and alert, attentive to Goody Jago's every word while his tail gently swept the planks.

"Do zumthing vex 'ee, my dearest?" Jago enquired solicitously of his spouse.

"Go sink a Dutchman, I surely do say I'm vexed, 'usband! I caught this light-fingered whisk cramming half of one of my new-made loaves into his pockets when he thought my back was turned!"

"But, Minnikins, why bring him here? Would a sound beatin' and a black eye not have zurved better?" Jago asked judiciously. "after all, the galley ... 'tis is your domain," he added warily.

"Why? Because the hammerheaded hackum thought to accuse Patch of pilfering! Patch; ship's dog and a hound of incomparable manners! The very crumbs of evidence were still clinging to this afflicke's own breeches! Pah!" She shook a log-like fist at the thief as she stamped a booted foot so close to his head that a small clump of hair came away, caught in the hob-nails under the sole. The accused whimpered, but wisely did not move a muscle. A low growl signified a hound's displeasure at such a foul slur on his character.

"Well, that will not do, my love! 'Twill not do at all." He turned to address the thief. Now, you ..."

Patch's gaze followed Jago's every move, but as he did something, someone caught his eye. There was a yelp; scuttling claws found purchase on wood, and the next thing I knew was that a bony body was launching itself at me and I was the focus of Patch's squirming, licking frenzy, a half-bark, half-whimper accompanying the tattoo of his tail beating the deck. It was a display guaranteed to draw attention and there was some consolation in knowing at least one individual was pleased to see me.

XXXII Hester: On the edge of rebellion

There was a story from Grace's book that seemed to have spies in every household and even a ghost peekin' in on folk in bed but there was nothing she'd ever read to me to guide a Devon matron on how to be when she was mired in secret doings. Day to day we went on as normal. Ben Burrell came around a bit more regular, and Little Hal made the most of his playmate. He sometimes got to sit atop Burrell's horse which I did think was bold, for he was only just two years old and still inclined to need his tail-clouts, and he still cried for his mama. 'Twas hard not to weep myself.

As April went on the messages we sent seemed to be more urgent. I was rarely told names of folk for Ben said that nobody should know every detail, for 'twould be like putting every egg in a basket. What would happen to a king's man if the plotting was discovered? They'd be like the basket of eggs, dropped, and from a scaffold with a noose about the neck no doubt.

Still, I could work things out for myself. I'd fathomed that along with uppity, unpaid army men in barracks all over England, there were pockets of king's men dotted all over the place. Burrell was in a chain of secrets that led from Mary's Cornish contacts right round Dartmoor and across Devon. They'd even managed to find a way to pass messages to the men in Wales who were of the same mind through a right good fellow in Coombe Martin. Tom Bushell he was called and he'd promised good silver from his mines to add to the funds too. Back a-whiles he'd had a small army of men holed up on Lundy island minting coin for His Majesty and it seemed he wasn't about to change his ways. Anyway, it didn't need a lawyer's mind to see that if we in the west and the folk over the Bristol Sea started firing the first shots, and if anyone else with an axe to grind joined in, then there would be a few great men in London uneasy on their Parliament perches. And here was Hester Mattock, in the midst of it all.

Matters were going according to plan, for in the middle of the month there was a letter from Mary informing us, in a round-about way, that Colonel Fortesque, who'd commanded Pendennis fort after the surrender, had taken some commissioners hostage a-cause they'd not been paid. 'Twasn't all about the troops wanting wages owed before they got sent home either. Local men were readying. There was a Colonel Bennett marching west to take matters in hand, but 'twas said Pendennis had declared against Parliament and were to be led by gentlemen as yet un-named, so I reckoned that would be Mary's Arundel cousin at the least. There was no word of Lewis Tremayne though.

Ben went to Tavistock market most weeks and to Ashburton or Totnes every other week so I nary expected to see him Fridays or Saturdays, but regular on a Monday he would be at the door. So, in the last week of April, when there was naught of him come Thursday I was a-wondering where he'd got to. There was a tiny alarum sounding but I'll admit I was missing his company too. When Sarah Beale swirled into the vat-shed in a flurry of skirt and shawl, her face furrowed with frowning, 'twas plain there was something amiss.

"Hester! Have you heard about Ben Burrell?" I tried to look blank. As far as I knew, nobody in Cornwood knew of the goings-on and since 'twas too early for customers, there'd been no gossiping at the 'Hands'. I just shook my head.

"Jet has just come back to the forge from some constable duty or other, and the vicar has heard that Cap'n Burrell was taken by the militia in Tavvy on Friday last and is held in the lock-up. They do say he is a spy and they be going to take him before Waller to be questioned!"

"What! They can't ..." I began, then bit back my words, a-cause I was about to let slip more than I should do,

"I mean to say, he was a soldier for the King but that was years ago! And his ma is a Buller and his cousin Francis be in Parliament too ..." My mind was buzzing like bees in a swarm, and though I was girt fond of Sarah I knew better than to tell her the truth, so I did what I knew would distract her and I burst into tears, crying,

"Not my Ben? Surely not! Oh, but what will us do, me and Hal, for he is so dear to us now ..." All the whiles I was looking under my lashes to see how Sarah was. The knowing look on her face was of a woman who had just had her suspicions of a romance confirmed. I felt ashamed at the deception but to be truthful 'twas not so hard to make the tears come, for I did have a soft spot for Burrell. With that and the imagining of some torture making him confess - and the fear of the aftermath - real tears came easily enough.

"There, there! I'm sure all will be well. If he has done nothing wrong then he'll be free as soon as they realise their mistake, I'm sure!" If I wanted Sarah's sympathy, I now had it sure enough.

From then on all the talk, hour on hour, was 'Captain Burrell this' and 'Ben Burrell that' and then we heard that half a dozen mounted soldiers had been sent to Burrell's father at Wadland and he too had been carted off. I had no notion as to what to do. My head told me to lie very low indeed though the bit of Hester Mattock that had never been truly affeard of anything was ready to hitch a ride on a wagon to see what I could discover for myself. A little play-acting; an abandoned woman seeking the man who had promised much might just touch the tender sentiments of the authorities. I decided against the plan for it was foolish to appeal to the feelings of any commander hunting rebels and anyway, it was just as likely to get Ben in more trouble with the strict Puritans for deceiving and fornication, even if 'tweren't true. Really what grated most was being in the dark.

I had another letter from Mary, and I quickly set to working out the news that Pendennis had been handed over to Bennett. Fortesque had secured the pay for his men and if there had been Cornishmen relying on the garrison to add might to their numbers they were going to be disappointed. 'Twas certain sure that Bennett looked as though he was in control. There was also word that I knew would have upset my friend, for Lewis was no longer involved in the plan, staying in France. Nonetheless, I did laugh at how Mary couched the hidden words, all wrapped in a damning tale about her youngest sister. There was no love lost there, I knew, but still 'twas funny to think that Mary had a kind of revenge a-cause she was revealing the nastiness of that twily madam at every place the message was seized. That was the only lightness I could take from the business. I had no idea where to pass on the information nor did I have anything useful to impart.

On May Day, although there was to be no proper marking of the start of summer a-cause Reverend Shute made sure of that with a hell-fire sermon against it the day before, a few of us women just happened to be abroad early enough to cut some boughs of fresh green with the dew still on them to make a garland for Nettie Pearce. Shute came across us chattering by the road before we went our separate ways, but we acted the innocents, crying 'Nay! For sure! She weren't a May Queen!' and 'Nomye, Sir! Would we engage in such heathenish vanities?' and ''Twas merely the maid's birthday and marking her turning sixteen was just a foolish female custom!' I was still chuckling to myself, and not far from my door, when a carter drove past, hauled on the reins and looked about, and bending down as if to see to his boots, hissed at me,

"Psssh ... pssssht...Mistress! You be she from the sign of the clasped hands?"

"Aye," I replied, wary, "and what of it?" I didn't recognise him as a regular traveller through Cornwood and I was certain he'd never been into the 'Hands'. He mumbled something, so I bent forward to hear, my hand on the footboard of the wagon. Quick as anything, he pulled something from his pocket then pushed the scrap of cloth into my hand. With no more explanation he clicked his tongue to the ponies and rumbled away.

On the rag was a badly drawn map of Cornwood, the river and the old bridge up by Wisdome Farm. Round the side of the map was scrawled 3, stone, right, tomorrow morn. 'Tiddn't no code, Hester,' I thought to myself, 'and tidn't clever neither. So, just the sort of thing an untaught brewster would be able to fathom then!' I recalled Ben's words. 'Twas no point in being offended and since the message had reached its mark, I thought I had best see what it betokened.

The next day I set Daisy to the scouring of a barrel or two and with the excuse of taking little Henry Charles for a walk in the spring sunshine, I set off up the valley. Tiddn't far to a humpty-back crossing over the river and though I had to carry him most of the way, in the dappled light under the bright green of the new leaves, Hal and I had a very pleasant time. I had burned the map but had guessed well enough what to look for.

Sure as eggs, as I was holding the lad up to toss pebbles into the water, I could feel that a stone, the third on the right hand parapet, moved beneath my hand. Hidden by Hal's clothes I could push the rock far enough and no further, until a curl of leather dropped into my hand. I slipped it up my sleeve and when Hal grew tired of the splashes I picked him up and hurried home as fast as I could. I saw nobody and was glad of that, for, though I was fairly sure my actions looked innocent enough, I was not sure that I could play-act quite so well if challenged and my poor heart was pounding fit to burst by the time I set Hal down at our door.

I had to wait until the infant was napping and Daisy on an errand before I could pick out the leather roll and unfasten it. Inside was a tiny scrap of paper. This was another message, as plain as the other but in a neat, clear hand. It read *Poyer defeated welsh body broken warn west*. I guessed what was expected but 'twas a tall task without Burrell doing the scribing

That night I managed something like a letter to Mary though the words I needed and our code were right hard to work up together. 'Twas near midnight when I finally scrawled the destination. I could only seal it with some candle wax, nothing fancy, just to close the pages. It would have to find its way to Heligan by the normal means, though it would not be swift, so the next day I handed my inky-stained package to our maltster who promised he would pass it to a fellow who would be heading to Saltash where it would await another carrier. The messenger who delivered it to Penwarne would be handsomely rewarded, I was sure. I could do no more.

As it happened though, there was naught more to be done, for late the next day a bedraggled Burrell rode into the yard. Even Hal's excited shrieks failed to raise a smile from his weary features. He was the colour of froth on wort so the scar on his forehead stood out worse than ever and he looked dog-tired. I sent Daisy to fetch some broth and bread, cheese and ale then more or less pushed Burrell to the settle by the hearth, and made him sit and eat before he said one word about what had happened. I was angsty to know but waited until there was a bit more colour in his features then I blurted out,

"Do they know about … things? Are you hurt? Have they tortured you?" For some reason that did make him laugh soft and low and I was relieved to hear it, though he didn't directly answer me.

"They might suspect, but, no, I do not think they know as much as they would like. It was not torture, Hester, just … troublesome. The County Committee arrested my father." I went stone cold.

"Does your pa …?"

"No, he knows nothing. He is an upright citizen who will comply with whichever authority has the upper hand. They questioned him of course, but he could tell them only what they already knew: I was a misguided young man who had fought for the losing side. Nevertheless, they have fined my father £500. They say it is an indemnity, to ensure this delinquent's compliance." What I wanted to say only came out as a squeak at first; I had to cough to clear my throat.

"Ben, 'tis such a sum! Can he pay it? What will they do to him if he cannot?" Ben's shoulders slumped.

"They will take him to Exeter, lock him away and sequester the estate."

"And what of your mother?" Ben looked at me. I could see his eyes wet with tears. Those tears were never shed but his next words brought a lump to my throat.

"She is dead. Ma took a seizure when they took my father away." He put his head in his hands, not weeping, just stone-still. My hand hung in the air over his shoulder. The Burrell I knew didn't seem the sort to need a woman's comforting arm. He would probably be mortified so I pulled back. I didn't suppose he'd have noticed, so 'twas well enough.

There was a rumpus outside the parlour, small feet kicking and a noisy protest and Daisy, her cheeks blotched with crimson flickets, lifted the latch and stuck her head around the door-jamb. Not a talkative maid at the best of times, she could barely stammer Hal's name, something about the poultry yard and pecking hens but gave up and fled when the tiddler swung round her skirts and hurled himself at us. He'd a runny nose and I thought him a tad hot but put it down to the tantrum we had heard. At any rate, me trying to clean his nose on my apron wasn't about to stop Henry Charles clambering on his best friend's knee to plague him for stories and games. Though he gently held off over a ride with the excuse that the mare was too tired and a good horseman like Hal must learn to take care of his mount, it was not long before a child's enthusiasm seemed to lift Ben's mood.

That evening the 'Hands' got busy, nobody buying much drink, but meeting to talk, the locals by turns angered or affeard about what had happened to the Burrell family who were quiet souls who had done no harm, and were well respected. The matter brought no glory to our great governors and the country's masters but there were few who would say so aloud and an uneasy feeling lingered in the parlour that night. Telling me he would come a-visiting on Saturday, missing the usual routine in town to avoid the authorities, Ben rode out towards Ivybridge before dusk.

I do wonder what would have happened if things had turned out differently. See, though we had a letter arrive four days after, on May 9th, telling us that six companies of soldiery were being withdrawn to Exeter, that their commander was lodged at Saltash intent on returning to Tavistock which would leave Cornwall wide open, it made little odds. And though the word came through that parties of men were readying across Devon to muster with the western men as the Cornishmen moved east, just like they did in our great grandfers' day nigh a hundred year ago, it mattered nothing to us.

Hal had come out in itching spots that quickly turned into blisters. The little lad was hardly out of sorts and made nothing much of it once I put mittens on his hands to stop the scratching but the next morning when I fetched him from his cot I was greeted with a serious look.

"Oh-dear no...see Hesser! Chick-ee-chocks! Hal see! See'em!" and sure enough, there were the tell-tale peck marks, just as if I'd been with a flock of fighting fowl. Lucky for me I wasn't truly sick. Taking cups of willow-bark beer helped, though verjuice dabbed on the scabs did sting enough to make me holler some. Still, it was miserable enough and though Daisy seemed well, I put a sign on the door and we did no brewing for almost a week.

When Ben found spots across his belly he took to his bed and was kept a-bed, for the pocks brought on a fever. Word came that his blistering had spread and that Burrell was proper poorly, with sores in his eyes and ears long after mine were dry and healing.

So for nigh on three weeks there was no spying to be done; no missives being sent, no hidden messages collected. If the rising of the Devon men should come to naught and a King be kept from his rightful throne, 'twould all be a-cause of a children's malaise - and the fault of one Cavalier captain and one Royalist spy, who didn't catch the chicken pocks until they were twenty-four.

XXXIII Mary: Undercurrents

Written this day 3ʳᵈ of May 1648
At Kestle Wartha
Heligan

Dearest Husband,
I sit in the garden, it is about 4 o'clock and I am watching
the children as they play in the sunshine. We have had such
foggy days that I wish to make as much of the brightness
while it is here. The winter seemed so long and spring has
been too wet. I pray the company you are in is congenial. We
do well enough here. John thrives and like his father enjoys
his food and is trying hard to push himself up and will roll
about if he cannot see his sisters who are both like little
mothers. They dote on him. He already has eight teeth. He
has the same redness that troubles Mary when she is cutting
teeth. John's is less on his face though his nose constantly
runs. His napkin rash wakes him and makes him testy. In a
few days I expect more to cut. I can feel them below the gum
if John will let me into his mouth. Such domestic joys you are
missing! Broken sleep and a dribbling, snot-ridden heir!
Damn the very arrival of teeth!
Do you recall the bad storms three months ago? It was most
terrible. That local man, Keigwin, was lost fishing?
Tomorrow morning I will arrange to ~~converse~~ ~~meet~~ visit Old
Jenny Keigwin, from by Gorran. Her daughter has just had
an infant and they have hit such hard times that I thought to
pass on some of the smallest baby clothes, for Agnes and
your sisters are always ready to make more should I need
new ones. God willing it will be so one day. Amen.
Their condition is at best tragic, their home is a hovel. If
there was a barn or stable at Penwarne or Heligan they
would be better housed. ~~It reflects badly upon the parish that~~

204

they do not offer assistance but we do know who is at fault there.

I had a missive from Hester. Her writing is improved as she learns. She yet needs the vicar at Cornwood. However she yet does not read well so she has a villager help when I write to her. She tells me that Hal sits a horse with confidence. He counts his numbers and is like Sark in looks, yet has much of Grace. He would make a good play-fellow for John. If only Devon were not such a distance.

I do miss company too. There is some good consolation in family. Especially ours. We are fortunate indeed. Apart from the one sister you know I cannot forgive. Loving hearts by side mine, and warm arms are near to bolster my low spirits. I sometimes wish that you were not such an honourable man. For then you would have lesser standards to bide with the new regime here and not your royal master. I would be selfish. I put my cause before that those of Parliament, Princes or King. I shall be sent to the Tower. I will be beheaded for such sentiment no doubt. No, the Commissioners would merely fine us instead though I am loyal just a miserable wife. Forgive my gloom.

There is little news to speak of yet it is a thin link to you. Written later. It is now the quiet of the evening. I have more equanimity.

Cook made little Welsh cakes, ultimately being defeated by the children. They begged and pleaded. It was her fault. She made them cakes when they played in the kitchen on the last rainy day. Now they always can beg sweet treats, expect them no doubt, no matter what! She claimed that there were no eggs. Nothing availed of that. Honor and Mary simply went to the chicken coop and brought eggs newly laid. I was no assistance. I was laughing too much.

Veritably this is a household led by the nose by its children and my mother and yours would no doubt be horrified as it is not as it was in their day.

Aunt Mary Arundel sent word in a very amusing letter that despite their straitened circumstances she wishes to mark Sir

John's birthday. Uncle John, in Arundel style, refuses any
participation on the day, 16th. He has declared that he will
bar the door to any guests. Any hint of celebration will be
curtailed. His age, he says, is not a matter for festivity as it
hampers him with aches, pains and infirmity. However, Aunt
Mary guaranteed that should there be nothing, he'd sulk. I
have seen such a mood in him. He is such a dear man that all
would forgive petulance. It seems so uncharacteristic as to be
comical.

Thus in a timely manner, the family meet, inviting Sir Charles
Trevanion, and our cousins Trelawny, who will be among
others who join us, along with Mary's Devon cousins. It will
not be a big gathering but should suffice. It will at least
soothe Sir John's pride. It is something to look forward to,
though much else is tightly restricted; food especially scarce
yet. I will make ready some pickled herring. It is an
acceptable gift. I am sure we have enough. I also know it is
Uncle's second favourite. However, it is Col.d Bream and
salted Pike Pie that truly stands his favourite. There is a
legendary fish in the ponds at Gwarnick it seems. I dislike it
for the meat is too muddy for my taste and ugly brutes. But
cheap! Aunt Mary is readying, with great zeal, to have her
cook bring a fresh pike in a great pastry st box, more a
cavern, to feed all men. I will be declining my portion, as you
may surmise.

I promise to write to tell you all of the festivities, whether
there be musicians or no, how many tall tales were told, so
that you do not feel left out. I will not take the babies though,
but father says he will travel if the weather be not wet.
Until then my dearest, I remain your loving wife,
Mary

 To await Colonel Lewis Tremayne
At Rue des Abbeyes
St Germain-en-Laye
or to the whereabouts of the Prince of Wales' retinue.

Written this day 12th May 1648
Written at Rue des Abbeyes
St Germain-en-Laye

Dearest Heart,
I write in haste and in some disarray as there has been word
that the Queen wishes the Prince to take ship from Calais to
Holland and thence to Scotland in the next few days, for
which I have been designated the comptroller of His
Highness' personal effects; an honour if you did not know the
chaos within which the household exists.
I would rather be a secretary or something far more lowly. It
remains to be said that we have had several such false starts
however, and this may be another. Her Majesty and the
Council seem to be divided and so policy swings from 'go' to
'stay'.
Yet this is not the matter on which I scrawl so inelegantly,
forgetting my duty in wishing you to lovingly commend me to
the little ladies and to my son, and to you.
While I was on envoy duties I was tasked to ride to Calais
where I was appraised of the latest situation in the
Parliament fleet. There is little you would find of interest
except one thing and it is as well to be forewarned: Captain
Bartholomew Fenwick's ship remains part of the fleet known
as the Irish Guard, which patrols the western seas, and is
once more reunited with that sea-devil Richard Swanley, who
commands the Charles. *Fenwick's ship will be part of the*
section overseeing the western coasts as far as Exeter. Their
task is to restrict the activities of the privateers, and to
harass any Royalist activity of course, and they have soldiers
to set ashore if required. It takes no great espionage agent to
fathom that and nothing of note if I tell you. I had hoped to
learn that ships would be taken up to the flotilla working the
Scottish coast, though for my peace of mind, Hell would not
be far enough away for either man.
It sickens me that I can not be in Cornwall to protect you but
my duty and honour lie here.

We must pray for a swift turning of fortunes. Or shipwrecks.
In haste for I am called away,
Affectionately as ever,
Lewis

At 2 hours past midnight, yet not abed so added a few words
I can only provide a small, insignificant vessel for to wholly
convey my news. If you were here I could speak from the
heart. What of my rising loneliness? I can only wait. And
watch the days slip by.

To my lady, Mistress Tremayne
At Portmellon. Or Kestle Wartha
In the parish of St Ewe
In the county of Cornwall

----

*The messages read thus:
From Cornish Royalists:
 Company in eight days to arrival will meet Keigwin at home.
Improved numbers. Sark has good side arms bolster cause of king.
News yet thin. Welsh defeated. Expect no assistance.
Arundel participation 16th guaranteed. Be timely meet Trevanion,
Trelawny among us. Devon ready. Colonel Pike stands ready to
bring in St Cavern [Kevern] men.

From exiled Royalists:
Can provide small vessel to convey news of rising. Watch days by
Portmellon.

XXXIV Grace: Obedience

If I wish nothing else for you, I pray that in your lifetime you find as good friends as I had on the *Dolphin* and know at least one indomitable spirit such as Goodwife Jago. For all that the reuniting seemed an inauspicious one, the moment when she discovered the identity of the latest member of the crew was marked by another bellow, though more screech than roar this time.

"By Neptune's fork! 'Tis Grace! Grace of Bristol, if I live and breathe!" Her hands grasped my shoulders, sizing my form. It was clear that I did not measure up,

"You'm all but skin and bone! Where've you been to all this time?" It was a rhetorical question and I could not have replied before she bawled across the deck,

"'usband! See who we have here, may the Lor' bless 'er! 'Tis Grace!" I noted that Pasco did not confess that he already knew of my presence, merely showed a beaming, white grin and nodded enthusiastically.

"Feels as if she be starved; at that mealy-mouthed Huntingdon hay-poke's say so, I've no doubt!" I guessed that she meant the notorious General Cromwell. Jago's response,

"A pox on living land-locked and by Parliament's yea-and-nay!" was met with an approving nod, but politics was not his wife's priority,

"This woman's in need of a good meal!" At that moment and to Goody Jago's apparent satisfaction, a strident clanging began,

"And timely, for 'tis the supper bell!"

Without further fuss, I was propelled to the mess-deck table, and quickly surrounded by hungry crewmen. A bowl of steaming fish and new-made bread was put in front of me as Jago diplomatically made the formal introductions, speaking of his great friendship with my father. I noted that our captain avoided linking Sark and I. There were a handful of men I recognised from my time aboard in '46. The others, including the mate, a grey-haired black-a-moor called Casso, seemed entirely at ease with a new, female associate. Only an oriental called Goemon looked wary. Later I learned his taciturn aloofness was a façade: he and Sark have much in common.

In a cheerfully chaotic fashion the crew told me of the vessel's exploits, men chipping in randomly when they thought significant details had been forgotten. Sark, sitting opposite, smiled occasionally but said nothing. Jago was one of a number of independent minded West-country seafarers who continued to support the King's cause, despite His Majesty's unfortunate captivity. Their exploits - and ports for refuge - had been restricted when the French had outlawed all privateers but when the Prince of Wales reinstated his endorsement of official piracy, the master of the *Dolphin* had managed to renew the letters of Marque, with the help of a convenient friend in the exiled English court in St. Germain-en-Laye. With an opportunistic flair they had been harrying any ship they could to the mutual profit of the crown and the crew. It had been in evading the patrol of a small Parliamentarian fleet that they encountered our smart merchant vessel and it was a matter of pride that the *Four Sisters* had not been able to out-run them.

The meal ended, I helped to scrub down the galley. I had yet to face the embarrassing matter of where to sleep. For all her forthright ways, Goody Jago was well-tuned to folk's disposition: she knew something was badly amiss. Over the meal, she had repeatedly glared at Sark, who blushed once, then refused to look up from his food. Now I discovered that she was intent upon resolving a situation which, to be truthful, would be difficult in a community ashore but was completely untenable on a relatively small vessel. We finished our tasks then, bidding me go aft to the poop, she stomped off purposefully.

Some time later she climbed to where, in effect, I was hiding. To my dismay, behind her was Sark. Impatiently she gestured him forward,

"Now then. Tell this woman what 'ee has just told me, word-for-word, or I tell 'ee straight I shall take umbrance at it!"

Sark looked like a small boy called to account over some misdemeanour and I found my wariness receding. He seemed to sense it, a small, wry smile just tweaking at the corner of his mouth,

"As I said, what man can pretend to know the riddle of a woman's mind?" He looked directly at me, his clear blue gaze holding mine. All levity gone, he spoke quietly,

"I never thought to see you again. Even in dreams I never expected to find you. Yet suddenly ... you were here, our minds in tune as ever they were and it seemed all would be well. You have ever been my sanctuary and I thought would be again." He glanced away, "Then you became so angry that I thought I must be mistaken. I felt a fool for hoping, and ashamed." The pause was leaden. "I will not beg."

I believed him yet I could not prevent the accusation slipping out,

"You abandoned me and our son! You gave no thought to my sanctuary. I have been like a shadow since you left and lived with constant despair, hopeless. How am I supposed to reconcile that in an instant?" Goody Jago coughed pointedly, arms folded across her bosom, and frowned first at me then at Sark.

"What wound did ever heal but by degrees?" she said. I must have looked askance. She shrugged her shoulders,

"The words be true even if 'twas a playwright set them down." She returned to her theme,

"Now, there be much that I ha' seen and heard in my life, and I heard 'ee both use the same word, hope. Surely then, that is what 'ee has now?" We were silent.

"Well then, so be it." Her foot was tapping the deck. "'Twas never my way to interfere in other folk's business, but a good match is rare enough that I know one when I see it. She pointed, arms crossing, to us, "I see it here," then coyly added, "and there be much in thee that reminds me of when Jago and me were a-courtin' ..."

After a moment of wistful reflection she stepped between us, put a weighty arm around each of our shoulders and pulled our heads together so our three brows touched.

"I don't say that such a match does all'us run smooth. But a few scrapes and skirmishes don't mean 'tis a war. Nor do posies and poems always betoken the deepest affinity." She looked from Sark to me and back,

"'Tis plain to see, you talk of much; share much; laugh much: these things are treasures of great worth. Just a-cause there be no embraces, donday hay moocho amor, no suelay harbah demasayda desen-voltura,, as that clever Spaniard penned." It was Sark's turn for raised eyebrows.

"This life is all too short. Take it from an old woman who knows; you found each other, and though a journey did part thee, the ocean did bring thee back together for a life to come. Journeys end in lovers' meeting, says the fellow on the stage."

There was gooseflesh all over my body at her words. I was beginning to feel giddy with emotion, but Goody Jago grabbed a clump of my hair with one hand, and Sark's ear with the other. Our resulting tears were not sentimental.

"And if yon pair of clay-brained, moon-phased ..." Goody Jago paused, momentarily at a loss. As one, Sark and I suggested,

"Oysters?" She nodded approvingly,

"Aye, if yon oysters are not transformed in right timely fashion then I shall take these thick pates and crack them together until 'ee are!" Neither Sark nor I were in a position to argue.

It was too soon to recover our former intimacy but Goody Jago seemed more than satisfied with the evidence of her eyes for we were spared any further castigation. On a small ship there was no room for personal quarrels, familiarity and meagre accommodation banishing any coyness. With Patch curled beside me, I shared Sark's cabin, the circumstances dictating it as pragmatic not romantic: there was nowhere else for me to sleep.

As if to put our concerns into perspective, I soon learned that the *Dolphin* and more specifically Sark and her gunners, were engaged upon a mission that, if successful, would open the west of England to a Royalist army intent on bringing together a disaffected nation with its allies in Scotland and Ireland. The task was dangerous; the risks enormous; the consequences of failure were not something anybody on board wanted to contemplate.

The first stage of the plan was to pick up a cargo, one which could legitimately take our ship into western Cornish ports. Jersey was still strong for the King's cause, and effective as a refuge. Sir George Carteret, the island's bailiff was, said Jago, as 'enterprising with his fleet' as Jago was with the *Dolphin*, though the word was that Sir Edward Hyde kept a close eye on activities. So the trans-shipment of a part cargo of sawn timber had been arranged, the wood disguising crates carrying muskets and a falconet. The small cannon would not be easy to man-handle and Sark had misgivings about the arrangements to provide the gun-carriage but had to trust that the network of conspirators in Cornwall had done their job. Barrels of salt filled the rest of the hold and gave us an excuse to call in to the fishing ports along the western tip of the Duchy. In the middle of each was a supply of lead shot. With the powder Jago had taken from Harman the arming of the King's new Cornish army had begun.

Before we left St Helier a messenger came aboard with word that the Pendennis Castle forces could no longer be relied upon as re-enforcements. It was clearly a major setback, but with plans so advanced it could not be allowed to thwart the rising.

"We are a small cog in bigger machinery," Sark reassured me, "and the impact nationally will be immaterial. It would have been better to have a garrison covering our back than at it, but ..." His shrug was eloquent. What could be done? Nothing. The machinery had been set in motion and on the next tide we set sail for Cornwall.

The *Dolphin* slipped into Mount's Bay at dusk on 9th May, Jago easing us into an anchorage on the western shore. The next morning mist shrouded us. It melted away as the sun climbed higher, until in a cloudless sky over a mirror-flat sea, there was only one ribbon of mist wrapping St Michael's Mount, creating an eerie illusion of the distant battlements appearing to hang in mid-air. With Pasco Jago, Sark and Casso in closed conference for an hour after breakfast in the tiny master's cabin, a sense of expectancy spread through the rest of the crew. Until now we had not been told any detail of the engagement in which we were concerned. I only knew that ashore there were men awaiting us. Calls from fishing boats passing within shouting distance may have been messages; all were in Cornish. I could make nothing of them but I'd heard the dialect used on board by crew and officers, Casso included.

My duties that morning included minding the fishing lines, a leisurely pursuit, if a responsible one; no fish meant no supper. Still, I was at ease as I checked the hooks and bait, with Patch lolling at my feet, sunning himself. Scanning the land I could see the platform of a battery of guns, the ant-like movements of soldiers about their business. As I watched Sark came to stand at behind me. He followed my gaze, answering my unspoken query,

"They're men from the garrison at the Mount, mostly the youngest recruits. They get sent over, are given a gun to man, but are never expected to use it. Will Keigwin has had his eye on them; there's little to fear. The guns cover this anchorage in Gwavas Lake. They and the Penlee battery further south were Queen Bess' reaction to the Spaniards who raided this shore fifty years ago, but they won't trouble us." We were in Sark's home territory and of course he knew this coast well.

"Is there any news?" I asked, "I have heard the fishing boats call up." Looking at me pensively, Sark was clearly in two minds as to what to say.

"Yes. Yes, there is. Jago asks that you come to his cabin." We tied up the mackerel lines, Sark directing a young lad to take my place. I bade Patch 'stay', wished the boy good luck and we headed below.

Inside, my eyes took a moment to adjust to the gloom, but on the table there were neatly arranged packets, letters and maps. Jago looked up as I entered, Casso nodding acknowledgment. Jago was business-like; gone was the affable sea-going buffoon. His West Country drawl was clipped, his language succinct,

"Grace, sit. Has Sark told 'ee anything?" I shook my head.

"Very well. You d'know of our cargo though and the cause we serve?" I nodded.

"Before dawn this day came the final particulars; so the enterprise begins." Such solemnity was unexpected.

"We had not looked to have a woman in our midst but, since you'm here, there's a role for 'ee. Are ye willing?" I instinctively looked to where Sark was leaning against the bulkhead, an open packet in his hand. I nodded again but Jago was not satisfied,

"I would hear thee, Grace, for it is not undertook lightly." My voice was clear, though I could feel my heart pounding as I replied: yes, I was willing.

The minutes and hours that followed were filled with details, observations, plans and contingencies. The scale of the rising surprised me; the extent of the network was far greater than I could have imagined, though logic told me that a Prince in exile, a King in captivity and a secret Royalist army needed to have substantial resources. What I did not expect was that our friend Mary Tremayne, that discreet, decorous wife and matron would be at the heart of the web of intrigue. The notes Sark was reading were in her hand, ostensibly an entertaining report on a gathering to mark Sir John Arundel's birthday, written for the benefit of Lady Ann Bassett who had been unable to attend. I did not ask why or how they came to be on Jago's desk. Nonetheless, the coded contents provided information as to the whereabouts of officers, arms and equipment and the finalized timetable of events. We had six days to wait, to unload the cargo under the watchful eye of the authorities and to rehearse, refine and render fail-safe the plan that Sark, his men and I would follow for now our very lives depended upon it.

Being born near Penzance, the mission with which Sark was tasked came with both its disadvantages and advantages. Naturally, he knew the area well, the landscape and the locality. Sark knew where would get support but there was an opposite side to that coin. He had returned home to pay his respects to his mother as and when he could, but not often enough for his appearance, especially at a time of unrest, to go unremarked. That might bring unwelcome attention.

So it was to be his task to assemble the network of small units of men, most consisting of no more than a dozen, in the small villages and hamlets between Penzance, where he was known and Helston where he was not. There the growing force of men from the Lizard peninsular would converge with Sark's to move east under the leadership of Arthur Bassett. The Arundel force would be mustered at the long-established meeting place of Castle-an-Dinas, near St Columb Major, and the combined army planned to move on Bodmin before the month was ended.

The guns and ammunition were to be landed at Cadgwith, and once that was done the *Dolphin's* pinnace would be made available where she could be most useful. With oars as well as a small sail she was light and fast, ideal for carrying messages across the bay, further if necessary. However, it became evident that, though the muskets and barrels could be managed well enough, the weight of the cannon would be problematic. It would have to travel overland. Time was of the essence; the gun needed to reach Helston to arm the Royalist force there, and soon. To Sark's amusement and Jago's discomfort, I suggested that my anonymity could be useful - along with a little more wood-work.

Our story would be that the body of my grandfather, who had died in St Helier, was being returned home to his family in Helston to be buried in his native soil. A coffin was hastily fashioned by the ship's carpenter. The bills of lading endorsed the story, and papers were forged for the coffin, for Sark and I. My role was to provide cover, the distraught grieving woman fetching the coffin home. The 'corpse' was the cannon, disguised in a canvas shroud, padded with wadding and wood-shavings. It looked convincingly gruesome with a stink from a rotting concoction of Goody Jago's devising adding a totally authentic odour. Nobody would linger long enough for a detailed examination. Despite all of this, Sark insisted that I should have some ability to defend myself so I spent some time with him and Goemon, who taught me the finer points of using a narrow steel blade - or something similar - at close quarters.

"Keep he close, pull ver' close before you use; like this!" Goemon demonstrated, hugging Sark tight and miming the stabbing action. I hoped never to need the skill but appreciated their efforts.

On May 15th the *Dolphin* anchored off St Michael's Mount and once more I put on my woman's garb instead of the old breeches and doublet I wore day-to-day on board. For the benefit of sharp-eyed lookouts in the fort the box was loaded into the little boat, the 'body' following. There was a short pull to the island harbour where the coffin was manhandled onto an old cart pulled by an equally elderly mule, for which we had paid an extortionate amount. I could still feel the rocking motion of the ship as we stood on the quay and it made me edgy and nauseous. Our nervous wait continued until the tide dropped, when we could cross the causeway across to Market Jew, slowly making our way through the rutted lanes past St Hilary to our first resting place, a small manor house at Colenso.

Five men were waiting and, after a brief evaluation of progress, two left with messages to Godolphin House and Tehidy Manor. Two others had instructions to gather men to cover the Helston road, moving west to reinforce the Penzance regiments in the assault on the Mount's garrison. Our host was to head east to beyond Helston, aiming to link up with Hannibal Bogans and a force moving to take the Dennis fort on the Helford. We would follow with our load as fast as possible.

The mule, called Jack, was fed, watered and the cart respectfully consigned to a barn. Keeping up the subterfuge, someone would 'watch', as was customary for a corpse and sensible for camouflaged cannon. The house, though a manor, was tiny so we settled down to sleep in whatever space the small rooms could afford.

It was first clear evening there had been for days. Smoking bonfires began appearing on hill-tops. As the sun set the sky turned scarlet over the moors to the west, it was as if the beacons had become one. Or as if Penzance was burning.

XXXV Hester: To recognise evil

So the great Royalist uprising passed over us and I d'think that the pocks may have saved Ben Burrell's life. From what we heard in the aftermath, there were plenty in '48 who joined my William and all the others who'd died for the King's lost cause.

The authorities were calling it rebellion, so more attention than ever was paid to regulations, the district seething with one county commissioner after another. I wondered if Ben brought trouble down on us a'cause his arrest marked Cornwood out as a bubbling cauldron of rebels. Still, every visitation brought extra business to the sign of the 'Clasped Hands', and our good ale and hearty food did all'us seem to go down well with the officials. They'd come, each with their armed guard, all wanting some vittles and they all'us paid willingly so I had no reason to complain.

I have often wished that I had the Sight like Loveday Yendacott, though I'm sure I'd have been affeard as often as enjoy it. But I will all'us keep asking myself, as I will ask St Peter at the gates of Heaven, should I have recognised the dangers?

'Twas the worst June we've had for years, with the fields sodden and over and over the growing wheat and barley was battered down by the weather which didn't bode well for the price of malt come autumn. The winds blew summ'at harsh, almost as bad as winter, so the logs in the hearth still needed lighting every evening. One filthy morn, with the hailstones still lying in the hedgerows, the door to the 'Hands' whipped open and three gentlemen and a handful of troopers with their captain stomped in from the mire. These fellows were to do yet more accounting, one of them just a spotty youth but with a girt leather bag across his shoulder big enough to hold the Bible on Reverend Shute's lectern. I was right glad that the

'Hands' was not like Roddy Rawle's place, with rooms and all, a'cause at least there was no need to find beds for any of them. They were lodged down at Fardel. I saw nothing of the gentlemen other than when they were at their task, but the troopers came to take a jug of ale in the evening and their officer came with them.

When it came time for them to do their assessing of the brew-house the gentlemen came asking this and that and wanting to see here and there. They demanded to see all my papers, even the pass from Pendennis, which the captain took an especial interest in, and they had a long look at Ma Mattock's last will and testament. Since I took on the place I had all'us been particular about keeping things straight, most especially in the way of money and all, double checking over and over in case my new-learned numbers had gone awry. I suppose it comes of not having anything for so long that I all'us worried about losing it again. At any rate they found nothing amiss.

I had laughed when Sarah called the captain, 'lanky-tall, mousey-locked with eyes the colour of dirty dishwater' but was true enough. She said he made her skin creep. I do reckon that most of the village felt the same a'cause when he and his men came into my parlour I could be sure that half the customers would up-end their ale-pots to drain their drinks and leave as soon as they could. If the soldiers wanted the settle by the fire it would all'us be free by the time their jugs of beer were poured. The only thing to recommend them was that they had coin in their pockets and were happy enough to spend it. I reckoned they thought 'twas better a dreary wet duty on Dartmoor than marching all the way to Scotland with General Cromwell.

The soldiers only ever called their officer by his rank, so 'twas all'us 'Cap'n sir'. On his part, he tried to seem friendly, but it wasn't fooling me. He was wooden and had about as much sincerity as our vicar but with even less charm. I tried to avoid him, a'cause when he looked at me with those eyes, they weren't like dishwater. Nomye, they were like cold, grey steel.

One day I overheard him asking Daisy if she was Hal's mama, but Daisy was all a-bivver, too affeard to answer. The boy was clinging tight around her neck, wary of the strange man frowning at him. The next evening I came upon this bothersome man trying to coax the child with a promise of a sit upon his great grey mare in the yard. With such a lure, Ben would have had Henry Charles at his side in an instant but instead our boy rudely turned tail and fled to me, hollering fit to burst so that I had to take him to the kitchen where his cries couldn't be heard by all and sundry. It was all I could do to soothe him, but I couldn't be angry. I think he and I felt much the same about that customer. There was a little alarum bell sounding, but I was trying to ignore it, just wishing for the day the book-men, the soldiers and their troubling officer rode off to do their work in the next town.

For all the troubles he had with the authorities, Ben would linger to talk and keep me company a'cause he knew I felt uneasy. Sometimes he'd come to help me with a letter to Mary, though now there'd be naught hidden in the lines. I was surprised that he would all'us pass the time of day with the soldiers, even bowing to the cold-fish captain character, but he reckoned it drew less attention to be civil a'cause all would seem normal.

They'd been in the area nigh on a fortnight, when one evening Ben found the soldiers on their own for a change. He began chatting to the lads, sharing a few battle-stories and the like. They were affable enough. One had even been a Royalist dragoon but a'cause he hadn't seen a King's shilling for months he'd been persuaded to fight for Parliament a'cause they promised regular pay. After a while, with the ale loosening their tongues, the red-coats began confiding. They moaned about missing home, about mealy-mouthed quartermasters and short rations. Then the turned-coat fellow, hunched over his tankard and the worse for drink, slurred,

"Anna-nother thing, gennullmenn, tell me if thou will, whhhaaas-it all about eh? Should us good ol' army lads have naval nobodies giving us orders? I sshhh-say 'twould be better to have a ruddy Royalist like yourself leading us than that toady-eyed sea-dog!" The others raggedly banged their cups on the table in agreement. Another jug was ordered and the story flowed with the beer.

It seemed this captain was not like Ben who had ridden with troopers and had a proper army rank. He was from the fleet. His ship was in Plymouth for a refit, so the ship's commander had offered his services ashore and the garrison, being short of senior men, snapped him up for a job that nobody else wanted. For himself, the captain had said he had 'old friends' he wished to revisit in the district, and Cornwood was top of his list. I was listening in, polishing pots that didn't need it so I could catch every word. I didn't like what I heard one bit.

In the middle of the next morning the captain arrived by himself. As a rule I didn't offer much during the day, only expecting the occasional tradesman. The captain was already bad tempered, looking for food to make up for a breakfast he'd missed and a'cause he could find nobody at hand, he was right angry when he called out for some service.

The thickness of the taproom door was betwixt us so the accent was a tad muffled. Yet I knew that sound and it recalled a night full of thunder and fear and shouting. I couldn't recognise a man I'd never seen and by his politest voice I wouldn't have known him but, angry as he was, I knew as plain as day, this was Grace's murderous husband and he was in my parlour.

I cannot say what would have come to pass if Daisy had been on hand to serve that morn, but there was naught for it. 'Twas me that had to face him. So, taking a deep breath and praying that my knees did not buckle, I grabbed a pile of wooden trenchers to look busy and bustled through with a,

"God give 'ee good day, sir!"

There was no time to say more. In the blink of an eye the atmosphere went from angsty to icy, as cold as if every bit of love or sunshine or anything good had been sucked out of my life.

"And I wish you a good morrow, Mistress Mattock." He gave a mean little bow.

"How opportune that I find you here, Hester. I may surely call you Hester for I feel ... Nay! I know ... that we are already well acquainted. Are we not? Hester." His tone was flat and cold. There weren't no point in pretence but I said as little as courtesy would allow.

"Sir, you have the better of me. You wished for food?"

"Indeed I did. But now I find the taproom fare less interesting. What suits me better is the prospect of your company without any drunken nolls or the wench and the brat about my elbows." His insulting tone riled me and with the memory of a chubby, frightened face clear in my mind, I felt my strength return.

"Master Fenwick. If you wish to talk, here I stand and I am listening." He leered horribly.

"Talk, Hester?"

Now I have been a woman long enough to be able to handle most slick-tongued fellows with hopes of a bunt or a fondle on the sly. But Fenwick weren't one of those and I knew too well how treacherous he could be. I was on my guard, but had to be sociable as a tavern-keeper ought or he could make trouble for the 'Hands'. I kept my mouth shut, biding my time.

"Cat got your tongue, woman?" he sneered. "Well, 'tis of no consequence for I will have the information I want from you." He pulled up a stool, set it down in front of him and pointed,

"Sit." There wasn't much else I could do, so I placed the platters on a table and did as he said. He strolled to the front door and slid the bolts top and bottom. Taking a clay jug from a shelf he smashed it against the wall, and taking a thick wedge of pot he jammed it beneath the door from the kitchen.

"There now, that's better. I hate to be disturbed, don't you?" I didn't reply. I think he guessed I'd not be too obliging.

"Now, Hester, our little tête-à-tête can go easily for you. Or it can go hard. The choice is yours. So, I will ask politely, where is my wife?" 'Twas out before I knew it,

"Why, sir, I heard tell she was dead these five years ..."
The slap knocked me clean off the stool, the sound ringing off the pots on their hooks. It felt like a trip-hammer was thundering inside the back of my head. A bony hand grabbed my sleeve and hauled me to the seat again.

"As I said, the choice is yours. Do not underestimate me, woman, nor take me for a fool." 'Twas not the word that I was considering. This man was more dangerous than an angry adder and cruel too. He looked me up and down.

"Not the rags you wore as you staggered to Arwinch Down, are they? A green skirt fashioned with a false petticoat, a pathetic attempt at a lady's finery, was it not? And that homespun rag of a shawl that the infant was swaddled in? Not fit for a whore's son ..." He laughed at my expression of horror.

Fenwick had been to Penwarne, I knew that much. But we had not known he had been so close as to spy upon us even before we'd heard him hollering at the church-house. That bolted door had only delayed this devil.

"Do you wish to answer civilly this time?" I nodded carefully. I told him what he wanted and what I knew about Grace's plans for the New World. He seemed persuaded.

"Good. Hopefully she will die of sickness which will save me having to go the trouble of disposing of her a second time. A pity though." I couldn't tell what he was thinking but I would wager 'twas a bad place to be.

"She has something of mine and like all my property, I want it back." I made a small movement, just to show willing, and he raised his fist a second time, readying to strike backhanded. I shut my eyes but instead there was a throaty cackle, a frog-croak laugh.

"Hester, Hester! I wish you no harm. Now, I have examined all the papers of which you are touchingly so proud. I did not see amongst them the item for which I seek; a book, leather bound, this big." He measured the size with his hands, though I knew full well what he meant

"I know it, sir, though 'twas so battered, all wetted, then faded so badly that I would hardly have known it as a book."

I hoped he might believe the thing was a rag, no use to anyone. From his expression, he was not taken in. I bleated,

"'Twas in Grace's baggage, sir, taken to the Americk lands. I will swear on my Bible it's not here!" He stood over me for some time, flexing first one fist then the other.

I stayed stone still. I could hear little Hal's laughter in the yard. He'd been promised a visit to see Ben's horse being shod if he helped Daisy feed the chickens. Ben had obviously come to fetch the child. I hoped that it would keep him out of doors and out of harms way. But 'twas as if Fenwick read my mind.

"Ah, the little boy! Tell me of him. He's a pretty one with his blue eyes and fair locks. But small for his age, though I suppose it must be expected when his mother has been a vagrant and living as a tavern drudge. I confess I am surprised that she carried to term after her Welsh swimming lesson." There was a pause then again he gave that sickening cackle.

"Still, the boy shows promise. I might have expected that bitch to name him for her imprudent father but to honour that man-of-blood, Charles Stuart was crass." Fenwick began to pace around and about, while I crouched as low as I could.

It took no wits at all to see that this man thought Henry Charles was his son. I couldn't be sure but I guessed that while he thought it to be so, Hal was as safe as any soul could be with a man as changeable as this one. But there was one thing about men, which I'd seen in my William and in Ben Burrell and now in Fenwick too; they were foolish about the basic rules of babes. Fenwick hadn't got the measure of a child who, if he really was the sire, should have been at least a year older. I tried an explanation,

"Sir, when his mother's milk dried I wet-nursed him and he …" I expected another blow, but instead the man actually shuddered,

"Gah! Enough about your disgusting paps! Vile harlotry!" His next words made the bile rise in my throat,

"It is of little consequence. Soon the brat's welfare will be no further concern of yours …"

A clatter of horses outside, the rattle of the latch and a pounding at the door cut short my ordeal as Fenwick muttered,

"God's teeth, what now?"

'Twas the commission men with their troopers, mounted up. It was plain they were ready to leave. Caught off-guard by his betters, Fenwick had no choice but to open the door. I stumbled out behind him.

The roadway was full but I could see Ben Burrell strolling from the direction of the forge, leading his own horse with Hal perched happily a-top. At his side was Jet Beale and neither man had any idea there was aught amiss in the cluster of men at my door.

One soldier held the reins of Fenwick's grey gelding. The captain snatched at them and after a tetchy exchange he climbed into the saddle. The riders jostled as Ben, just as he all'us did, bowed dutifully to them then cheerily turned to me,

"Hester! Hal has been a right clever lad this morn and has shown himself to be a true horse-man! Make a guess at what he has done!" I shook my head. The warning that hung on my lips had to go unsaid. Ben grinned at Jet, who nodded cheerfully,

"He picked up Bessie's hooves for Master Beale to shoe her!" I tried to smile, tutted at the dirt on Hal's clathers, scolded the men for letting him do something dirty and all the time wondering why the riders didn't move off.

I'd never had any call to tell Ben the true facts about Grace. He knew that she'd not had a long and happy marriage; that her boy was a beloved memory of his father. Nobody in Cornwood knew Grace by any other than the name she took on when she marched out of Pendennis Castle. How was anyone to know the misery one little word would bring.

Jet chuckled as he lifted Hal from his perch,

"Down 'ee come, young cavalier! 'Tis a great shame that Mistress Sark b'aint here; your mama would be right proud o' her lad!"

Horses snorted; commands were called. Amidst the clopping of hooves, the jintle of bits and bridles, the jantle of stirrups and spurs, had Fenwick heard it? For just like the playwright said, 'twas all in a name; for Grace and Sark; for Fenwick and Grace. The future of a boy-child depended on a name: a name, a book and a man with no scruples, no feelings, nor a heart.

I prayed as the horsemen cantered away. I prayed by my bed and as I worked. I prayed on my knees afore, during and after every Sunday service and a few more time besides. I prayed Fenwick hadn't heard the name Grace had adopted.

But I don't think the Lord can have been listening.

XXXVI Mary: Uneasy Cornwall

Written this day 23ʳᵈ May 1648
Kestle Wartha
Heligan

Dear Hester,
I have no time on my hands but will write, brief and in haste,
for I was troubled to hear of the pocks afflicting poor baby
Hal and then your good neighbour Burrell. It is an illness I
recall well. When I took the chicken pocks I was perhaps
thirteen years of age and felt poorly enough. But I have seen
grown men and women collapsed and weeping with the
misery of it. I have not yet seen the spots and blisters in my
own babes, but as it is said that small children suffer less
with it than older patients then I would wish it came here
sooner rather than later.
I can put nothing in my missive to offer any help for here
there is nothing but a skin salve, which I will write out for
you. Perchance it will help.
Make an ointment using hops, new leaves and marigold
flowers if you have them.
Bruise the leaves in a mortar and beat in some hog's grease,
put in a stone jar and leave in the sun for three days, though
if we shall see sun this summer I shall be surprised, so by the
fire where it may melt will suffice. After three days, take it
and in a pan boil it a little and while it is hot strain it. Repeat
this, adding the oil you have made to the mix. You may do it
three or four times. When the grease smells strong of hops,
boil it hard until all the hops are crisped then strain and the
oil may be mixed with bees wax to make an ointment. It is
effective rubbed onto itching spots to stop the scratching
when the wound is nearly healed.

Though I send this recipe which my mother made, I think that Hal might be well by the time you have made such a salve. I shall send some ready made that I know to be in the still room at Penwarne.
When I have more leisure to frame some cheerful gossip I shall sit with my pen again.
Until when I remain,
Your friend,
Mary

To Mistress Hester Mattock,
At the sign of the Clasped Hands,
In Cornwood in the county of Devon

P.S The carrier will not take the pot of salve for which you have my apologies for my promise.

[N.B. This recipe is for the purposes of this fiction only and has no medicinal benefits.]

Written this day 23rd May 1648
At Kestle Wartha
Heligan

My dearest husband,
I have just come in to the house, it is gone three o'clock. This morning I went to Heligan to your father and thence to Penwarne and have stayed with papa. He is no better. The old complaint has reoccurred, that same one that has troubled him ever since he lost his hand fighting alongside Sir Francis Vere's forces in the siege at Ostend. As you know the false hand will sometimes make a sore which even my

best salves cannot heal. The only good thing is news from Antony. The surgeon who has tended my aunt has offered to see papa. He comes well recommended by Aunt Carew and by many of her circle. His travelling west is as yet undecided though. We must hope that he can be released from his duties sooner than later, for papa's comfort and well-being. The canker on his wrist looks particularly angry and although I do not mind attending to the bandages, neither Agnes nor Bridget can bear to look at them.

Reverend Trewick, St Peter's beloved ~~ives~~ incumbent has been threatened ejection. We hear many such cases now. Some good men are accused of trivial nonsense such as playing a game of chance but mostly the charges are for using the Prayer book, which we have been comforted by since King Edward's time. Many have held fears, fuelled by rumours, that St Peter's is or will have ~~ben~~ without rector for too long. Mevagissey folk worry that they will be like Gorran and have nobody to tend them. The revenue from the tithes, £100 at Gorran in each year they say, is always sequestered by the County Committee who have no care for folk's souls. The new authorities ride roughshod.

It makes me feel most terribly sad. It has destroyed so many friendships. Edward Herle, Sheriff of this county, tries conciliation. Yet he was ever the gentleman. And much goes against his nature. His role, troops of soldiers, of militia and horse, troubles him. He was looking very ill at Easter certainly. I wonder his wife has not taken to her bed with worry as she was always nervous.

I am occupying myself sewing. The mercer in the town had no linen. Truro had none. So to Helston I must! Or else we shall all go without undergarments for there are darns on the patches already darned. You must not look for new shirts. Domestic economics forces my hand there; there's no more Holland cloth for anything than napkins. Can you buy fine linen and send it to me? Or would it be simpler to purchase shirts in Paris? Expense is expected I suppose. But for a wife *not to be able to make shirts for her spouse - these are indeed hard times.*

More home news which I have been told I must tell their papa by delighted twins.
They saw dolphin, swimming about off rocks in Portmellon, 'tis no lies! I tried to tell them it was a sea monster and they should beware but they did not believe me. Obviously I have too honest a face to tell lies, even as tales to entertain my offspring. They wanted to see more, wait all afternoon. Does more than one dolphin swim together? I said that I would ask you, their illustrious papa, for you were certain to know for I have never seen any, even on my voyages.
When your news comes they will be elated, send to me soonest you may. Two children will otherwise be watching for messengers every day and I shall have no peace!
But, I shall close for now as there is nothing more of note from your home other than that we miss your presence every moment of every day.
Your loving wife, always,
Mary

To await Colonel Lewis Tremayne
At Rue des Abbeyes
St Germain-en-Laye

*The second letter contains a message which reads:
No good news from west yet. St Ives been held by St or ben [St Aubyn] for authorities. Sheriff County troops of horse occupying Helston. Forces there more than expected.
Dolphin off Portmellon lies to wait news. Will send soonest.

231

XXXVII Grace: The dangerous truth

There will be times when your instincts move you stronger than logic, or even loyalty. My advice to you is to always follow your instinct, though I doubt your father would have endorsed that view in May '46.

On 16th we woke to a low fog clinging to the landscape, veiling Godolphin Hill. We knew that farm hands from St Buryan, miners from St Just would be mustering, converging on Penzance, to be led by a former Royalist, Major Grosse. Sark's confidence was vested in another of the leaders, Martin Maddern. He and Sark had known each other as boys before Sark's life had taken him to sea. Maddern had led a unit under Sir Richard Grenvile with Lewis Tremayne and had kept up a correspondence with our old friend while he had been in exile. It had been some of Martin's correspondence with Mary that I had seen on Jago's desk.

"I would trust him with my life" Sark had declared. It was exactly what we were all doing.

The state of the roads was dire. The wagon was fragile, our progress painfully slow. Having done barely four miles we stopped at Germoe to let the mule rest. As I knelt in the church, an opportunity to think as well as keeping up the appearance of a mourner, a black-robed figure knelt beside me. My heart sank; I did not need the well-meaning ministrations of a conscientious cleric.

"Rev'rend sends his deepest condolences. And this." A small note was thrust into my hand. The man rose, bowed slightly to the altar and left as quietly as he had arrived, his muddied boots dropping clods of wet earth in the nave. I followed him as fast as I might, having struggled to get off my knees, but he had already disappeared. Unfolding the scrap of paper I read, 'St Aubyn forewarned, leading militia to Mount. We will face arms at Market Jew.'

"Did you see the curate?" I asked Sark as I reached the cart. "He passed me this!" I handed over the paper.

"I doubt if that was the curate," he said, reading swiftly then tearing the message into tiny pieces "but the information seems credible enough." Tossing the shreds into the swiftly flowing stream, he stood for a moment, pensive. Making up his mind, Sark took Jack's reins,

"There is little we can do back there and men depend upon us keeping to the plan. Come along, Jack! Let's have a bit more enthusiasm for the King's cause or it's to the glue pot you go!"

With Sark hauling at the head-harness we had struggled from Germoe and had just passed the road down into Porth Levan when the mule pricked up his ears, planting his hooves four-square in the mud, refusing to budge an inch further. What he had heard soon became evident, a large party of soldiers, pikemen and musketeers, making their way briskly towards us.

The Colonel had to work hard to prevent his horse cantering headlong into chaos. There was a lot of noise, with bellowed commands passed back through the ranks and Patch adding his voice. I leashed him quickly as the Colonel sidled his mount past,

"Confound it, man! Get that wreckage ..." he began, but as the cargo - and the smell - became evident his furious tone changed, moderated considerably through the leather of the gauntleted hand he put to his nose and mouth,

"Lord 'a mercy! My respects to you, ma'm, and to the deceased. However, you are blocking the highway to men on the official business of the High Sheriff of Cornwall! Can you not ..." but he couldn't finish his remonstration.

Drums, strangers, a stallion in the vicinity and the clattering of armour had pushed Jack to the limit of his nerves. With an unexpected surge of energy the mule, bucked, kicked and sidled, twisting in the traces and knocking the cart sideways. The ancient wheels had quite literally rattled themselves to bits and, like Jack, had reached breaking point. One spoke snapped followed by the total collapse of the wheel nearest the wall, leaving the cart, coffin and a braying mule in a mass of wood in the road. My heart missed a beat as the heavy box slid heavily across the bed of the toppled wagon, coming to a thudding stop against the stone bank.

"Colonel Bennett, sir! Shall we clear this ..." asked a burly but benign sergeant of pike,

"Get on with it! We will wait ... over there!" replied the Colonel and rode on. At a gesture from their officer the musketeers shuffled past, with their ensign riding behind. They gathered along the road, clearly glad to be upwind of the accident.

The carpenter's work had been solid and as Sark and a half dozen unhappy pikemen shouldered the 'body' nothing looked amiss. As I unhitched the trembling mule, another group stacked the remnants of the cart against the wall. The coffin was placed on the verge and with the roadway cleared, the sergeant strolled up.

"Where d'your papers take ye?" I dreaded an inquisition but he didn't wait for an answer, merely observing helpfully,

"We've not long passed a blacksmith, back away there in Breage. I'd say he could fix you up even if there's no wheelwright locally". A shout went up from the Colonel,

"To me! Form up! That's enough time lost! There are rebels baying at the barricades of Penzance and Colonel St Aubyn awaits us!" The sergeant leaned on his halberd, glaring at his commander. Then, resigned to the inevitable, he clicked his tongue, sucked in a deep breath and turned to his men,

"Right, you, you ... and you two. Late for Colonel's inspection, you were, so here's your punishment detail. Give this lady and gentleman a hand, and carry their dearly departed to Breage church. Then catch up with the rest of us, double quick! And you," he said, pointing to three others, who were sniggering at the back, "can carry their pikes. Come on, you lucky lot!" he said to the remaining men, "Order-r-r your pikes!" as his unit picked up their weapons and reformed,

"Shoulder your pikes! March on!" The drum beat a brisk rhythm and, with a respectful nod to me, the sergeant marched his men the way we had come.

With no burden to pull Jack was happy enough to be led by me so I followed the bearers along the road. They moved at an enthusiastic pace, no doubt eager to get the task over, so we were in Breage in no time. There we found the church warden attending to the hinges of the lych-gate. Explanations were given and the 'corpse' was set to rest in the church. With the church warden keen to ensure that the deceased would be removed before the services on Sunday, we were promptly directed to the smithy at the edge of the village.

A blackened face turned from the hearth at Sark's salutation.

"Ayee! By God's teeth …" It was an unorthodox greeting, even given the strange circumstances. The man's eyes were wide in amazement, the whites stark against his grimy skin. When he was sure we were flesh and blood the soot-encrusted craftsman took his tongs from the fire and setting his work aside, strode across and hugged Sark in a bear-like embrace.

"Well, rip me! If it b'aint our Sarky! What in the de'il's name brings you here?" He peered around Sark's shoulder,

"By Beelzebub's ars…rear-end!" he quickly corrected is colourful language, "Mistress Grace? Can I believe my eyes?" He rubbed his fists in his eye sockets, as if to wipe away a vision, leaving two circular smears.

"Emmott Robbins, you old rogue! Your command of English hasn't improved any!" Sark chuckled.

Emmott, permanently grubby, usually cheerful, and always busy, had been armourer to Lewis Tremayne's regiment and one of the few to march out of Pendennis Castle in the summer of '46.

"Are you making arms for the other side now then? Or sticking to nail-making and coat-hooks?"

"Cheeky bastard!" laughed Emmott, thumping Sark's shoulder, "I'm making what I'm told to make. If they pay, I won't say nay. I've Jenny, my wife and our child to support now, I'll have y'know!" and as if he'd realised some enormity of lapse in manners, Emmott grabbed us by the elbows and steered us to a small but tidy cottage tacked on to the back of the forge. I left Jack tied to the gate happily munching dandelion leaves while Patch, on his best behaviour, stayed close by my skirts

The Robbins' hospitality was as generous as their home was immaculate. Jenny quickly relaxed in our company and when the infant needed nursing, shyly took her leave and went up the narrow steps to the bedroom. Solicitous for her safety, Emmott carried his son up for her. Closing the door at the top of the stairwell, he returned to the table, and keeping his voice low, resumed our conversation with a very different tone.

"So, reminiscing over! I sense there's a deal you ain't telling me, Sark. Out with it!"

The smith's instincts were sharp. I watched Sark gauging the situation very carefully. His next words made no sense to me at all,

"With the dog locked in the kennel and the young whelp abroad, who's to go hunting?" Robbins' reaction was instant,

"The man, and the man, and the very man until the hound is at his hearth again." The men clasped hands across the table, a particular grasp, elbow to elbow.

"I couldn't be sure, Emm, I'm sorry. How many do you have?" Evidently something of significance had passed.

"Two score, maybe more. We've been waiting. Yet I never expected *you*! How come?" Emmott spoke quickly, keeping his voice low.

"It's a long story. We'd a cargo, and one part wouldn't go ashore where we planned, so ..." Sark shrugged, "there's a small cannon stinking your parish church to high heaven, and it's supposed to be in Helston by Friday!"

Robbins' roar of laughter must have startled the suckling baby, and his wife's reproving call made him sheepish, but from that moment his goal was to find a solution for our lack of transport.

Arriving in Helston too soon was as problematic as being too late, but as the tavern-keeper in the next village was one of Emmott's following, it was decided that we would lodge in Sithney. The body would be carried by a borrowed cart to that church until early on Friday morning. In the meantime, Emmott would endeavour to collect and repair our own wagon and bring it to us so that we could take our load into the town as planned. It was just a matter of waiting. The trickle of news kept my nerves on edge, giving me the sense that this countryside was simmering, frothing, ready to bubble over like a pot of boiling cream.

At daybreak on 19th, as we took breakfast with the taverner, men began to gather, gradually setting off in small groups, carrying commonplace tools or baggage, heading in the direction of Helston. Three men stayed with us, ostensibly to help Sark take the coffin from the church, the smell now so bad that they needed to muffle their noses and mouths.

The roads were steep and busy, the stinking wagon trundling in their midst raising groans of complaint from several travellers. From the reports Sark had received, we expected some army presence, but overnight a nervous mayor, with endorsement from the same Colonel St Aubyn who was now combating the Penzance rising, had persuaded a unit of soldiers to remain in the town, effectively doubling the guard. More troops were expected, both cavalry and infantry. The uprising needed to progress swiftly if anything was to be achieved and weapons were the key to success but getting the Royalist forces armed was becoming more complicated by the hour.

Our objective was St. Michael's Church, set above the town, looking out over the valley. However, a picket had been set on all the routes into Helston, one where each individual had their papers checked and their identity noted. The stink from the coffin was now drawing very unwelcome attention. As we approached the soldiers I spotted two officers standing back from the barrier watching the proceedings. They eyed the cart and I bowed my head, warily eyeing them from beneath my mourning veil. However, when our turn came to hand over our passes, Sark was waved through with the wagon but the soldier on duty insisted I lift the gauze. I think he was less officious, more roguish; teasing a shy female was a welcome diversion in a boring routine. He nodded for me to move on but as I did there was a shout,

"Hey! You! Woman with the veil! Halt! In the name of Parliament!" I stopped dead in my tracks, glancing at Sark who stood by the mule's head. He nodded very slightly, gave a small smile to encourage me.

"Turn about, madam, and kindly remove your veil completely." When I did I was faced with a man no older than me, swarthy, with dark eyes. From his uniform I supposed him to be at least a sergeant. When he spoke I recognised his accent, so similar to the North Devon burr that Hester could mimic. His tone was formal.

"I am sorry for your loss, madam, and I apologise if I alarmed you, but I have some questions I need to ask. You would, I believe, be more at ease if we were in a less public place." I tried hard not to panic, but instinctively reached out toward Sark, something not lost on the officer.

"Madam, your companion is welcome to accompany you. I will assign one of my men to tend your wagon. Leave the dog, if you please. Both will remain here until your return. Come!" He crooked a finger at Sark, and waved a guard forward, giving his orders. He indicated that we should follow him. I tied Patch to the cart then Sark gently took my arm in his, giving a reassuring squeeze.

We turned away from the church, through narrow lanes between workmen's cottages, towards the centre of Helston, stopping at the first of the townhouses. The officer politely indicated a ground-floor room, evidently now a militia office with maps, papers and reports in sheaves across any flat surface available. He cleared a chair,

"Please, take your ease, ma'm. I hope not to keep you long, but they are difficult times in which we live and this is a sensitive matter." I remained on my feet but the tension was taking its toll. My anguish did not need to be play-acted.

"Sir, I beg of you. Why am I here? I have sad business enough. My papers are in order, I assure you. I do not know what you want!" His response came as a complete surprise,

"My name is Daniel Edwards, Ensign to Colonel Eure. While you do not know me, I do know you. Your name is Grace Sark." My knees gave way and I sat down with a thump.

"You left the fortress at Pendennis on the surrender of the Royalist garrison on August 17th 1646, walking out alongside another woman. Her name is Hester, Hester Mattock, and she has a son." There was no question of rebuttal; he was making a statement. My false documents were not worth the ink with which they were written.

"I cannot deny it, sir, and must throw myself upon your mercy." His eyes widened then he frowned, his head cocked slightly to one side.

"I cannot think, Mistress Sark, why you think that would be necessary but since you clearly have something on your conscience …" I closed my eyes, took a deep breath and when I opened them discovered that he was smiling, eyes sparkling with mischief.

"Let me suggest we proceed in a civilized fashion. I will call for refreshments, then first I and then you will speak plainly. No dissembling. While we are in this room you have my word; you are safe, so you may put aside your sword, sir." Sark politely slipped off his sword and baldrick.

Food and some stale beer arrived, and as he cut bread and carved cold mutton Ensign Edwards talked.

"It seems an age away now, but for a while at least, Hester and I were sweethearts. In Bideford." He pursed his lips into a wry expression. I could see how young Hester might be charmed by this man.

"Well, I had hoped 'twas so when I marched away, assigned to the Queen's Guard. When I found myself back in my home town, under a different flag and in Parliament's uniform, I looked for her, but she had gone. There were rumours of witchcraft; others told me she'd run away to Barum. It mattered not how, I had lost her" He flushed, and taking a deep drink of the beer, grimaced, and pushed the rest away. I guessed that the distraction had given him a moment to regain his composure.

"You know how military events unfolded. Eventually my regiment was assigned to Fairfax' army. We were deployed to raise the siege at Pendennis, and so I was in the guard that lined the route from the fort at the hand-over. When I recognised Hester it was as if years had fallen away. I made it my business to seek her out, baby or no." He chuckled,

"The paperwork is a nightmare, but if you want to find someone, have even a single clue and an officer's authority, then Parliament's administration makes it simple. It's time consuming but straightforward enough."

Sark caught my eye. I could follow his thoughts without words for I was sure they mirrored my own: Fenwick.

Edwards continued,

"I recognised you today only because you marched beside Hester and I recalled your name as it was listed beneath hers. One day I may get to Cornwood. I doubt Hester will remember me. I should just like to see her, to know she is well."

In the confidential quiet my nerves had subsided marginally, but Ensign Edwards had one more surprise in store.

"Mind you, I must suppose that you are quite the enigma, madam, for another gentleman was ardent in his enquiries about you. He was hard to ignore and a little less than polite. I hope that you will not have been inconvenienced as I may have caused him some delay in his search when I ... mislaid ... some documents he was seeking."

Now I was convinced his charming grin was sincere. I smiled back,

"You could not have done me a better service, sir." I heard Sark's boots grate on the stone floor; he was understandably uncomfortable here. We had a mission to complete but our host could not be harried without raising suspicions.

However, he had not forgotten the circumstances, or our arrangement. In a bizarre turn of events our fate was put firmly into my hands when he said,

"Now. Your turn."

I hardly knew where to begin, so started with the commonplace,

"The babe, sir, is not Hester's but my own. I was too weak so she carried him and they assumed he was hers in the listings." Ensign Edwards' eyebrows twitched in interest, but now was not the time for Hester's life story.

Then, in a flash of the waywardness to which I have sometimes been prone, I made a decision; impulsive, reckless, deadly even: I told the ensign the truth.

As I spoke, Sark stood, stock still and pale in the dim light, one muscle twitching below the scar on his left cheek. When I finished the silence seemed interminable, Edwards staring at me, leaning by the unlit fireplace, lips pursed, arms folded.

His next move was cat-like; a reaction to a noise, a deep rhythm that, at first was barely perceptible other than the vibration of the panes of glass in the casement. The sound quickly grew to the distinctive rumble and thump of the drums of an army and its ordnance, cannons on heavy wooden carriages being hauled through narrow streets. After the heavy plod of oxen pulling artillery, came the confident, brittle crunch of hundreds of well-shod men, scarlet-uniformed soldiers flooding the narrow lanes and market place like blood in a slaughterhouse. Orders were called and repeated, echoing round the walls. The press of animals blowing, stamping, and whickering added to the growing chaos outside. Within minutes our privacy was shattered by the arrival of a number of officers, all of whom recognised Edwards. Salutations over, they milled about the room, their immediate concern being the frenzied business of billeting a militia.

If ever there was a point at which Time stood still, I believe that was the moment. Our past was catching up with us; our future hung in the balance.

Picking up pen and selecting two sheets from a pile, when Edwards spoke, his manner had become stiff, formal, as if concluding some business,

"I see. Well, I can provide the requisite papers." He wrote for some minutes, signing, drying and setting his seal to the papers before folding them. However, he made no sign of handing them over. Instead he stood up, leaned out of the door and called to a passing corporal.

"I want you to find the constable with all haste. Bid him seek the vicar and the sexton. Tell them it is a matter of great urgency and that I will explain when we get to the churchyard. On your way!" The man snapped to attention, and promptly disappeared into the crowded lane.

"With your permission, madam, I will oversee your sad mission personally. Come with me and, sir, don't forget your sword!" It seemed here was another individual adept at play-acting. There was no option but to comply though we had no idea what to expect next.

Outside the smell of massed humanity was overpowering, with gunpowder and sulphur adding an acrid tang to the air. We pushed through the throng, past horses drinking from the fast-flowing kennels at one end of the street and several soldiers shamelessly relieving themselves into the same stream at the other. Eventually we reached the cart. Despite the crowds there was a sizeable clearing around the wagon. Edwards strode up, dismissed the soldier from his guard detail and waved Sark and I forward. Retrieving Patch, he handed me the halter, walking beside me as Sark persuaded the mule up towards the church on the hill.

"Sir, I have no words to …" I began.

"Then say nothing. I know too much as it is. My priority is to get you away from what I can assure you will be a debacle; a dangerous, disastrous calamity for the rebels and for the King."

Sark replied quietly,

"Ensign, we owe you our thanks. But I would ask two questions if I may." Edwards nodded.

"How much do you know of the Royalist's plans?" When it came, his response was stark: all of them. Hands clasped behind his back, Sark slowly drew a deep breath, keeping his gaze firmly on the ground.

"And your second question?" Edwards said with the merest hint of wryness. Sark looked up, one eyebrow raised,

"If that is so, why help us?" The tone was as quizzical as Edwards' reply was wistful,

"For the mutual love of a woman. To make amends. To banish regret, perhaps," he sighed. "If you had lied to me matters would have gone very differently. But you did not. When - if - we meet again I would like to greet you as friends."

"So, how do we get the gun ..." My question was cut off by a calloused finger across my lips.

"Grace, there is no gun. A corpse, unexpected and in need of a quick and decent burial will be interred in St Michael's graveyard. Then the man's grieving relatives will have papers under my authority allowing them to travel without let or hindrance, by whatever means they choose, to Cornwood, Devon. There may well be a vessel in Helford passage with orders for Plymouth but I can assure you it would be prudent to avoid that part of the Lizard peninsula in the immediate future. On the other hand, there is a small boat at Porth Levan which I hear is ... accommodating."

Within the hour the interment of the coffin took place, a hasty committal into a grave prepared for another soul. The weight of the casket as Sark, Edwards, and the sexton struggled to lower it with appropriate dignity suggested he had been a man, hearty in his appetites, well-built but perhaps slim. Only five individuals were there to mark his passing.

After, as we stood at the church gate, Edwards handed over the packet of documents to Sark. Holding out his right hand he clasped Sark's in the same clasp as I had seen at Breage and Sithney. His words were spoken softly, but he was clear and emphatic,

"Until the hound is at his hearth again. Farewell!"

In Porth Levan that evening, a pinnace waited as dusk fell. On board, the sailor in charge, Sark's oriental friend Goemon, might have aroused the curiosity of the Cornish fisher-folk, but wary, he had kept to the shadows. The boat had lingered all afternoon but as dusk fell had been about to pull away from the quay when Sark whistled his signal from the cliff path as we hurried towards the harbour. We boarded quickly and the pinnace made its way to rendezvous with the *Dolphin* off-shore. Once the anchor was raised, Pasco Jago set a course for Portmellon Cove, by Mevagissey.

Be it Royalist uprising or Cornish rebellion, we were to play no part in the events unfolding in the lanes, farms and villages of the Lizard that night.

XXXVIII Hester: The evil that men do

For ages after Fenwick left I was edgy, panicked when I heard unexpected footsteps. Ben all'us used to tell me when he planned to come a-visiting, which was kindly, and most customers had something about them, a whistle or a way of walking, that meant I knew who was about but Captain Fenwick had had this way of creeping up on you. Even so, as days went by life returned to the ordinary routine. There might be the occasional excitement of a traveller with the latest doings in the county or sometimes further afield but 'twas all'us wonderous fine when I had a packet from Mary.

When I was a maid back in Bristol, I never, ever thought I would read or write. 'Twould have seemed silly. A girl like me doing penmanship and all that? Never. Not till sows could flit like sparrows. But there, see what 'tis come to now: me getting letters from a lady of a great family and me penning back. I keep every letter in a bundle, tied up with a bit of green ribbon left over from … a long time ago.

All things considered, for a miner's daughter from Radstock, there's been much in my life that pen and paper has marked a record of, for posterity, as my William used to say. I asked him once what the word meant and he said he thought 'twas so folks would remember us. 'Tis why we wrote the dates in the great Bible that I keep by my bed; a marriage, a birth, two deaths already, all penned to keep the memory of us when someone reads it. I suppose one day it will record my passing.

Anyway, the day the letter about Grace came I felt like running round the village singing, a'cause there she was, not in the Americk lands but in Cornwall! At least, she was when Mary sent the letter. Grace put in a page to reassure me all was well, just telling in a few words how she and Roddy Rawle had gone their separate ways. I thought Grace being

245

reunited with her man was close to a miracle and summ'at so very fine that the playwrights ought to put it in a story.

She said naught about how it was between them both but since she said naught about wanting to return to Cornwood either, I guessed it couldn't be too bad. Anyway, I was content for things to stay as they were, me keeping Hal safe. Grace knew that better than anyone.

Neither Mary nor Grace penned anything about the outcome of the great spring rising of King's forces, except Grace said she and Sark had reason to thank an old friend of mine for their safety, which is all very mysterious and for sure I can't think who she might mean, but as she said it was too long a tale to relate on paper, perhaps it b'aint so significant.

Grace wrote about how their boat had been given a job to do, to wait by the coast near some little fishing port until a messenger would bring them word to take to some important men who she dared not name. 'Twas a quiet private cove they were anchored by, so Sark had asked permission that he and she could row ashore one afternoon. All was well until unexpectedly a woman with small children came around the rocks, and Lord a'mercy! There stood Mary Tremayne! Now that was happenstance enough, but when she saw them, Mary cried out,

"Grace? Can it be? Oh, Grace! Come! Come here to me!" Grace said she remembered the words most particularly. 'Twas most strange for there were Goody Yendacott's words again. Since that day on the moor the thought of her has been enough to give me goose-prickles at the best of times, but now I can only think that there is much in this world and in Heaven that is beyond anyone's explaining.

Slipped into my letter, was a little picture of a boat Sark had drawn for Hal, so I nailed that to the wall by his cot so he can see it every morn. Grace had put in a little book for her lad, four tiny folded pages with a story she had written in simple words about a ship and a rescue from pirates. I have read the tale every night before I tuck Hal into bed. Daisy likes to listen in; she's all'us been fond of stories.

One day, very shy, she said she'd like to learn her letters. Perhaps I will try with her when I have time to hand. She didn't have the best home, with that ma of hers and we didn't get off to a good start together when I first came to Cornwood, but now she works hard. She'll make a man a good wife one day and it won't hurt for her to know her letters and numbers.

In July we began to hear that, even though the King's men achieved nothing in the west, there had been much to-doing up north. The Scots were marching south to support His Majesty and on the other side of the country there was even more trouble, with some dire happenings in a place called Colchester, a place full of Royalists all up in arms. Into August, after my birthday but just before the men started to gather in the pathetic harvest, there came word of more battles. I thought then, may the Lord help us, for surely there've already been enough men lost.

The talk in the 'Hands' was of blood spilled, and Cromwell; of the King and lost causes. One fellow even blamed the King for the bloodshed, though his notions were roundly scoffed at by most other customers, with Jet saying he was full of 'daft ranting'. But at the harvest-home supper, when Tinker Luccumbe brought the terrible tale of Colchester town, where the folk ate their dogs and cats and horses before they had to open their gates to Lord Fairfax, it took me right back to Pendennis, so awful and sudden that I burst into tears, right in front of all and sundry, and had to be taken home to my bed until my sobbing had stopped.

A letter from Grace in September must have come by a long route as it took an age to get to me. This time Sark had sent a picture of a fort, a star shaped castle with little guns and men all scurrying about, and ships in the harbour below it. Hal's pa said that this was what he could see from the top of the hill on the island where their ship was now sheltering.

In a funny turn of events, when naught was going well for the King in his business anywhere else, it seemed that far away on the islands they call the Sorlinges, the garrison had been so angered at getting no pay and having scant supplies that they locked their commander in the church during the Sunday service, and declared the islands to be for the King once more. And not one shot was fired! Now, Grace said, there were ships a-plenty like *Dolphin* supplying the place and keeping the western seas in the King's interest, so at least the soldiers would get to eat. Not that it made any difference to His Majesty.

There was snow on the ground and the top of the well was frozen on the day we learned the King was dead. The walk up to the church that morn was bone-chillingly cold, with the air so icy that it felt as if blades cut your throat with every breath but on Dartmoor it wasn't out of the ordinary. I had bid Daisy stay home by the hearth with Hal, who was full of sniffles and I got a scolding by the church warden. I was putting Daisy's soul at risk and he looked grim, but 'twas a normal reproof and I just bowed my head dutifully and meekly begged his pardon. Cornwood had seen no signs or portents; aye, there'd been word that there was turmoil in Parliament. And Christmas had been just another day, if you did as you were bidden. The terrible tidings were all the worse, for we did not expect it.

That morning Shute's sermon was summ'at horrible to hear. He ranted and raged, with spittle flying, crying out in the most gruesome manner against kings and princes, blaspheming so zealously that even the Savery family from Slade, the pa being probably the staunchest of any Parliamentarian in our district, got up from their pew and walked out.

When Shute finished there was a leaden silence, then came the weeping - and not just from the women neither. My legs were like a quaking pudding and I felt sick. Even though snow began to fall, folk stood around long after the service, murmuring, consoling one-another. We were all trying to fathom how to it had come to be that men, ordinary men, some only come to importance a'cause of being soldiers, had cut off the head of the King. A king: crowned and signed with holy oil; the son of a King; with queens and kings for years uncountable before that. 'Twas all so unthinkable. As I made my way home I pondered on how the world was turned over and about and no mistake, aye, and fetched inside out too.

I had told those I knew would commonly have called in that the 'Hands' wouldn't open that day. Though 'twas tuning off business, folks just nodded in agreement and I didn't think I would be any the worse for showing a bit of respect. Yet when I got home there was a horse in yard, and pushing open the door into the candle-light, after the bright of the frost and clear air, it took me too long to see that the rider was sitting on the settle at my hearth with Daisy cowering, just behind his shoulder. The man had Hal on his lap, the lad jabbering away to his new friend as he played with a dagger, twisting and turning it this way and that to watch the steel sparkle in the flames from the fire. It was Captain Bartholomew Fenwick.

"Have a care that you don't cut yourself, my boy!" said he. 'Twas wicked, that jiggling Hal up and down. But it made the child chortle as he brandished the knife about like a sword.

"You! How did you get in to my house?" 'Twas all I could do to stop myself from leaping forward to snatch the weapon.

"Good day to you too, Hester!" he said, scornfully, for I had forgotten the first rule of an alehouse keeper, to all'us mind your manners and greet your customers civilly.

"I trust you enjoyed the ministration of the church this morning. I am sorry to have missed Reverend Shute's beneficence but Daisy has been most accommodating since my arrival - I believe it was just after you left for your devotions. I had hardly expected such hospitality."

Daisy hunched her shoulders and her head sank low, something she all'us did when she'd something to be ashamed of. I tried to seem unflustered, though 'twas hard when all I could see was that blade likely to snick off a tiny finger, or worse.

I could not imagine how this creature had charmed our little lad, when Hal had been so wary when Fenwick had been here before but the reason was soon clear enough.

"We have been talking a great deal about young Henry Charles' love of horses, have we not my young friend? He is most eloquent on the subject and knowledgeable for his age. I have told him that I have a pony for him in the stable in my fine house in Bristol. He is keen to go to see him, aren't you, Henry Charles?"

Seeing me, the child's attention wavered and the dagger dropped to the floor with a clatter.

"That is most kindly, Captain Fenwick. We have no stable here for a pony." I could see worry beginning to flicker across Hal's face a'cause I was not his usual, bright Hester. I wasn't as cheery with this man as I would be with his friend Ben Burrell, or Jet, or even the maltster or Tinker Luccumbe.

"So you ought not to tease the boy with promises I cannot keep." I tried to keep matters normal. I couldn't reach Hal and I did not want to frighten him more than he was already. He knew something was very wrong, even though the grown-up people around him were all saying the right words. But when he tried to wriggle free an arm clinched him tighter. Then a sparkle of tears rimmed his eyes. He put his thumb in his mouth and sat very, very still.

"Oh, but the pony won't be here. He will only have his pony when he arrives at his new home." I couldn't stop myself, a girt gasp as what I was hearing.

"You can't take him away from …"

"Why not? He is my son, Hester. Of course I can take him. I shall give him everything that he, as a young gentleman, requires."

Stupid, stupid Hester. For all my learning, I fell right into the trap, too late to see that Fenwick had been baiting me all along.

"He's not …" I cried, and in the moment before Fenwick began to laugh I knew that if Beelzebub had been in the very same room, this man would have proven crueler, more evil than the very devil himself.

"He's not my son, were you going to say?" It took every bit of courage I had to look into his life-less eyes. I tried to speak, but my mouth had gone dry. There were no words.

"Yes, I know that now. Your friend's little blunder only confirmed my suspicion. You and his dam thought to dupe me, eh? Oh, but you were trying to be too clever, you scheming trollop, you and his mother, that faithless harlot! The whelp's life is worth nothing, less than nothing! And yet …" he stroked Hal's curls from about his face, "and yet I am willing to overlook that."

"No!" It came out croaked, "Take me too … he needs me, he is young, barely more than a baby. I am all he has …"

"You? What for? I shall be doing him a great honour. Now he will have his own maid and an excellent tutor, in a moneyed household. He will have all a boy needs to become a suitable companion … for I find I like the company of a well-brought up boy … he is yet young …" The next words brought my stomach to my mouth, the bile rising so fast that I thought I would choke.

"He is so much younger than his father was, but then, I believe there is much pleasure to be had in the anticipation. With time I shall mould him to serve me well. There is a delicious irony in the situation. Sark made me a cuckold; I shall …"

That was when I screamed. I would not, could not hear such vile corruption spoken. But I'd not see Grace's boy, my dearest Hal, to fall into the clutches of this animal. I had to do something; I would do anything for the life of our darling boy.

I walked towards the man and baby, holding out my hands, looking all the while into Hal's fear-filled eyes, trying to keep my voice steady, calm, to reassure his quaking trembling. Fenwick began his raucous, jeering laugh. I tried to shut my ears to it, tried once more,

"Please … This is the only home he has known. You do not know how to soothe him when he is poorly, how he likes his oats and milk and honey … Don't fret, chicken, this horrid man can't hurt you, Hester's here. Hester's here …" Fenwick stood up, and with Hal grasped tight to his side, bent down to pick up the dagger.

"I think, Mistress Mattock, you forget yourself." The knife was glinting, aimed at me,

"You cannot take him!" The tears were streaming down my face, and Hal was crying silently, huge gulping sobs wracking his tiny frame,

"Oh, Hester, I think I can, for you cannot stop me."

In a village on the skirts of Dartmoor, in a small alehouse, two women face peril. One cowers, unable to prevent a whimper escaping her lips. The other stands rapt, intent upon the face of a little boy in the hands of man with eyes as cold as ice. She once vowed that she would give her life to protect this blue-eyed infant, another woman's son.

A door opens. Her attention is only fleetingly diverted. In a single heartbeat, a swarthy stranger assesses the scene then gallantly steps forward to protect the girl he loved long ago.

He is too slow.

Unwaveringly, a blade smudged by an infant's finger-marks, slashes high and hard at the woman with dark hair and eyes the colour of honey.

Blood-stains spread across scrubbed granite slabs. A door closes, deadening the sound of swelling screams. Then a murderer, with the shock-silenced child in front of him on the saddle, rides unchallenged from the scene.

XXXIX Mary: The missive and the messenger

Written this day 4th February 1649,
With King Charles II,
At the sign of the Golden Key,
Molestraat,
At The Hague.
Holland

My dearest wife,
His Majesty is dead. Long live the King.
In my life this day is the saddest I have seen. Has word
reached you of affairs in London? I cannot bear to think that
I should be the bearer of such appalling tidings.
These last seven years my heart and my conscience have
been with the King, believing in his cause. Now it is a blow
most horrifying to learn how the matter has come to an end.
First came a travesty of a trial, the legality of which is
nominal at most, for who should try a king, who is God's
anointed? And then the axe.
Oh, God forgive me, for all the love I had for His Majesty, I
could not have stood with him on the scaffold. The very
thought makes me shudder. How can people have watched?
Perhaps to see the evidence with their eyes for who would
believe it could come to this?
If Bevil Grenvile still lived, I think his heart would have
broken at this outcome.
We have had some indication of the individuals who put their
name to a warrant, a contemptible sham to signify that the
execution was legitimate. For myself, I am sickened by the
men who could fabricate such an event, among their number
your cousin, John Carew. I cannot imagine how your poor
grandfather would have reacted, God rest his soul. It grieves
me to think that I must continue to converse with John for I

have asked something of him with regards to a certain individual's past conduct though I can say no more for now.

Since November when I was requested to come to ~~His Highness the Prince~~ His Majesty there has been much to be done but that was as nothing compared to the frantic activity between ambassadors and diplomats once the army made their objective plain - to condemn and then to kill Charles Stuart. It was all in vain, but the work continues on the new King's behalf and I am likely to be part of that.

But Mary oh, my dear, you would have wept to see him for it has been the days since the last communiqué that have been hardest.

It was heartbreaking to witness the anguish of His ~~Highness~~ Majesty, Charles, trying to maintain the dignity and calm of a Royal Prince and yet never knowing for sure what was happening. And in the event, I can hardly believe that the story came through nothing more than a newssheet. What insolence!

The chaplain, Doctor Goffe, finally broke the news, and there could have been no easy way but, with kindness I think, he approached Charles with the respect due, and, kneeling, addressed him as Your Majesty.

How does one comfort a King or a Prince of the Realm? The tears were those of a son, imagining the horrors of his father's killing, but they were also those of a young man, one who has such weighty dilemmas, responsibilities and principles now thrust upon his shoulders. He is but eighteen. His father may have advised the way of peace and forgiveness, but can one do that now?

I am sure that I could not be gracious in the same circumstances.

I cannot imagine any monarch on the continent being less that revolted by the events in England. A Scot here, I think him to be Agent to the Marquis of Argyll, though I forget his name, declared that they had cut off the King of Scotland's head, without due consultation with the Scottish Estates

which are like our Parliament. The despicable man was less offended by the act than the omission!
It is a very bad business indeed.

My dearest, for the foreseeable future it may be that your letters will not reach me here for it is likely that I shall be dispatched to accompany one of the many diplomatic missions which are inevitable now. For myself, I hope not to be sent too far for the distance from Kestle Barton is already almost unbearable. Ireland may be a possibility.
I know that soon I have to travel to Amsterdam, to meet with Sir Richard Grenvile, though I can say no more about my instructions, but after that I am at His Majesty's disposal.
It pains me to write such unhappiness, and politics, but I have nothing jovial to report this day and my spirits are so low that only you could comfort me, yet are so far away.
Give my love to the children and my respects to your father. I am pleased he is keeping so much better.

You are, as always, the pole star to which I navigate.
I am your loving husband,
Lewis.

To my lady, Mistress Tremayne
At Kestle Wartha
In the parish of St Ewe
In the county of Cornwall

Written this day 7th February 1649
Your home at Kestle Wartha
Cornwall

Dearest husband,
I received yours this very morning from the Dolphin, *also*
seeing Grace for a brief interlude. Your friend Jago again
allowed Sark to bring her ashore to the cove to deliver the
package. It was a most timely arrival though one which
would meet with such unhappy tidings as I must now
recount.

Long live the King. And may God rest his father's soul.
We had indeed heard, in church, of what folk here are
already calling the martyrdom of His Majesty Charles I. It
caused dire distress amongst the congregation, two women
fainting, and many tears being shed. What is the world come
to, kings executed for treason; husbands and wives parted by
politics. It is a world gone mad.
I hope that your meeting with Sir Richard achieves its
purpose and that he is in one of his affable moods.

However your letter only piles misery upon an already
cheerless situation for a rider came late yesterday, mired in
muck, Benjamin Burrell, lately a Captain in His Majesty's
army. He was charming and polite and his reason for
travelling so far to Kestle most considerate. He hoped that I
would not be offended at his impudence coming here for he
had grave concerns and felt it his duty to convey the news in
person because he had for some time now had the pleasure of
Hester's friendship.

Lewis, he came to tell me that Hester is like to die, and it is
Fenwick's doing.

I will try to write of it plainly, though I am so agitated I can
barely hold the pen. Firstly he introduced himself, saying
though we had never met, we had corresponded indirectly.

*Did we? I do not know. Do you know him? He implied that
you did.*

*Should I have recognised him? I fathomed he is the man that
helped Hester write to me, to us ~~in that way~~ but I should not
know him by looks should I?*

*You know my terror when Bartholomew Fenwick came here?
I know now that later he went on to Cornwood for the demon
has been hunting Grace. He kept his identity hidden and
despite not finding her he did deduce far more than anyone
would have wished, though he did not at that time know that
Grace had taken ship.*

*Then on Sunday last, Fenwick went again to Cornwood. He
entered the 'Hands', uninvited and unannounced, whilst the
villagers were at church. Hester returned to confront the
villain but the child is now a hostage to fortune as Fenwick
also wants the return of the book, the rutter, the one piece of
evidence which would condemn Fenwick to the gallows, by
his very own words.*

*However, this is but part of the miserable intelligence these
pages bear. It is why Burrell came in person rather than
simply put pen to paper.*

*Hester tried to prevent Hal's abduction. Benjamin said that
she had been like a wild-cat, and flung herself at her
tormentor, but she was badly hurt, stabbed by Fenwick as he
made his escape. The wound is deep. Hester is very weak.
She is likely to die.*

*Burrell tried to reassure me that there may yet be hope. If the
injury can be kept clean, he said he has known men's with
wounds very similar to heal and be well again in time. He
said that in the care of Daisy the good friends she has in the
village, Hester will have the very best attention available.
And he himself had engaged the services of a surgeon from
Tavistock. He could not tell me the surgeon's diagnosis.
The Hue and Cry was raised thanks to the timely arrival of
another man. He was seeking Hester, a fellow claiming to be*

a friend from Hester's years in Bideford I think, but when Burrell left nothing had yet been found of that devil or the boy. Oh, Lewis, what am I to do? Should I go to her?

All of this I told to Grace, and she listened in silence, still like a rock. I think she will be strong, for she has survived much. Sark vowed that Fenwick would be found; that his son would be safe, for he would move heaven and earth to do it, and would kill Fenwick or die.
But Grace replied in a voice that made shivers on my spine,
"No, no you will not. I know not when or how it will be, but here and now I vow on everything I hold true, good and holy, that I will make myself a widow." And I believe her, every word.

They left immediately after, so this letter comes by another route and I hope the carrier does not tarry for I have paid him well.
Lewis, I have never wanted to add to your trials but I find more and more that I cannot bear this life apart, the fear, the loneliness. Always I despair when there are troubles, but even when there are pleasant happenings I find myself desperately wishing you were here. Please, husband, please, look to your family, over your duty. Please, Lewis, come home to me.
I will send this now, though it is not how I would wish, but you would want nothing less than honesty.
In haste,
As you are my dearest love, I remain,
Your wife,
Mary

Written this day 29th March 1649
At Kestle Wartha
In the parish of St Ewe
In the county of Cornwall

My friend, my dear Hester,
I write once more so that, even if you are weak, you might
hear this when it is read to you, and know that I think of you
and pray for your recovery daily. Captain Burrell sends word
to me of your progress so that I know if you are doing as you
should.
So little happens here that I can only write of day to day
matters, but they might give you cheer and bring you back to
us. Grace has been here again as the ship plies her trade
between this coast and France, to Scilly or the Channel
Islands. You will have heard from her I think. It would be
such a delight to think that maybe one day we might all be
reunited.

Do you remember when you came here first, that wet day,
drenched and shaken from riding pillion with your husband,
Will? I think neither of you liked horses. ~~And for a woman~~
~~expecting her first infant in your condition~~ *It cannot have*
been easy. But it was soon as if we had been friends for many
years.
So, to tell you of my days. Well, the children I wrote of in my
missive yesterday, so I shall say less of them.
Today I have been supervising the spring clean. There has
been a little whitewashing of the parlour in the last week,
though to move the furniture is a bind as much of it is old,
from my father-in-law. To budge the cupboard for example,
which was made at the time when Queen Bess' reigned is like
trying to shift a mountain.

My sister Agnes and I have set to the mending of some old
hangings for the second best bed, though they will barely
serve to keep the worst of the cold out. I would like to be able

*to afford new wool, but our budget cannot stretch. So
mending will have to suffice.*

*The chickens have begun to lay again, which bodes well for it
is early. I dearly hope that this summer is better than last* ~~for
folk here are finding it exceeding hard. Corn has been so
expensive. Did the poor harvests affect your malt? I know
that you had concerns last year~~. *But you must not worry
yourself.*

*We have some lambs as well. There is one which the children
are hand-feeding as the little orphan was refused by its ewe,
and our shepherd could not get another to accept it. I
remember as a child escaping from the schoolroom,
preferring to spend time tending birds with broken wings or
baby animals. It seems my offspring have inherited that at
least, though their father's intelligence and grace would be
more useful to them.*

*Hester, you must eat well if you are to recover so I send some
cream, some of our bacon, and a little cake of fruits which I
think you will like to eat. It is one we have made at Penwarne
for many years. There are also some salves which I hope will
help the wound.*

*Let this letter find you in much improved health for that
would give me the utmost joy.
So I remain your friend,
Mary*

*To Mistress Mattock,
At the sign of the Clasped Hands
In Cornwood
County of Devon*

Written this day April 12ʰ 1649
Old Court House Inn
St Brelade
Jersey

My dearest wife,
Let bells be rung, for I have high hopes that this may be the
last letter I write from exile, and God be praised but also His
Majesty and Sir Edward Hyde, for it is to him I owe this. At
his suggestion did I apply to come home, to submit to the
Committee for Cornwall.

I understand that a recognisance of good behaviour may be
issued, which will enable me to come home. Mary, my love, I
shall be in Cornwall, at your side and by my own hearth,
perhaps by this time next month. I shall be recalled to
Pendennis first, for interview and to be given my papers.
That is a bitter-sweet paradox, a journey come full circle.

I continue to follow instructions from Sir Edward, but he
feels that my presence in His Majesty's retinue can offer no
assistance to the King, while, at home, I may do so much, and
Heligan and Kestle, and perhaps Penwarne would benefit
from a gentleman returning to live as quietly as may be, with
his wife and family.

Also, I have received word from John Carew at the Inns of
Court. He considers that Fenwick may well be brought to
answer for his crimes. He will consider taking the evidence
about the villain to the appropriate authorities. There is
much to be done yet but we have to place our hope in this
new England, this Commonwealth, in which we find
ourselves.

I have had no letters reach me from you, so cannot know how
Mistress Mattock fares. I pray for her recovery.

I will dispatch this with Jago on the Dolphin *whose service I do at least know to be reliable and quick so that you may know as much as I do as soon as possible.*
No more for now though as I write with all speed, but dearest chick, you know that very soon you are to have your happy ending,
Your loving and returning husband,
Lewis

To my lady, Mistress Tremayne
At Kestle Wartha
In the parish of St Ewe
In the county of Cornwall

XL Daniel: Epilogue or Foreword?

I loved a girl once; a lass with raven dark hair and eyes the colour of warm honey. I gave her a ribbon. Green it was, to tie up the silky hair that used to escape from her cap when we went a-walking along the banks of the river Torridge.

I have often wondered whether she still has it, the ribbon. Or, when I marched away as young men do, did she tie it as a charm somewhere, like the tokens at the wishing wells, so that the pain of the memories would ease as the coloured threads faded.

Years passed, as they will. Then, one day I saw that very same girl, unmistakable, alive, mingled amongst a thousand luckless souls, the rag-taggle Royalists who marched out of a Cornish fortress on the Fal. She did not see me. Once again, she slipped through my fingers.

But from that moment I vowed that, come what may, I would seek her out. I will ask her about the ribbon; is it lost or has it faded? If she so wishes, I shall buy her a new one.

Then once again, perhaps she will walk out with me along the Torridge to the seashore.

THE END

Newlyn, Cornwall

February 16th 2016

Author's Notes

THE MAIN CHARACTERS

Fictional characters are those indicated by an asterisk. All others in the novel are historical individuals. Where my fictional characters meet real ones, I have tried to make the situations in which I have placed them plausible. Personalities are based on research where possible but where the characters are fictitious any resemblance to actual people living or dead is totally coincidental.

*Grace Fenwick, born Grace Godwynne, in July 1625, an intelligent and pragmatic red-head, is the only daughter of a successful Bristol merchant. She might be expected to make a good marriage, being educated by a liberal-thinking father, applying her skills to running her own household. At her father's death however, she had no choice as her inheritance would pass to her husband.

*Hester Mattock, Born Hester Phipps in Radstock in August 1624, the daughter of a miner, Hester has always expected to make her own way in the world. Shrewd and resourceful Hester may not have had an education but she is astute and quick witted. Black hair and light hazel eyes give her a swarthy, gypsy appearance and perhaps her capacity to adapt and think on her feet stems from some Romany in her ancestry.

William Mattock, a Royalist soldier listed as one of Colonel Lewis Tremayne's men at Pendennis during the siege in 1646. The document T 1621 at the Cornwall Record Office (CRO) lists his home as Cornwood, a village on the skirts of Dartmoor as well as his true fate though no record states that he married a girl he met in Barnstaple

Mary Tremayne, born Mary Carew, 22nd January 1624 (this is a fictional date for the purposes of the novels; it has not been possible to identify her actual date of birth). The eldest daughter of John Carew of Penwarne, niece to Sir Richard Carew of Antony, she is a gentle soul, a romantic dreamer born into the privileged elite of Cornwall, who marries her childhood sweetheart

Lewis Tremayne, eldest son of John Tremayne of Heligan. Royalist Colonel

*__Pasco Jago__, master mariner of Dartmouth

* **Goody Jago**, his wife. Nobody except her husband knows that her Christian name is Hepzibah.

***Bartholomew Fenwick**, master mariner

***Tremenheere Sark**, Cornishman, master gunner and seafarer

John Carew of Penwarne, Mary's father, 'Carew the One Handed'

John Carew Mary's cousin, the eldest son of Sir Richard Carew and his second wife. This Carew signed the dearth warrant of Charles I. At the Restoration of Charles II in 1660 he was arrested, put on trial and found guilty of regicide. He was hanged, drawn and quartered in October that year.

Agnes (some records show Ann), **Bridget, Grace, Candacia**, Mary's sisters

Sir Richard Grenvile, Royalist commander. (In some histories: Grenville)

***Loveday Yendacott**

***Jehoshaphat and Sarah Beale**

Reverend Henry Smith is a man history records as a good man, ejected from his parish and arrested.

Reverend Walter Shute

* **Grand'mer Toms**

***Roderick Rawle**

William Keigwin   ) These were all leaders of the West
Christopher Grosse) Cornwall rebels in 1648, with
Martin Maddern   ) gentlemen like Richard Arundel
Captain Thomas Pike) ready to lead them if the rebellion had succeeded.

Colonel Bennett led troops, via Helston, to tackle the western rebels in May 1648 having been in the West Country since 1646

Emmott Robbins, listed in CRO document T 1621 as armourer to Lewis Tremayne's regiment, there's some evidence to suggest that an Emmott Robbins baptised a child in Breage in 1648.

Benjamin Burrell of Cornwood

*Daniel Edwards of Bideford.

Richard Wiseman was a noted surgeon who served with Hopton and the Prince of Wales both before and after their exile in 1646. As such he was not present at the siege; that is my fiction. There is no evidence to suggest that he was involved in any Royalist plotting, but was with the Prince in 1651.

Surgeon John Haslock was the Parliamentarian doctor tasked with seeing to the welfare of the troops at Pendennis. He is known to have tended Sir Henry Killigrew. Sadly Killigrew's wound proved fatal. Haslock left a list of the Royalist officers at the surrender of Pendennis Castle. None of the 200 women/children were named.

Historical Details

For readers who like a little background, here are a few historical snippets that might be of interest. There may well prove to be inaccuracies in this novel and historians are constantly researching; new facts come to light to provide new perspectives. I am always learning and need correcting if there are errors! If you would like to get in touch with me there is a contacts page on my website: www.stephhaxton.com

A real code: In the Cornwall Record Office is a document which, like the surrender documents for Pendennis, set me off on a creative journey. It is numbered T1763/1-2 and is in Lewis Tremayne's own hand. It gives the details of a cypher or code. The terms included in the encryption are not domestic, they are military. Lewis was more than just a respected Royalist Colonel.

It is thanks to a descendant of Lewis Tremayne's appearance on the BBC TVs 'Antiques Roadshow Detectives' that I tracked down the truth about Lewis Tremayne. Since he does not appear in any records before 1649, I strongly suspect he was in exile with the Prince of Wales. Why he returned when he did remains a topic for the third novel in this trilogy.

Captain Benjamin Burrell: his memorial stone is in Cornwood parish church, but as his wife was Dorothy, anyone who suspected a romance between Hester and the Cavalier spy was always going to be disappointed. He died in 1715.

Cornwood Vicars: There is some interesting information on the incumbents of Cornwood parish:
http://www.cornwoodchurch.com/index.php?page=history
"Henry Smith, who had been instituted shortly before the rebellion against Charles I "was treated in a most Barbarous and Inhuman manner... his House was also Plundered by a Party of Soldiers from the Garrison of Plymouth, who did not so much as leave him a Dish or a Spoon. At the same time

they Plundered him of his books also ... himself, his Wife and five or six Children were all turned out of Doors and substituted for some time by the Charity of the neighbouring gentry (his estate was sequestrated) ... He was ... sent to a Common Jayl in Exeter, where he died soon after the Martyrdom of his Prince.

Walter Shute was [made incumbent] at the vicarage. He is said to have preached a blasphemous sermon, in which he derided Kings and Princes, on the anniversary of the martyrdom of Charles I. However he was conformed at the Restoration and was allowed to continue in the living, being properly instituted on 8th November 1662. He it was who allowed the Church to be abused, the rood loft to be pulled down and the painted and stained windows to be broken."

Chicken Pocks/Pox This childhood disease was recognised in the seventeenth century, but was called 'pocks' or 'pecks' as the initial rash looks as though the patient has been pecked by chickens.

Post 1646: After the end of the first Civil War the system of county Committees was firmly established. However, there was so much work to be done that the administration seems to have been quite chaotic in places. Surviving records are limited but the Church Court to which Hester would have had to apply for probate was replaced by a civil board just at the time she needed it. Records do show that in this period individuals applied both to the church powers and then to the civil powers to confirm the legality of their claim.

The financial hardships suffered by the West Country post 1646 are well documented. Poor harvests exacerbated a tax system that imposed much heavier penalties than in the pre-war period.

1648 Rebellion in Cornwall is a much forgotten episode in Cornish history. For anyone wanting more information, I would recommend reading Mark Stoyle's book *'West Britons'*.

The Sorlinges is the old name for the Isles of Scilly. The islands were regained for the King's cause by a bloodless coup in September 1648. When the islands' commander, Buller, and his officers were at church Parliament soldiers (by then in severe arrears of pay) mutinied and with many island people (suffering the billeting of troops on them with no reparation of costs) declared for the Royalist cause. The Colonel and his officers were dragged to Star Castle, stripped of money and clothes and threatened with the dungeons if they did not declare for the King. The islands were a strategic post between Ireland and the Channel Islands and France. The Royalists were quick to take advantage and Prince Charles sent the 20 year old John Grenvile, son of Sir Bevil Grenvile and nephew of Sir Richard Grenvile, to command the garrison. He arrived in February 1649, days after the execution of Charles I and immediately declared the Prince of Wales as Charles II. Royalist naval forces under Prince Rupert had significant supremacy of the sea and Hopton patrolled the western approaches with 20 ships, harassing Parliament shipping and foreign vessels alike. The islands remained a base for a Royalist fleet of privateers until May 1651.

Translations and quotations
Eagle eyed fans of Shakespeare will be able to locate the quotations I have used. Sark and Grace have a favourite play, *Twelfth Night*, but Sark's greeting I found in *Hamlet*. The beard reference can be found in *Troilus and Cressida*; the reference to eyes is in *Coriolanus*. There are others so seek them if you will!
Goody Jago's pseudo-Spanish quote translates as 'where there is great love there is often little display of it' and is borrowed from *Don Quixote*, by Cervantes

The trial and execution of King Charles I
There isn't enough space, nor is there any need, for me to detail the events that led to the execution of the King on

January 30th 1649. The Army, one of whose leaders was Oliver Cromwell, believed that the rebellions of 1648, known as the Second Civil War, were at the instigation of King Charles and consequently the blood shed in the conflict was his responsibility, an act against his nation and therefore treason. If the King would not compromise then the only way forward was to remove him. A tribunal 'tried' the monarch and inevitably found him guilty. Many historians note that his speech during the trial was perhaps the finest he had ever made.

And finally ...

If Daniel's epilogue leaves you anxious; if Sark's history intrigues you; if Fenwick's perfidy has you raging about retaliation, I aim to restore my readers' equanimity with the third in the 'Pendennis' trilogy which I hope to have available in Spring 2017.

Acknowledgments.

Firstly, I must apologise to Mr and Mrs J Tremayne because in order to get my plot to work I had to slightly adjust the dates/details of the birth of Lewis' children, Mr Tremayne's ancestors.

Thank you to everyone who has encouraged me as this book took shape. Perhaps the biggest thanks should go to the readers who were adamant that they wanted to know what happened to my heroines, an insistent voice being Sue Lewington's.

Megan Nelhams has been brilliant - adept proof-reader and one of those indomitable readers, along with Pauline Hope and Pat Kelly, Karsten and Judith Nissen, and Nigel and Heather at 'Mr Billy's', the top on my list of coffee shops in Penzance.

Helen and an anonymous historian at the Yealm Harbour Office helped with information about Hester and Grace's destination.

Chloe Phillips at the Cornwall Record Office has always been happy to delve with me into documents and has patiently listened to a lot of ramblings.

Claire Chamberlain has done a beautiful cover - again.

Roger Alway was the fount of seafaring advice; he and Laura gave the perfect early critique. The finished book is better thanks to them. Thank you Claire Alway for helping to sort out the Spanish translation.

In Yokohama, Peter and Tamiko Empson and their colleagues helped with a legendary Japanese name thus potentially giving Sark another dimension and an even more interesting history than I expected.

Hannah and Magda at TJI Printers have been superb ever since *Exposed to All Villainies*.

Thank you as ever to Wendy Smith, Helen Thomas, Kathy Jesson and Ella Westland, John Hurst and John More.

Thank you to other authors, especially to Angie Butler who understood about characters voices and didn't think I was mad; to Mel Logue, with her parallel passion for the 17th century, who bribed me to get this finished; to Angela Stoner,

Helena Paterson and the Society of Authors Cornwall chapter - to name but a few.

My lovely Mum has suffered for my art practically every day for nine months and was also an eagle-eyed editor, sharp on continuity. Thank you.

Fern and Stuart both encourage me above and beyond anything I could ever expect, prodding me along and getting excited with me; thank you for listening to me no matter what.

Ultimately, my love and thanks go to Ramsay who built me the best 'shed' ever, a writing retreat at home, proving more than anything else could do just how much he believes in me. Thank you.